D1010049

ALSO BY DONNA GRANT

LOOKING
FOR A
COWBOY

DONNA GRANT

St. Martin's Paperbacks

This is a work of fiction. All of the characters, organizations, and events portrayed in this novel are either products of the author's imagination or are used fictitiously.

First published in the United States by St. Martin's Paperbacks, an imprint of St. Martin's Publishing Group.

LOOKING FOR A COWBOY

For information, address St. Martin's Publishing Group, 120 Broadway, New York, NY 10271.

www.stmartins.com

ISBN: 978-1-250-25006-3

Our books may be purchased in bulk for promotional, educational, or business use. Please contact your local bookseller or the Macmillan Corporate and Premium Sales Department at 1-800-221-7945, ext. 5442, or by email at MacmillanSpecialMarkets@macmillan.com.

Printed in the United States of America

St. Martin's Paperbacks edition 2020

10 9 8 7 6 5 4 3 2 1

Prologue

It had been a long night on patrol. Marlee removed her hat and smoothed back the curls that just wouldn't stay out of her face. She'd had a bad feeling all day that she couldn't shake. She blew out a breath as she replaced her hat and waited for her partner, Ron Carter, to park the car. No sooner did he shut off the engine than she was out of the vehicle and making a beeline for the precinct.

"I won't take offense," Ron hollered good-naturedly after her.

She lifted a hand and threw a glance over her shoulder at him. Ron had been on the force for over twenty years, but he loved what he did. And he was a good cop. "Sorry, Carter. I've had enough of your face today," she teased.

His laugh followed her into the building as she finished the last of her duties and hurried to change so she could get home. Halloween had always been a special time for her and her twin sister, Macey. For as far back as she could remember, the two of them had always dressed up and given out candy. It was a Frampton family tradition that their parents had passed on to them.

Marlee pulled up to the small house she shared with

her sister. She couldn't stop smiling as she grabbed the bag next to her purse. Marlee glanced inside at the tiny costume within. It was the first of many she intended to buy for her future niece that was due in a month.

She had a hop in her step as she walked to the back door of the house. When Macey had gotten pregnant, and the father wanted nothing to do with her or the baby, Marlee had insisted that she and Macey should raise the baby together. As twins, they were rarely apart. It was the perfect solution. Macey had agreed, and from then on, they hadn't looked back.

"Mace, I'm home!" Marlee shouted as she turned the locks behind her and then tossed her keys in the bowl next to the back door. She set her purse down as well as the bag. "Mace? You in the bath again? I bet you're stuck. Again," she said with a chuckle as she walked through the kitchen and living room to the stairs.

When there was still no answer, Marlee frowned. "Macey?" she shouted again.

Fearing the worst, Marlee ran up the stairs and looked in all three bedrooms as well as the bathroom, but there was no sign of her sister. Marlee took in a calming breath and realized that her twin had probably been unable to sleep again and was out front.

Marlee made herself calmly walk down the stairs and open the front door. But the second she found the chairs on the porch empty, her heart began to pound with dread. She closed and locked the door and ran to her purse to look for her cell phone, hoping against hope that her twin had sent a text and that Marlee had somehow missed it. Maybe Macey was in early labor. It happened.

"Please let it be something like that," Marlee murmured to herself as she dug out her phone, though the knot that had been in her stomach all day intensified.

There was no text from Macey.

Marlee's hands shook as she called her sister. It rang and rang and rang before going to voicemail. Marlee called three more times before she gave up and dialed the hospital. She heard what felt like an eternity of rings before someone finally picked up. "I'm looking for my sister, Macey Frampton. She's eight months pregnant, and I need to see if she's been admitted."

Marlee closed her eyes, that bad feeling from earlier intensifying with each second, and every beat of silence on the other end of the line.

"I'm sorry, ma'am. There's been no one admitted by that name," said the woman.

Marlee disconnected the call. Her heart thumped so loudly she could feel it slamming against her ribs. She looked down at her phone and dialed the precinct. Their town was small. There was crime, but nothing like in the big cities.

Why then did she feel as if that were about to change?

"Sergeant Adams," said a deep voice when the line connected.

"Hey, Sarge. It's Marlee. I'm probably freaking out for nothing, but Macey isn't home or at the hospital. I—"

"Frampton, I need you to listen to me carefully."

The moment Adams spoke, the room began to spin. Marlee had been a police officer for three years now. She knew exactly what those words meant.

"Marlee? Can you hear me?" Sergeant Adams' voice pierced the fog descending around her. His tone held a note of anxiety—and sorrow.

She swallowed, grabbing hold of the table that held her purse. Macey had found the console at a garage sale and lovingly sanded it down to the bare wood before painting it with swirls and stars. Her sister had a gift for sure. She could pick up a paintbrush and create anything.

"Yes," Marlee answered, realizing she had to reply.

"Ron is out front, Marlee. You need to let him in."

The phone dropped from her numb fingers as she looked through the house to the front door. The outline of a man could be seen standing there as blue and red lights flashed behind him, shining through the windows to dance on the walls.

The last thing Marlee wanted was to answer the door. She wanted to rewind the day and start again, this time listening to that feeling within her so she could change whatever this was.

But she couldn't do that.

Marlee made her way to the door as if walking through quicksand. Her hand was clammy and slipped on the knob as she tried to turn it. Finally, the door swung open, and she looked into her partner's brown eyes.

In that instant, she knew that this wasn't just bad. It was the worst kind of horrible. Her knees started to buckle, and Ron was instantly beside her, his arm wrapped around her to hold her up. Marlee squeezed her eyes closed against the tears that threatened.

"I tried to stop you before you left," Ron said. "But you were already driving off."

It took her two tries before she found her voice. "What happened?"

"You should sit down," he urged.

"What happened?" she demanded, her voice louder as she leaned her head back to look at Ron's aging face.

His brown eyes lowered to the floor for a heartbeat before he drew in a deep breath. "Macey was attacked."

"Attacked? What does that mean? Is she hurt? What about the baby?" There were so many questions, and she wanted all the answers immediately.

But Ron didn't answer. He just looked at her.

Marlee shook her head and tried to pull out of his arms, but her partner wouldn't let her go. "I'm sorry, Marlee."

At those words, the dam burst, and the tears fell. She hated herself for them because she needed to be strong right now. She was a cop. She knew exactly what was going on, but not even that could help her rein in the bone-deep sorrow that filled her.

"Take me to her," Marlee demanded as she sniffed and looked at Ron through her tears.

His dark brows snapped together as he shook his head. "You don't need to see her."

"Take me to her, or I'll go myself."

"Goddamn stubborn woman," Ron mumbled under his breath.

But his hand was gentle as he placed it on her back and led her out of the house. Marlee spotted another patrol car, and two more officers guarding her place. They wouldn't meet her gaze. She kept her attention on putting one foot in front of the other to get to the car, but once inside, her mind raced with the kinds of horrors that could've befallen her sister.

The ride to the crime scene was short—and silent. Ron kept glancing her way, but she remained facing forward. She spotted the flashing lights well before they got close. As much as she wanted to know what'd happened, she was also terrified of the knowledge.

In the short time she'd been a police officer, she had witnessed all kinds of things—including stabbings, shootings, and murder. She didn't know most of the people, but occasionally, she found herself at a house with someone she knew. Those were the worst calls to take. And it was the reason she didn't want to get out of the car now.

"You don't have to do this," Ron said as he shut off the engine.

"Yes, I do."

Before she changed her mind, Marlee opened the door and stood. The cool night air brushed against her tear-streaked face. She dashed the drops away, but more took their place. Marlee walked to Ron, who waited on her at the front of the vehicle. Together, they approached the scene. Yellow tape was everywhere. Marlee spotted four different detectives talking to people and taking notes.

The cops on scene went silent the moment they spotted her. She steeled herself as Ron lifted the tape, and they ducked under it.

"Sorry, Frampton," someone said as she walked past.

Others also spoke, but she stopped hearing them the moment she saw the white sheet covering the body on the ground. She stumbled, but Ron was there to keep her up-right. Those standing around Macey's body moved away. The forensic team stopped snapping pictures and gathering evidence.

Marlee halted before she got too close to her sister so as not to contaminate the crime scene. The sheet didn't cover the blood that had seeped out to pool around Macey. The streetlight nearby blinked, and a breeze rushed through, lifting the edge of the sheet near Macey's head to reveal a long, auburn curl.

"How?" Marlee asked when she found her voice.

Ron swallowed. "This can wait."

Marlee speared him with a look. "How?"

"Evidence is still being gathered, but from what has been pieced together so far, your sister went for a walk. A witness said a van pulled up beside her and yanked her inside. Then, her body was found here."

Macey wasn't stupid. She wouldn't have left the house after dark—or without her cell phone. "She was taken during the day, wasn't she?"

"A witness told us it was about two hours after you went to work."

Marlee's stomach roiled at the thought, recalling the dread that had overtaken her all day that she had pushed aside. "What did they do to her?"

"They took the baby then slit her throat," Ron said, his voice low and filled with misery. "Her phone was with her, but just out of reach. It appears she tried to grab it, but the blood loss likely made her too weak."

The fury that welled within Marlee was staggering. "And the baby?"

"We've put out an APB and given the information to the Feds, as well."

That got Marlee's attention. "The FBI? Why?" Then it hit her. "The infant kidnappings in LA."

"We think it might be connected," Ron said. "Over the past three weeks, two other pregnant women were killed in the same way as Macey. Their babies were also taken."

His voice faded away as Marlee returned her attention to her sister. The image of her twin lying dead upon the street with a sheet over her would be something forever stamped in her mind. Marlee was going to have to tell their parents and make funeral plans, but really, all she wanted to do was find the bastards who had killed Macey and tore her baby daughter from her womb so violently.

Marlee had a mission now, and nothing would dissuade her from it.

Chapter 1

Present day
Clearview, Texas

Damn, it was a cold one, and it was only November. The worst months had yet to come. Cooper blew warm air onto his hands and rubbed them together as he finished changing the tire on his mother's car.

"I told you I could get someone to come out and do that," Betty Owens said from the front step, huddled in a jacket.

He glanced at his mom. "I'm more than capable. There's no need to waste money when I'm here."

"But you have a life, Cooper."

He finished tightening the last lug nut and straightened before he flashed her a smile. "What? You don't want to see your handsome son?"

"Oh," she said with a roll of her eyes as she scoffed at him. "Get inside. Your breakfast is getting cold."

Cooper put away the tools and hurried into the warm house. He watched his mom moving about the tiny kitchen as he removed his coat and washed his hands. It was the same house he'd grown up in. He'd pushed her to make some improvements over the years to keep it up to date, and though she'd put up a fuss, she was also glad when the upgrades were done.

"What happened this time?" He pulled out a chair at the bar and eyed her, knowing his mom.

She shrugged. "It was a nail."

"I saw it. I'll take the tire over to have it patched."

His mother sat beside him and began spreading strawberry jam on her toast. She took a bite and swallowed it before she set it down with a huff. "Fine. Last night, coming home from work, I swerved when an owl flew across the road."

Just as he'd suspected. He put his hand on her arm. "Mom, I love animals as much as you, but you need to be more careful. If it's your life or theirs, then I'd rather you be safe."

"Your father used to tell me the same thing," she replied with a sad smile. "I'll be more careful."

"Thank you."

Cooper went back to eating, shoveling the eggs and bacon into his mouth. He could cook, but there never seemed to be enough time. More often than not, he stopped off at the café and grabbed his meals. It was just easier that way. But, man, did he miss his mother's cooking.

He was lucky enough to be close friends with Brice and Caleb Harper, as well as their sister Abby, who was married to Clayton East. The Easts had the largest cattle ranch in the area. Luckily, Abby loved to cook, and there was always food whenever he and Jace dropped by. Which was often.

"Anything new going on in your life?" his mom asked.

It was her not-so-subtle way of asking if he was dating. "Still single. I've got too much going on to find time to date."

"Life is too short, honey. You should use your time more wisely," she admonished.

He grinned. This wasn't the first time she'd told him such things. He could throw it back at her that she had been single for over eighteen years now, but he didn't. His father had been the love of her life. And even though it had been many years since his father's death, Cooper remembered how good life had been back then.

Being a single mom wasn't easy, but his mother had never complained. She picked up and carried on. Though she'd cried in her room at night, thinking Cooper hadn't heard her. He never told her he knew of her suffering, and he never would. She had wanted to carry that alone in silence, and he gave her that.

"If I'm meant to find someone, I will," Cooper said.

His mother's green eyes met his. "Son, you're a good man. There is absolutely someone out there for you."

"If you say so."

"I do." She finished the statement with a nod of her head.

Cooper went back to his meal. He was nearly done when the back door opened, and Jace walked in. The two had met in kindergarten and had become immediate best friends. The friendship had lasted through high school, college, and even the military before they both returned to the small Texas town and their two other best friends, Caleb and Brice Harper.

"Mornin'," Jace said and flashed Cooper's mom a bright smile.

Her face lit up at the sight of him. "Jace. I've fixed plenty, so you should have enough to eat."

It was a well-known fact that Jace ate everything in sight. He was always eating.

Jace gave her a kiss on the cheek before he grabbed a plate and piled it high with food. Then, he sat and jerked his chin to Cooper. "Hey."

Cooper swallowed his bite and lifted a brow. "Well?"

Betty's eyes widened. "Well, what? I know that tone from Coop," she said with a pointed look at Jace. "Does that mean you had a date last night?"

Jace shrugged and began shoveling food into his mouth.

"It does," Cooper said with a sigh.

Betty smiled. "That's great. Did it go well?"

Again, Jace shrugged—which was code for *I don't want to talk about it.*

Cooper drank down his orange juice and reached for the coffee. "Mom swerved to miss an owl last night. I've got to take the tire in to be patched. This is the second one in four months. At this rate, I should just buy stock."

"Sounds like it," Jace said with a chuckle.

Cooper looked into his friend's hazel eyes that crinkled in the corners. Jace had been down of late, and no amount of prodding made him give anything up. Cooper was really worried about him, but if Jace didn't want to talk, Cooper could do nothing but be there when his friend needed him.

Jace pushed his clean plate away and poured himself some coffee, dumping copious amounts of sugar in. "You know what today is, right?"

"I do," Cooper replied.

Betty perked up. "Is it today? I must have gotten my dates mixed up. I thought it was tomorrow."

"Nope," Cooper said with a smile. "It's today. You going out to the Rockin' H later? Or would you rather I pick you up?"

Betty rolled her eyes and got to her feet. "I don't need to be driven around. Not yet, at least," she stated with a wink. "And, of course, I'm going to the ranch. After everything Brice and Naomi have endured, I'm happy to celebrate with them."

Cooper and Jace shared a look. They'd both been with Brice and Caleb last night. Brice was excited but more nervous about the possibility of the adoption falling through. His and Naomi's attempt to have their own children hadn't worked out, but they still wanted to bring a child into their lives.

"Are you going there now?" Betty asked.

Cooper nodded as he rose and rinsed off his plate to put in the dishwasher. "Brice and Naomi already left, but Jace and I are going to help get the house ready for them."

"Isn't the baby's room finished? I thought the girls went shopping already?" Betty asked.

Jace choked on his coffee. "If you call what they did shopping. I didn't realize women could buy so much in one day."

Betty chuckled and shook her head as she leaned back in her chair. "You boys have a lot to learn about women."

"I know all I need to know," Jace stated and quickly got to his feet.

The uncharacteristic anger from his friend caught Cooper's attention. He shrugged when his mother gave him a questioning look because he had no idea what was going on with Jace. Surely, it wasn't about Jace's ex. That had been over for some time now. By all accounts, Jace had moved past that, but this comment made Cooper rethink things.

"You boys leave the dishes," Betty said when Jace began cleaning. "I've got a couple of hours before I open the salon. I can clean."

Jace shot Betty one of his bright smiles. "If my momma taught me anything, she taught me that I always help clean after someone fixes me a meal."

"One of the many reasons I love your mother," Betty replied.

Cooper joined Jace. Before long, the kitchen was cleaned. He wiped his hands on a towel to dry them and then looked at his mom. Betty Owens was the strongest woman he knew. But he worried about her. He didn't like her living alone. His father might have been her soul mate, but that didn't mean she couldn't find someone else to love.

"See you tonight," Cooper told her before kissing her on the cheek.

Jace followed with a kiss on the other cheek. "Bye, Mom."

It was a running joke that they had been friends so long that it was like having two sets of parents. Cooper even called Jace's parents Mom and Dad. They were all that close.

"Be safe, boys," Betty called as they walked out.

Jace was still smiling while walking to their trucks. "You've got a great mom."

"So do you."

"Oh, I know, but Betty is truly something special. She handled both of us on her own when my parents sometimes didn't know what to do."

Cooper laughed as he recalled some of their rowdier antics. "That's true. But we also gave your parents more of a hard time because there were two of them."

They reached their vehicles. Instead of getting in, Jace smiled, a faraway look in his eyes. "The world was so simple back then."

"It stopped being simple a long time ago," Cooper stated.

Jace shrugged. "I suppose so."

"You okay?"

"Yeah. Of course," Jace said, shrugging off the question. "I'll follow you to the Rockin' H."

Cooper wanted to say more, but when Jace decided to clam up, there was no getting him to talk—about anything. Cooper got into his truck and started the engine.

He waited for Jace, then he backed out of his mother's drive before heading down the road.

He glanced to the side and looked at his mother's house. After the work accident that had killed his father at the sawmill, the company had given Betty a large sum of money. That, along with the life insurance, had left them sitting very pretty. She could've moved into a bigger house, one the size of the Easts', but she had chosen to remain here.

She had paid off bills, settled the mortgages on the house and the hair salon she owned, and began investing. Cooper had always known things were good for her financially, but he hadn't realized how good until a few years ago when he resigned his commission in the Air Force and returned home. That's when his mom had transferred most of the investments into his name. Cooper had gotten a look at just how good his mother was. She had tripled the money.

It meant that neither she nor Cooper ever had to work again. That knowledge relieved a lot of Cooper's worry about his mom. If nothing else, she would never have to be concerned about money.

He drove down the road toward the Rockin' H horse ranch that Brice and Caleb owned together. Brice had an eye for picking horses, and Caleb could train any equine. It was a match that brought in a ton of business for the brothers.

They, along with Cooper and Jace, had spent years on the rodeo circuit. Brice and Caleb did team roping, while Jace had chosen steer wrestling, and Cooper calf roping. They had all been very good at their chosen sports. Even after Brice and Caleb walked away to open their ranch, Cooper and Jace had continued.

But Cooper was ready to hang it up. Not that he didn't

enjoy it, but it didn't satisfy him like it used to. Nothing did anymore, if he were honest. He worked jobs at the East Ranch and helped Caleb and Brice when they needed it. Hell, a year ago, he helped Danny Oldman, the sheriff, out with a sticky situation.

Cooper needed to find his direction. He just wasn't sure where that might lead. He was finished with the military, and he was done with the rodeo. He enjoyed helping his friends, but there had to be more.

A *FOR SALE* sign caught his attention. The overgrown pasture had been on the market for years. And this was the fourth time it had caught Cooper's attention. If he told his mom, she'd say that it was a sign he should look into it.

Maybe she was right.

Once at the Rockin' H, Cooper parked and turned off his truck, but he didn't get out. Instead, he grabbed his cell phone and called the realty company. As he spoke to someone on the phone, giving the location, he watched as Caleb handed Jace a handful of ribbons attached to balloons. There were so many, Cooper was surprised that Jace didn't float away.

It took both men to get the balloons into the house. Cooper pulled the phone away from his ear, put the call on speaker, and recorded the hilarity of the situation. It was like watching a silent movie between two of the Three Stooges. Cooper kept his laughter silent as he got the information from the realty company and stopped filming.

He watched the video again. This time, laughing out loud.

Chapter 2

It never ended. Marlee had thought that after ten years, she would make some kind of dent in the never-ending—and growing—pile of cases for kidnapped babies and children. It might have begun with her sister, but it had become Marlee's passion, the thing that consumed her.

One agency, in particular, had caught her attention. She couldn't prove it—yet—but she knew the Family First Adoption Agency was moving children illegally. She'd done her own investigation into them, so she knew how legit they looked.

She watched the comings and goings in the small Texas town from the driver's seat of her economy rental in a parking lot outside of the courthouse and police station. The vehicle was so small, she felt like she was in a clown car, but she had to stretch her budget. Besides, she'd gotten used to driving such vehicles a long time ago.

It felt like another lifetime when she'd tried to get as much car as she could afford—and always spent more than she should. Now, she spent her days in rentals that could be labeled kids' vehicles, they were so tiny. She had stopped buying cars for herself long ago. The used Volvo parked in California had been paid off for some time, and she was just fine with that setup. Because it allowed her to spend more of her money on her investigations.

Which was what had brought her to Texas.

Her client was searching for his missing newborn son. That had Marlee hunting in Texas, particularly near Dallas since it was the closest city to the family. She had gotten a tip and was about to disregard it when something had caught her eye about the young couple. On paper, they looked normal. All the I's dotted and T's crossed. For all she knew, they were everyday folks. Yet, she'd learned the hard way that people were rarely who they appeared to be.

Brice and Naomi Harper were young and seemed in love. Marlee had been following them for two days now. Their family and friends were numerous, but that didn't mean the couple wasn't involved in something nefarious. People always did crazy things when children were involved. A woman desperate to have her own would do anything for a baby. Marlee had stopped hoping that the people she investigated were good and that there was no reason for her to be looking into them. But that was never the case. It wouldn't be here, either.

She blew out a breath and reached for the cup of coffee that had gone cold. That was another thing she got used to—cold coffee. She could drink it hot, cold, and any way in between now. Gone were the days when it had to be hot in order for her to get it down. Then again, it wasn't as if her line of work allowed for a lot of niceties.

She hadn't had a home-cooked meal in ages. She couldn't remember the last time she had been to a gym. Or the movies. Shopping was done by necessity only—and usually then for equipment to make her job easier. She racked up loads of frequent flier miles and points at hotels. At the rate she was going, she could take a year-

long vacation on some tropical island and not pay for anything.

Not that it would happen. Every time she thought
about taking some time off, she thought about the families that'd had their babies or children kidnapped. She
thought of the children yanked away from those that
loved them—and she continued working.

Marlee yawned and looked at the last half of her gas
station sandwich with distaste. She'd love a hot meal.
Ohhh, even better, a long shower. But it would be hours
before she got that. She leaned her head to the side and
stretched her neck before repeating the movement on the
opposite side. A knot had formed in her shoulders. If she
didn't get that seen to soon, she'd be unable to turn her
head, which would make her work even harder.

She grabbed her phone and searched for local massage
places. Unfortunately, she couldn't book anything since
she had no idea when she'd have any downtime. For the
last thirty minutes, she'd been waiting for the Harpers
to walk out of the police station. She had been shocked
when they pulled into the parking lot and climbed out of
the SUV before opening the passenger door and taking
out the baby carrier. Marlee hadn't gotten a glimpse of
the infant within since it was swaddled against the cold,
and the cover was pulled over it.

Her search for masseuses ended as she went back to
reading the file on the Harpers on her tablet. Brice Harper
owned half of the Rockin' H horse ranch with his brother,
Caleb. Naomi was a photographer who sold most of her
work online. The couple had been married for four years
and were both successful in their businesses. They were
also connected to the Easts.

Marlee scrolled through the information on her tablet
until she got to Clayton and Abby East. Years ago, after
his parents died, Clayton had inherited the East Ranch,

the largest cattle ranch in the area. He and Abby were well known in the community. They did a lot for the area, including charitable work and making large donations to various nonprofits.

Everyone related to the Harpers and Easts, or friends of the couples, looked like model citizens. That included the local sheriff, Danny Oldman. Marlee wished her view of the world hadn't been tainted by rich people believing they could buy whatever they wanted with their money or do whatever they wanted, including having a baby cut from a mother. She wished she didn't know how often the authorities were paid to look the other way. Or, worse, were in on the crimes.

But she did.

She was waging a one-woman war on the world of kidnapped babies and children. She had victories, but there were more defeats than wins. She'd been beaten down many times to the point where she wasn't sure she could get back up. Then she'd remember the sight of her sister on the street that horrible night a decade earlier.

Marlee would then get back on her feet and take on the next case.

It would be easier if she had a team, but no one seemed to work as hard as she did. Or wanted resolutions as much as she. Only those who had been touched by the same tragedy fully understood it. And only those who got it truly wanted to work the cases.

She sat up straighter when Naomi and Brice walked out of the building, smiling. Behind them was none other than the sheriff. He held the baby carrier this time. Danny Oldman was careful as he put the infant into the car. After a few words to the couple and hugs for Naomi and Brice, the sheriff waved and walked back inside the station.

Once the couple was in their vehicle, Marlee started her car and put the heat on full blast. She sighed at the feel of it warming her. She was used to extreme temperatures, and she didn't let a car idle unless she didn't have a choice.

She made sure to keep as much distance as possible between her and the navy Mercedes SUV. There wasn't a lot of traffic, so she used that to her advantage and put even more distance between them. Based on the map she'd memorized of the area, as well as the few days she'd spent in town, the couple was headed back to the ranch.

The SUV didn't stop again until it reached the Rockin' H. Marlee couldn't travel down the drive to follow them, but as she passed, she saw the house in the distance and the number of cars parked there. No doubt there was going to be a party.

Under any other circumstances, Marlee would have said it was indeed a day for celebration. But she knew the awful truth of many of these matters, and she could find no joy in it whatsoever.

She kept driving, letting the entrance to the Rockin' H—and her quarry—go for the evening. The couple was home now, which would make things much easier. She dialed her connection in Dallas, the one who had agreed to watch the adoption for her so she could stay in town and do more scouting of the area and its inhabitants.

Marlee waited for John Leon to answer. Even before she met him in person, she'd known he was a big man. John was a six-foot-five, two-hundred-and-fifty-pound black man with a look that could stop people in their tracks. He was, in a nutshell, not someone you wanted to fuck with.

"Marlee. How are things?" his deep voice asked when he picked up the call.

She meandered her way back to town. "As good as you can expect. Tell me about the adoption."

"It was with the Family First Adoption Agency, just as you said it would be. And they beefed up security."

That made Marlee frown. "What do you mean? You've had dealings with them before?"

John sighed loudly. "They landed on my radar once before. When I began closing in on them, the agency suddenly shut down. This is them, just with a new name."

"What?" Marlee asked with a shake of her head. "You didn't say any of this when I called last week."

"Because I wasn't sure," John told her. "I didn't have enough on them the first time to get the authorities brought in, but I sent what I did have to a friend in the FBI. The next day, the company was gone. For the last two years, I've been looking to see if they reopened. I started to think they were gone for good when I went to Family First for you. This time, they were in a secure building. When I reached their floor, someone at the elevator asked my name. I pretended I'd read the wrong floor for where I was going, but I'm not sure the guy bought it. I recognized him from the old company. He probably recognized me, as well."

"Which means they could close up this one also," Marlee said and slammed her hand against the steering wheel. "Dammit. I'd love to take them down."

"You've got to get the new parents first. That way, it won't matter if the company folds, the Harpers will have information on them that we can give to the authorities."

Marlee rolled her eyes. She had given up on the FBI doing anything about these crimes. They might claim to care, but no matter what evidence she brought them, they never followed up. Apparently, they were too busy for such things.

"Did you have a family you could push into helping you last time?" Marlee asked.

"No."

One word. That's all she would get. But that's all she

needed to know that it had to do with his grandson's kidnapping.

"Tell me about the Harpers' visit then," she urged.

John said, "The couple arrived early. As I mentioned, I tried to follow them up, but since I suspected I was being followed myself, I went two floors above them and made an appointment at the acupuncturist there. Then I left. I waited in my car for the couple to return. It took nearly three hours before they walked out with the newborn and got into their car to leave."

"Thanks, John. I appreciate the help. You should have the payment for your fee. I sent it earlier."

"I got it," he said after a long pause. "Marlee, you've been doing this a long time, just like me, so please hear me when I say that I've got a bad feeling about this. You need to be careful."

She scrunched up her face. "I think if anyone needs to be careful, it's you. I'm not the one who went to the agency."

"Be that as it may, heed my warning."

"I'm not walking away from this case. The mother was killed the same way as my sister. This baby might not be the one I'm looking for, but the dates all line up. And whether this child was cut out of its mother or not, we both know the agency isn't on the up and up."

John grunted. "That's the thing. I've been doing some research on them while waiting for you to call. They look legit. The kind of lawful that they weren't before."

"Then maybe it isn't the same company."

"I think it is, but I think they got smarter this time around."

"That one guy you saw . . . He's probably security and moves around a lot."

"I don't think so," John said. "This company—"

"Is moving children off the books," Marlee interrupted him. "I know just how freaking legit it appears. But I also found at least ten adoptions over the last year that were done *off* the books. There's more. I know it."

John let out a string of curses. "You need to be careful. These people are dangerous."

"I'm well aware of that."

"And I thought I was in this too deep. I know you want answers to what happened to your sister. I know you want to help all those who have lost children. And I know you want to return babies to their parents. But you can't go up against someone like Family First on your own."

"Why not? Someone has to. I'm tired of going after the crumbs. I've got my sights set on the entire cake."

Chapter 3

It was a good day. Cooper stood against the counter in the kitchen, a bottle of beer clasped in his hand as he watched Brice and Naomi with their new son. After all the heartache they had been through learning that they couldn't conceive, they had found another way to have a family.

And Cooper couldn't think of a more deserving couple.

"Ever think you'll have one of those?" Jace asked, jerking his chin to the infant.

Cooper shrugged, twisting his lips. "Kinda hard to do when I'm single."

"Pfft. Single people do it all the time."

Cooper glanced at him with a frown. "I saw firsthand how hard it was for my mom being a single parent. And that's when I was older. I can't imagine doing it with a baby."

"That was stupid. I shouldn't have said that." Jace's gaze dropped to the floor before he took a long swig of beer.

Cooper studied his friend. "I know you didn't mean anything by it. I just have some pretty harsh views on the subject. What about you? You want kids?"

"I do."

"You've never told me that."

"It's not something guys talk about with each other," Jace said with a shrug.

Cooper took a drink of beer and let what Jace had told him sink in. Then he said, "I can see you with kids. You'd make a good dad. But only because you're just a big kid yourself."

Jace laughed and then covered his mouth, nearly spitting out his beer. He swallowed then punched Cooper in the arm. "I can't even say anything because it's true."

"So true," Cooper replied with a smile.

Caleb walked up then, grinning. "I'm not even going to ask why Jace nearly choked just now."

"It's nothing, really," Cooper said, still grinning as he glanced at Jace. "I just said he'd make a great dad since he's a big kid himself."

Caleb licked his lips to try and hold back his grin. "I already feel sorry for the woman. She'll think she has just one kid to take care of, but she'll actually have two."

"Hey, now," Jace said, acting insulted, but his grin ruined it. "I can't help who I am."

The three laughed, then grew silent when the baby began to cry. Brice took the infant from his sister, Abby, and rocked him until the baby went back to sleep.

"He's a natural," Caleb said.

Cooper nodded. "When are you and Audrey going to have little ones running around?"

"In a few years. We're not in any hurry," Caleb answered.

Jace finished his beer and quietly set the empty bottle on the counter. "I'm glad this turned out well for Brice and Naomi."

That made Cooper frown. "Why wouldn't it?"

Jace rolled his eyes. "You really need to read the news."

"Why? Not only is it damn depressing, but how can

you believe any of what's said? It's all about who is report-
ing it. Same with history. It's written by the conquerors."

"Save me," Caleb said with a dramatic sigh. "I can't
hear this argument for the millionth time."

Jace nodded excitedly. "Exactly. Look, even Caleb
agrees with me."

"Hold up," Caleb said and held up his hand. "I never
said I agreed with either of you. I simply said I didn't want
to hear the argument. But, for clarity's sake, I don't listen
to the news either." He then turned to Cooper. "However,
I do get breaking news alerts on my phone. You might
want to at least do that."

Cooper scratched behind his ear. "Fine. I'll bite. Why
should I be listening to breaking news?"

"You kill me. You really do," Jace said as he squeezed
the bridge of his nose with his thumb and forefinger. He
then sighed dramatically and dropped his hand. "There's
been a rash of murders in several states involving pregnant women. The women are killed. The babies taken."

Cooper was taken aback. "Who would do such a dis-
gusting thing when there are plenty of women giving up
children for adoption?"

Caleb turned and looked at his brother and sister-in-
law. "You want to know why people would kill a pregnant
woman for her child? All you need to do is look at Brice
and Naomi."

"No," Cooper said, not buying it. "There has to be
something else going on. Like I said, many women give up
their children for adoption. That's how Brice and Naomi
got little Nate."

Jace shot him a perturbed look. "And how many people
aren't accepted by the adoption agencies? How many can't
afford it?"

"So, you think there're people out there stalking pregnant women, killing them, and hoping nothing is wrong

with the infant so they can sell it to someone looking for a baby of their own?" Cooper asked.

Caleb nodded, his brows raised.

Cooper set his beer on the counter and gaped at his friends. "Have both of you lost your minds? No one can just pop up with a kid nowadays. There are social security numbers, fingerprinting, and too many other things that identify someone."

"You seriously need to watch some crime TV, because you have no idea the lengths that some will go to," Jace said. "As for everything you mentioned, if someone has the means, anything can be done."

"Right," Cooper said. "Money. Something you say these people with money don't have to do is go through a regular adoption agency."

Caleb held up a hand, halting them. Then he looked at Cooper. "Do you know what Nate's adoption cost? It was over sixty thousand dollars."

"Okay." Cooper nodded, his mind working. "I was thinking around that amount."

Jace gave him a pointed look. "How many people do you think have that kind of cash lying around? Some save their entire lives for retirement and never even get close to that amount. And, usually, it's young couples who want kids."

Cooper held up his hands. "Okay. Okay. I get the point." He bit his lip, still thinking about the murders. "If someone is taking those infants from their mothers' wombs, wouldn't they charge *more* than an adoption agency? Not less? After all, they're expending a lot more effort."

"Audrey and I talked about that last night after watching the news," Caleb said. He looked at his wife and shook his head. "I tend to agree with Cooper. These people have to be charging more. It means they have a certain clientele."

Jace squeezed his eyes closed. "Fuck me. You're talking outside the US."

"Yep," Caleb said as he looked at his friends. "How many infants outside of America have been adopted by residents here? It's a lot. Because those adoptions are typically a little cheaper."

Cooper felt sick to his stomach. "And if you find someone who doesn't do things by the book, then it could be even cheaper. Damn. I didn't even think about that."

Caleb shrugged. "But there's an argument that these killers are taking the babies and selling them cheaper right here in the States. Either way, it's making headlines."

"I don't need to ask if the adoption agency Brice and Naomi used was reputable," Cooper said.

Jace snorted and nodded his head toward Clayton and Abby, who were gazing adoringly at the baby while their three children seemed more interested in eating cake than seeing their new cousin. "I've no doubt that Clayton had the company investigated. We all know how protective he is of the family."

Caleb smiled before he lifted the beer bottle to his lips and drank. He lowered it and said, "Actually, he didn't. At least, not that I know of. I'm pretty sure Abby told him that Brice and Naomi could do it on their own."

"Good for them," Jace said.

Caleb elbowed Cooper and shot a covert look toward Jace when he turned his head. Cooper shrugged, letting Caleb know that Jace had said nothing about his date the previous night.

"So," Caleb said, getting Jace's attention, "how was the date? I hear you took her to the steakhouse."

Jace blew out a breath and looked at the ceiling. "I knew I shouldn't have told y'all I was going on a date."

"Actually, you told us you signed up for online dating," Cooper said with a wide grin.

Jace pointed at first one then the other. "Y'all are ass-holes. You know that?"

"Come on, Jace," Caleb called with a laugh as Jace turned to walk away. "We're just joking."

Jace halted and pivoted to return to them. He looked at Caleb but shifted his attention to Cooper. "I can't say anything to Caleb 'cause he's already got Audrey, but I can, and will, with you."

"Say what?" Cooper asked with a shrug. "I can take whatever you want to throw at me."

"Is that right?" Jace asked, a sly smile pulling at his lips.

Caleb groaned with a roll of his eyes. "Aw, shit. Why'd you have to go and say that, Coop?"

Cooper was asking himself that same question. And by the look on Jace's face, he was in for it.

"This is going to be great." Jace rubbed his hands together. "Tell me, Coop, when's the last time you were on a date?"

"I don't know," he replied hesitantly.

Jace's face lit up. "I do. It's been over six months. You know, Danny and Skylar's wedding is coming up. You said you'd have a date for that."

"I will," Cooper stated. If nothing else, he'd bring his mom.

Caleb dashed that when he said, "Betty doesn't count. It has to actually be a date. And Jace is right. I remember this bet. Both of you agreed to have a date."

"Hey, I'm trying," Jace said and threw up his hands.

Cooper winced as he remembered that night while playing cards. He'd won a lot and had entirely too much bourbon. He wasn't sure, however, about everything that'd happened after they stopped playing poker. "Dammit."

"Ryan recorded it just in case," Caleb announced.

Cooper was really stuck if the police chief, Ryan Wells,

had recorded the vow. He looked between his two friends and shrugged. "Looks like I've got to start searching for a date."

"Did someone say date?" Audrey said as she walked up and put her arm around Caleb. "Because I hear there's a new woman in town. From what everyone is saying, she's a looker. You can't miss her. She's got curly, auburn hair."

Jace cut his eyes to Cooper. "I caught a glimpse of her the other day at the gas station. She's a looker for sure."

Cooper tried not to appear interested but damned if he wasn't. Because he definitely had a thing for redheads.

Chapter 4

Marlee straightened from leaning over the sink in her motel room and looked at herself in the mirror. The dark circles under her eyes spoke of yet another night with only a few hours of sleep. She braced her hands on either side of the sink and let out a long breath.

She craved to be able to shut her eyes and not see her dead sister. It got worse when she finally did go to sleep and had the same nightmare—looking for her niece, only to hear a baby crying. Each time, she followed the sound, but never got close. It was the same dream, night after night, and only stopped if she drank enough or took a sleeping pill.

Even though Marlee knew her niece would be ten now, she still heard a baby in her dreams. It was unsettling, but more than that, it was a reminder that no matter how hard she looked, no matter what she did or the contacts she made, she had yet to find her sister's baby.

And she likely never would.

That had been the hardest thing to accept. Though, in all honesty, she hadn't truly accepted it because she still looked for her niece. No doubt she would continue to do so until the day Marlee breathed her last.

Her phone buzzed, drawing her attention. Marlee looked over her shoulder to see the reminder to call her parents. She ignored it and turned on the faucet to toss more cold water on her face in an effort to get rid of the dark circles and bags beneath her eyes. When she couldn't stand the cold anymore, she stripped out of her tank top and panties and jumped into the shower.

She took her time lathering her hair and body. Her shower was really the only time in her day that she took for herself. She stood beneath the spray much longer than necessary, but the hot water did wonders to ease the tension in her shoulders. It reminded her that she needed to get a massage before the knots got any worse.

With her shower finished, she turned off the water and toweled off. She wrapped her hair in the terrycloth and walked naked out of the room to her suitcase, where she found clean clothes and got dressed. Only then did she let her hair down and face the mirror.

"Ugh," she said to herself as the dark circles appeared even more prominent.

In the past, she would've pulled out a huge cosmetic bag and quickly gotten to work disguising them. But she hadn't worn makeup in over four years. She still had it, but she only used it on rare occasions. And bringing it on her work trips? Yeah, that took up room in her luggage that was better used for equipment.

She did, however, still have enough vanity to use some products in her hair. Otherwise, the curls got out of control. She opted to let it dry naturally and used that time to check her emails. Really what she was doing was putting off calling her parents. But, eventually, that task could no longer be ignored. She didn't hesitate because they were horrible people. Quite the opposite, actually. They supported her fully in whatever she did. The fact that she wasn't home more often left her feeling guilty.

Marlee steeled herself and picked up the phone. As usual, her mother picked up on the second ring. "Hey, M—" Marlee started, only to realize it wasn't her mother's voice. It was Pam, the nurse she'd hired to live with her parents.

"Marlee?"

Fear zinged through her, causing her heart to pound. "Yes?"

"I called you several times yesterday, but I couldn't leave a voicemail because it's full again."

Marlee squeezed her eyes closed. Shit. She really needed to go through and delete those. She'd been so intent on her quarry she hadn't even noticed the calls. That wasn't fair to her parents or to Pam. "I'll get that taken care of today. And I'm really sorry for not realizing you called. What happened?"

"When I listened to your mom's lungs yesterday, I heard some crackling. It was enough to cause concern. It took a little doing, but I convinced her to go to the doctor and get checked out."

Getting Marlee's mother away from her father literally took an act of God. She was impressed that Pam had managed it. Marlee opened her eyes. "That's good. Did the doctor find anything?"

"She has pneumonia. You know Diane. She's not happy to be in the hospital, but she's getting excellent care. In fact, she should be home in a few days."

"Again? She just had pneumonia a month ago."

"It happens," Pam said in a gentle voice. "Especially in the elderly. It's why I make sure and check every day."

"Do I need to come home?"

"We're fine. Your dad is watching one of his old westerns. He understands that your mom isn't well, and that's why she's not here at the moment. I've got it under control."

She'd never forget the night she'd told her parents about Macey's death. Her father had suffered a stroke just moments later, and he hadn't been the same since. He couldn't talk, and he was paralyzed in his left arm. Since her parents were getting on in age, and her work took her all over the country, Marlee had hired a nurse to be with them. Pam was the best thing that had ever happened to the Framptons. They both adored her and did everything she asked of them—the exact opposite of what they did for Marlee.

"How do you do it?" Marlee asked. It wasn't the first time she'd posed the question, and she knew it wouldn't be the last. "These aren't your parents. I just—"

"We've had this discussion before," Pam said, a smile in her voice. "This was my calling. I love it, as odd as that sounds to some. You have your purpose, and it's one that does a lot of good. If I can help make your life, as well as your parents' lives, easier, then I'm happy."

"I honestly don't know what I'd do without you."

"You just take care of you. If I've learned anything about you over the last five years, it's that you don't take care of yourself enough."

Marlee chuckled. "Point taken."

"I get updates on your mom every couple of hours. I'll make sure I pass those on to you."

"You're amazing, Pam. Thank you."

She made a sound. "Just eat. You've lost too much weight. And please tell me you're getting a massage. You know what happened last time."

Marlee winced, remembering the pain she had suffered from the knots in her neck. "I'm getting one today. Promise."

"Good. Talk later."

After she hung up the phone, Marlee immediately went to make an appointment with a masseuse. She was lucky enough to get one a couple of hours after lunch. It gave her time to sort through some emails and do more research. In an effort to take better care of her body, she even put in an order for a salad to be delivered to the room for lunch.

She drank the motel's horrible coffee made from the beat-up pot in her room and downed a bottle of water as she looked through the various photos she'd taken of anyone around Naomi and Brice. Marlee hung them on the wall, looking at each one in detail. She always got consumed by the task, which was why she often forgot to eat. Time got away from her while looking for the bad guys.

When she moved to the next photo, one of Cooper Owens, she hated to think that anyone who looked that good was one of the villains. But she knew all too well how often that was the case. Though, from what she'd discovered, Cooper Owens was a good guy. So, maybe he really was. She'd probably never know.

By the time the knock on her door came, she was famished and in need of some time away from the computer screen. She pulled up one of her audiobooks and hit play as she settled in to enjoy her salad.

Her greatest joy—and something she and Macey had gotten from their mother—was romance novels. While her mother preferred historicals, Marlee loved them all. There wasn't a sub-genre of romance that she didn't devour. As she listened to the narrator, she allowed herself to fall into the world as she ate.

Finding time to read was difficult. And while she still loved books, when she was traveling, packing, following someone, or even digging into their lives, her audiobooks became a necessity. They were her escape, the things that got her through each day.

She listened far longer than she should have. When she glanced down at her salad, it was gone. She had become so engrossed in the story that she hadn't realized she'd eaten the entire thing. Then she looked at the time and gasped.

"Dammit," she said as she stopped the audiobook and jumped to her feet.

Marlee hurried to put on her boots before she grabbed her jacket, purse, and keys and ran out the door. It wasn't until she was nearly at the massage place that she looked down and saw that she'd left her phone behind. There was no time to get it now. It'd have to wait until later.

She'd just put the car in park when it started to rain. Marlee grimaced as she got out and ran to the building, a shiver running through her. She preferred the moderate temperatures of California. While she had gotten used to hot and cold places, she didn't particularly like them.

Marlee paused when the hairs on the back of her neck rose. She swallowed, the feeling that someone was watching her too strong to ignore. She glanced over her shoulder as she opened the door, but she didn't see any-one. A receptionist greeted her when she walked into the building, and she smiled, though she kept glancing out the door to see if she could locate what had alarmed her.

She was filling out the paperwork for her visit when the door opened on the side of the room, and the massage therapist walked out with her client. They spoke briefly, and Marlee waited until the client made her way to the counter to pay before she glanced up. Her eyes landed on none other than Abby East.

"I hear congratulations are in order," the woman behind the counter said, a wide smile on her lips.

Abby laughed and nodded enthusiastically. "It's taken Brice and Naomi so long, but they finally have a child. We spent yesterday with them."

"It's all anyone can talk about around town. What did they name the baby?"

Abby beamed with pride. "Nathanial, but they're calling him Nate."

The worker cooed. "That's adorable. Don't forget to remind Naomi that she still needs to take time for herself. She shouldn't pass up her monthly massages."

"Trust me, we're all reminding her of that. She's just so taken with Nate that it might be a while before she gets back to normal. Brice, too, for that matter." Abby shook her head, her brunette locks secured in a ponytail. "Although, I can freely admit that Nate stole my heart the moment I saw him. He's adorable."

The worker handed Abby the receipt to sign. "How are your three liking their cousin?"

"Wynter and Brody couldn't care less. But Hope is utterly enthralled. She cried when we left yesterday."

Marlee finished her paperwork and rose to hand it to another worker. By the time she answered all the questions posed to her, Abby was gone. They brought Marlee to a waiting room with soothing music that was likely supposed to relax her. Instead, her mind was focused on her current job. If she were just anyone, she'd probably think like everyone else and be happy for Naomi and Brice. But Marlee knew the ugly side of adoptions.

There was no way she would be able to relax enough for a massage. She had a list of things she needed to look into. She got to her feet just as a tattooed man with a long beard and perfectly coiffed hair called her name. Since she was the only person in the waiting room, she couldn't ignore him.

"That's me," she said.

He held out his hand. "I'm Chris. I'll be your therapist today. Tell me what you'd like to work on."

She shook his hand. "I've got some pretty bad knots in my neck and shoulders."

Chris led her into a room. "I can definitely take care of that. I'll let you get undressed, and I'll be back in a moment."

Even as Marlee removed her clothes and got on the heated bed and beneath the sheet, she wondered if she was wasting her money on the massage right now since she was too wrapped up in the case. At least that was her thought until Chris began to work out the knots. It wasn't long before her mind quieted, and she was able to relax.

In a blink, the massage was over. Marlee actually groaned when Chris said that the time was up. She needed another few hours at least. After Chris left, she dressed and then met him in the hall where he handed her a cup of water.

"You weren't kidding," he told her. "I'm surprised you can move at all. Your muscles are locked."

She twisted her lips. "It's something I deal with daily."

"You shouldn't let that happen. I suggest you return in two weeks."

"Thanks. I'll see," she said with a smile before he led her out to pay.

As she stood in the same spot that Abby East had, Marlee's mind went right back to the case. She got the attention of the worker who had checked Abby out. "This might seem rude, but I overheard the conversation you were having with the lady before I went back for my massage. She's Abby East, right?"

The woman looked suddenly leery. "Yes."

Marlee grinned. "I thought so. I've not met her yet, but I knew about Naomi and Brice bringing home their new baby. I was supposed to go to the party, but I had to work, and I didn't want to just walk up to her."

"Oh, you should have," the worker said, now relaxed after seemingly coming to believe Marlee's lie. "Abby is the sweetest woman I know. And her husband?" The woman fanned herself. "He's to die for."

Marlee had seen a photo of Clayton East. He certainly was handsome. "I know."

"Y'all can have Clayton," another woman said, this one younger as she came around the corner. "Personally, I'd take Cooper."

Since Marlee knew everyone associated with Brice and Naomi, she immediately knew that the woman was speaking about Cooper Owens. Who, if Marlee were looking to hook up with anyone, would be who she chose. There was something about his eyes and that heart-stopping smile.

"Do you know Cooper?" the younger woman asked.

Marlee just smiled. "Doesn't everyone?"

She finished paying and walked out of the building to find that the rain had stopped for the moment, and the temperatures had dropped even more. This time, nothing made her think that someone was watching her, so she chalked it up to being hyper-sensitive before. She shivered and jumped into her car to start the engine. On the way back to the motel, she pulled into a nearby gas station to fill up. She wasn't on empty, but she never knew if she would need to drive a long distance at a moment's notice, so she always kept the tank filled.

Before opening the door, Marlee tugged on her coat and reached for her wallet. She shoved the hair that the wind kept blowing into her eyes out of her face and got the gas going. Most people ignored others filling up near them, but not Marlee. She always listened in because you never knew what kind of gossip you could pick up.

"You're new."

The male voice took her by surprise. She turned to find herself staring into faded blue eyes and a face weathered by age and the sun. White hair poked out from beneath the cowboy hat situated atop the man's head. He looked her up and down.

Marlee gave him a nod. "I am."

"It's your hair."

She quirked a brow. "I'm sorry?"

"There ain't too many natural redheads in this town."

Marlee smiled and turned back to the pump, but it was obvious the man wasn't going anywhere. She sighed and turned back to him. "You know everyone in the area?"

"Of course," he stated as if she had asked if the sky were blue. "I've lived here my entire life. The young'uns always move away, but eventually, they make their way back. It's rare for someone like you to come here. What are you after?"

No one had ever put it quite so plainly before. Marlee leaned her hip against the car. "Why do you think I'm after something?"

"Like I said, we don't get those like you here."

"I feel as if I should be offended."

"Mac doesn't mean anything by it," said a deep voice from behind her. The sound made her stomach do somersaults as if butterflies had taken up residence there. She didn't move because she couldn't.

The old man, Mac, ran a hand over his whiskered jaw and looked over her shoulder. "Wondered how long it'd take you to get over here."

"I think just in time," the man behind her said with a chuckle.

Mac tipped his hat to her and walked away. Marlee wasn't sure what was wrong with her. She was used to dealing with all sorts of people. It began when she was still a cop, and that training had come in handy more times than she wanted to admit, both then and since.

But no one had ever affected her in such a way.

"Ma'am? You okay?"

She nodded and pushed away from her car. The pump had finished, which gave her something to do. She pulled out the nozzle and replaced it on the hook. As she turned to put the cap back on her gas tank, she saw that a large hand was already doing it.

Her gaze traveled up the arm encased in a dark brown coat. Slowly, her eyes moved to his neck and then landed on his face. She knew him instantly. How many times had she stared at his deep green eyes in the photographs she had? His black Stetson hat was pulled low, but she still caught sight of the dark brown locks that were a tad long—though she preferred it that way.

He had a shadow of a beard on his handsome face, as though he hadn't shaved that morning. It accentuated his amazing jaw. She found it sexy as hell, which only irritated her more. Then she made the mistake of looking at his lips. They were wide and on the fuller side. And as she stared, they curved into a grin.

"I'm Cooper Owens," he said and stuck out his hand.

Marlee glanced down at the hand and blinked. It took her a second to reach for the proffered palm. The moment his long, lean fingers wrapped around hers, something warm and electric rushed through her. Her eyes snapped to his, and by the small frown on his brow, it seemed he'd felt it, as well. Marlee wanted to yank her hand from his hold, but she couldn't seem to make her body obey.

Cooper tilted his head to the side, concern in his eyes. "Did Mac say something rude?"

"No," Marlee croaked. She shook her head while clearing her throat. "No, no. Everything is fine."

"You had me concerned for a bit." He smiled again.

Damn him. Didn't he know what that did to her?

"I don't suppose I could get your name, could I?"

The last time Marlee had acted so stupidly was in junior high when she tried to talk to a boy she liked. It had been a disaster. One she had worked hard to never repeat. And yet, here she was, doing it again.

"Marlee Frampton," she told him.

"Nice to meet you, Marlee."

She was drowning in his green eyes as his thumb rubbed gently across her hand. Marlee knew she should get away from him immediately. Whatever was going on with her spelled trouble. She knew it, but it did no good.

"It's nice to meet you, too."

Chapter 5

My God, she was stunning.

That thought kept going through Cooper's head as he held her hand. Her auburn curls danced in the wind while her eyes, the color of bourbon, watched him. She had a delicate face that made a man think she needed saving. But one look in her eyes and a person immediately saw the steel within her.

That didn't make him like her any less. In fact, it made him more interested. That, along with whatever it was he'd felt when they first touched, had him slack-jawed. His first impression of Marlee Frampton was that everything was there for someone to see—if they only looked.

And he was certainly looking.

"What brings you to our fair town?"

Her gaze slid away as she pulled her hand from his. "Business."

"Here?" he asked. There wasn't much going on in the area that didn't revolve around ranches. While he imagined that Marlee could fit in anywhere, he didn't peg her for a rancher. "You in the ranching business?"

She swallowed. "No."

No further explanation came, which meant she didn't want to discuss it. Cooper couldn't blame her. He was a stranger asking probing questions. "I hope to see you around again."

The smile she shot him didn't quite reach her eyes. She turned and walked around to the driver's side of her car before getting in and starting the engine. Cooper remained where he was as she drove off. A dozen questions rushed through his mind that he wished he would've asked her, but he'd been too blinded by her beauty.

"Well, son, I think you need to brush up on your wooing skills," Mac said as he came to stand beside him.

Cooper couldn't disagree. "I don't think I've ever been so drawn to a woman before."

"Hmm. Those are the ones you've got to look out for."

He turned his head to look into Mac's faded blue eyes. "Why do you say that? Seems it'd be the type you'd want to find."

"Pfft," Mac said and waved aside Cooper's words. "You've obviously never fallen hard for a woman and not had her return that affection."

"I've had my heart broken before."

"Not like what I'm talking about. Just watchin' you told me you're half in love with her already, and you just met. She's the kind who'll destroy your heart, son. Trust me."

Cooper glanced down the road to where Marlee had disappeared. "Or, she could be my soul mate."

"There's that chance, I suppose. I took that gamble once, and it didn't turn out so well for me."

"That was her loss."

Mac smiled, showing several missing teeth. "Exactly. I would've loved her like no other." The smile died then. "What I'm tryin' to say is that you can't make someone love you. Just be careful."

Cooper waited until Mac was in his old Ford pickup

and driving away before he made his way back to his truck and climbed inside. He started the engine and debated if he should go in the direction Marlee had headed to find her. But what would he say? She'd likely think him a stalker. He needed to come up with another plan.

Cooper blew out a breath and turned in the opposite direction. He finished his errands and found himself headed toward the police station. The officer at the front gave him a wave and a nod as Cooper rounded the desk and waited to be buzzed in. Once he passed the locked door, he made his way to the chief of police. The office door was open as Ryan Wells read over something.

Cooper knocked on the frame. "Hey."

Ryan's head snapped up. "Hey. I wasn't expecting you today."

"Surprise visit." He walked into the office and sat in one of the chairs.

Ryan sat back so his chair leaned back some. He quirked a brow. "What's on your mind?"

A woman, but Cooper didn't want to tell him that. He and Ryan were friends, and he wasn't going to abuse that friendship by asking Ryan to look into Marlee. "Just finishing up some errands."

"You're still bored."

Cooper shrugged. "I'm happy helping out on the side for you and the department."

"My dad would say you're rudderless, that you're going in whatever direction the wind blows you."

"He wouldn't be wrong." Cooper laughed softly. "I've got this feeling that there is something out there I'm supposed to do. I've just not found it yet."

Ryan twisted his lips. "You'd make a great cop. I've told you that before. I saw your and Jace's skills when you aided Danny and Skylar last year. I'd hire you in a heartbeat."

"I appreciate it. I like helping out when I can, but I don't believe being a police officer is my destiny. I know that makes it sound like I don't want to work, but I do."

"You might not have a regular job, but you work harder than most people I know." Ryan sat up. "Now, how about you tell me the real reason you're here."

"I just wanted to talk."

"We've known each other long enough that I can tell you not to bullshit me. Spit it out, Coop."

Cooper rubbed his palms down his thighs. "I don't want you to do anything. Maybe I just want to talk."

"All right. Talk," Ryan urged.

That's all it took for Cooper to tell the chief about Marlee Frampton. The more Cooper talked about her, the more he wanted to see her again.

The more he craved her.

"I think you should ask her out, man," Ryan said with a shake of his head. "You've got it bad."

Cooper grinned. "Yeah."

"What the hell are you doing here talking to me? Get your ass out there and find her," Ryan said, a smile on his face.

Cooper jumped to his feet. "I think I will."

Chapter 6

Marlee shut the motel room door behind her and leaned back against it. She closed her eyes and pressed the backs of her hands against her enflamed cheeks.

"Holy shit," she murmured.

She'd shot the pictures of Cooper herself. She'd seen him alone and with his friends, but nothing, absolutely *nothing* had prepared her for an up-close and personal meeting. Charming didn't even begin to describe him. He was . . . she sighed and banged her head against the door.

Those eyes, that mouth.

His voice!

She dropped her arms to her sides and opened her eyes. "This can't be happening."

Or could it? She could use Cooper to get close to Brice and Naomi and talk to them.

"No," she said with a shake of her head. "That's crossing a line I've not done before."

Then she thought about the man with two young kids who had buried his wife and was in turmoil about his missing baby. The timeline for the kidnapped boy and Nate coming up for adoption was too similar.

Marlee had followed Brice, Naomi, and their friends and family for nearly a week. She knew their habits and frequented locations. She didn't want to use Cooper because . . . well, she knew it was morally wrong. She didn't want to hurt anyone, but if it stopped pregnant women from getting murdered with their unborn children cut from their bodies, then she'd do whatever it took.

Even if it meant using Cooper Owens.

Marlee warred with her internal moral compass for another thirty minutes. No matter how she tried to spin it, she wasn't comfortable using Cooper. But she didn't have a choice. She needed to get the baby back to his rightful father—even if that meant tearing the child out of the arms of his adoptive parents.

She'd done it a few times before. It was one of the hardest things she'd ever done. Some of the parents understood why the baby was being taken away by the authorities, but others had fought tooth and nail to keep the child.

What few understood was that Marlee felt everyone's pain. The family of the murdered mother and the missing child, the new parents who thought they had finally begun a family of their own. And even the authorities, who stood in the middle with her, making sure everything was done properly.

She worked for the families devastated by such tragedies, and those yearning to find their missing children. That's who paid her and came to her for answers—and closure. She didn't work for the police, the FBI, or the adoptive parents. She had to remind herself of that sometimes because it was easy to get caught up in all the emotions. Because all of it was emotional.

Marlee might not like some of the things she had to do, but she did them anyway. And Cooper would be one of those things. She was eager to speak to him again and it sent all kinds of warning bells off in her head. She would just have to be careful. No matter how she felt around him, or how he made *her* feel, nothing could happen. He was merely a means to get what she needed—which was a baby returned to his rightful family.

With her decision made, Marlee took off her sweatshirt and jeans. She rummaged through her suitcase until she found the gray V-neck sweater that clung to her breasts. Together with the black jeans and boots, she looked passable. She'd learned to make sure she packed one outfit that was nicer casual for just such instances.

She looked at her hair in the mirror and grimaced. The wind had wreaked havoc on her curls, making them frizz. She used some more product to tame the worst of it but also pulled back the sides to get it out of her face. It didn't look too bad. Not great, but not horrible either. She shrugged and glanced at the clock by the bed.

Her best bet for running into Cooper was later that evening, so she had a couple of hours to kill. Marlee first cleared out her voicemail box, then she went to her laptop and opened it. She answered some emails, but it was the one to Bill, the father of the missing male baby, that was the worst to answer. He wanted an update, and unfortunately, she didn't have much to tell him.

Giving families false hope was something she desperately tried not to do—ever. Marlee presented facts and always cautioned the families about being unrealistic regarding the outcome, and how long these investigations took. Not that they all listened to her, but she made sure to tell them anyway.

Marlee also called the hospital to get an update on her mom. The nurse let her speak to her mother briefly. Diane was a fighter, always had been. Her father had often called his wife a firecracker, and she was that. Not just because of her auburn hair but also because she never gave up on anything important. Marlee got all of that from her mother.

"You doing all right, pumpkin?" her mother asked.

Marlee had stopped lying about her jobs in an effort to save her family because her mother knew the truth. "This is a hard one, Mom."

"Did you find the baby?"

"I'm ninety-five percent sure."

"I know these jobs take a toll on you. I hear it in your voice, and I see it on your face when you come home." Her mother sighed. "But this is your gift. As hard as it is, you have a knack for knowing where to go and who to see. Don't ever forget that."

Marlee smiled. "Thanks. I wasn't really looking for a pep talk."

"Sure, you were," her mom stated. "You just didn't know it."

Marlee laughed, but it soon faded. "I'm sorry I'm not there to take care of you."

"Don't you dare. I don't need you to take care of me. I need you to find those missing babies. I know how those families are suffering. So do you. That's what makes you so damn good at your job. Don't think about me, sweetheart. Your father and I are fine. Pam is wonderful. Just come home every now and again so I can see you. But I want you to know that we support you."

"I love you, Mom."

"I love you, too, pumpkin. Now, go get to work."

Her mother ended the call, and all Marlee could do was shake her head. Her parents put up a good front, but she knew that their health wasn't good. It tore her up to be away from them. After this job, she was going to spend a few months at home. She needed it, and they needed it. And if luck was on her side, Marlee would have this job wrapped up before Thanksgiving.

She was about to shut her laptop when an email alert came across her screen from John in Dallas. Another child had been taken. Less than a week old, an infant girl had been snatched from a woman who was putting the car seat into a vehicle at a shopping mall. Two cameras—each with a different angle—caught the entire thing. However, there wasn't a clear view of the two individuals. Making it even more difficult was the fact that they wore ski caps, covering their hair and most of their faces.

This wasn't the first time a baby had been snatched in such a way, but it would take some work to see if the case matched others over the last couple of decades. Investigators like her would be working quickly to try and get a jump on the kidnappers and figure out where they might take the baby.

Usually, Marlee joined in on the hunt, but she'd been on this job for a long time and felt confident that she could wrap it up soon. She might not actively join the others in the search, but she'd keep her eyes peeled since Clearview wasn't too far from Dallas. The more eyes, the better on such cases. That's why Amber Alerts were so successful.

Kidnapping was a tricky business. Taking a young child or a baby made it so they didn't remember their families, which sometimes made things even harder on those searching for them.

Marlee shut her computer and got to her feet. She was more determined than ever to close her current case. It affected her more than usual. That generally meant it was time for her to take a break and recharge. There were other ways outside of traveling for her to help the investigators. And that's precisely what she was going to do once she got home to her parents.

She put on her coat and grabbed her keys and purse before heading to her car. The restaurants were filling up with customers wanting dinner, so Marlee headed to the local café, which happened to be Cooper's favorite based on her reconnaissance. There was no guarantee that he'd be there, though. If he wasn't, she'd try later. If he was . . . well, then she would proceed with her plan.

Marlee parked and walked inside. She never minded eating alone, but doing so resulted in being stared at by others. She never understood it, but she had learned to ignore it. The café had an old-time diner feel to it. She had been in here for breakfast before and had sat at the bar then. This time, she chose a booth and faced the entrance. The seats were powder blue, and the table white. Both had a classic look, but they were brand-new.

The waitress walked over and handed her a menu as Marlee took off her coat. The waitress was in her thirties and had her blond hair up in a bun. She wore a dark blue fifties-style waitress uniform, complete with white sneakers. "Evenin'. What can I get you to drink?"

Marlee looked at the choices of beer on tap. "I'll take a Yuengling, please. And water."

"Comin' up," the waitress stated with a grin and walked away.

Marlee went back to perusing the menu, trying to decide between a burger or something a little healthier like the grilled fish and veggies. The café might look like a diner, but it had an assortment of food for everyone. Suddenly, her hair rose on the back of her neck again. She stiffened and slowly turned her head to look out the window, but once again, she couldn't locate anyone.

"Well, hello."

She recognized Cooper's voice immediately. Her head snapped around, and she found herself smiling before she knew it, her possible watcher forgotten. "Hi."

"Not sure if you've been here before, but the food is excellent. You can't go wrong with any of it," Cooper told her, his eyes crinkling at the corners. "And I can say that honestly because I've had everything on the menu."

Marlee laughed softly. "Have you?"

"It's my favorite place to eat."

"Then you must have a favorite meal."

His grin widened. "The blackened crab nachos. They're out of this world. Trust me."

She nodded, spotting the nachos on the menu. "They do look good."

"Marlee," he said and cleared his throat as he glanced around to see if anyone was listening. "I'm sorry about earlier. I didn't mean to freak you out."

"It's fine. Really."

"It isn't. We don't get many new visitors in town, and you're a beautiful woman. I'm sure you get approached all the time."

She never got approached, but she wasn't going to tell him that. "Thank you for the compliment."

"I just want you to know that I'm a good guy. Promise," he said with a smile.

Marlee held his gaze for a heartbeat. This was her chance. It was now or never. She took a deep breath and said, "Prove it. Have dinner with me. We each pay our own way, and we share some conversation."

"All right," he said without hesitation. "I'm game."

She motioned to the seat opposite her. Cooper removed his coat and tossed it into the booth before he slid in. Marlee got a view of his cute ass in his jeans, but the broad shoulders showcased by the blue and green plaid flannel shirt he wore really got her attention. Near his throat, she glimpsed a black thermal shirt.

He filled the booth and took all of her attention in the process. Her training as a police officer made her aware of everyone and everything. Not so when Cooper was near. He was all she saw.

I can't do this.

But she had to. Whether she wanted to or not, people were counting on her. No one had ever made her second guess herself before. Or maybe she just didn't want to cause Cooper any harm because he was genuinely a good guy.

That was it. She'd met so few people in her life that were decent human beings. She wasn't sure what to do with one, even when he was seated across from her.

Liar. You know exactly *what you'd like to do to him. Beginning with stripping him out of those clothes.*

Marlee swallowed and pushed up the sleeves of her sweater as heat filled her. Her nipples hardened, making her want to reach up and cover them so they'd stop tingling. But Cooper was there, looking at her with those gorgeous forest green eyes of his.

"You sure about this?" he asked, a worried frown filling his face.

She nodded her head—a little too quickly. "Yep."

Marlee inwardly winced at how high-pitched her voice was. Given Cooper's expression, he wasn't buying her lie.

"I won't hurt you," Cooper said. "You don't have to be afraid of me. I won't even walk you out to your car when you finish eating if you don't want."

He finished with a grin meant to ease her mind. If only that were the issue.

Marlee made herself relax. "I'm sorry."

"No need to apologize. I'm sure being a woman isn't easy. My mom used to get asked out all the time. She was afraid for herself at times, so I'm keenly aware of how you might perceive me," he told her.

"Your mom is fine, though, right?"

Cooper chuckled. "The woman is amazing. My dad died when I was thirteen, and she raised me on her own. She faced any hardship that came her way with her back straight and chin raised. When she feared for her life, she took self-defense classes and honed her shooting skills. But she did teach me how to respect women and know when to back off."

"She sounds wonderful."

"She is," he said with a smile.

Marlee nodded her thanks to the waitress when she delivered Marlee's beer. Cooper ordered his own. When they were alone again, Marlee asked, "So, the two of you are close? You and your mom."

"Very. She owns a hair salon on Main Street."

Of course, Marlee knew that. Just as she knew that Betty Owens had raised Cooper on her own. However, Marlee hadn't known the Betty that Cooper spoke of so highly. Research only showed you so much about a person.

"What about you?" Cooper asked. "You have family?"

Marlee dreaded this part. She often left talk of Macey out, altogether. Not because she was embarrassed but because people genuinely didn't know how to react. She was saved from answering when the waitress returned with Cooper's beer and waited for them to order.

Cooper looked at her, still waiting for her to tell him about herself. How Marlee wished she could gloss over this part.

But it wasn't to be.

Chapter 7

He could look into Marlee's soft brown eyes for eternity. She had a wall up, a formidable one at that, but Cooper didn't begrudge her for that. He had no idea what she'd suffered in her past. All he knew was that he wanted to get to know her. She was the only thing he'd thought about since meeting her at the gas station.

That five-minute meeting had left a lasting impression for sure.

And then to find her at the café? He couldn't believe his luck. He'd thought to just stop by and say hello, maybe talk to her a little more so she wouldn't run from him. The next thing he knew, he was sitting with her for dinner.

She observed him when he spoke as if she were interested in every word he said. Yet the minute the conversation switched to her, that wall rose a little higher.

"My parents are still around," she finally said.

He wanted to probe for more, but he sensed that was all he was going to get out of her. "I'm sure you've been asked this a lot, but are you visiting or moving to the area?"

"Just visiting."

Damn. Getting information out of her was like pulling teeth. However, Cooper wasn't put off by it. He smiled. "I hope you'll be in town for a bit. Clearview might not look like much, but it actually has quite a bit of character."

"It's quiet. Reminds of me of where I grew up," she said.

The moment the words were out of her mouth, it appeared as if she regretted them.

Instead of asking her where she was from, Cooper said, "I volunteer at a sanctuary nearby. They take in all kinds of animals, but mainly, it's for horses. If you have some free time, you should check it out."

"That sounds nice. I might do that. I think I saw a sign about it a few days ago."

And just like that, Marlee seemed relaxed again. Cooper inwardly patted himself on the back. This woman got more intriguing by the moment. She was like a flower. If he wanted to discover anything about her, he needed to go slow and allow each petal to open so he could learn more about her.

"One of my best friends' wife is an equine veterinarian. Audrey takes care of the horses at their ranch, the Rockin' H, as well as at the East Ranch. In between all of that, she tends to the animals at the sanctuary."

Marlee drank some of her beer and put her forearms on the table, leaning forward. "The East Ranch? That's a prominent place around here."

"Yep. You'll never meet nicer people than Clayton and Abby East. They'd give you the shirts off their backs. Abby has two younger brothers, Brice and Caleb. My best friend, Jace, and I befriended Brice and Caleb at a young age and found ourselves at the ranch all the time. Abby and Clayton took full advantage of us being there and had us helping out all the time." Cooper smiled, thinking back to those days. "We've remained close friends ever since."

"It must be nice to have people you've known for that long."

"It is."

"But," she paused, her brow furrowing, "does anyone ever really know someone else?"

Cooper wrapped his fingers around his cold bottle of beer and brought it to his lips as he regarded Marlee. He didn't answer until the bottle was back on the table. "I think it depends on the people you let into your life. For me, Jace, Caleb, and Brice, we're brothers. We've had each other's backs for years, and that won't change. Ever."

"People say they have others' backs all the time," she replied with a shrug.

"Maybe. But can they say they've joined forces with the local authorities to bring down a ring of individuals who were making the women in the rodeo pageants nothing more than prostitutes to win the crown and the money? Can those people say they joined the local authorities to stop a veterinarian from killing horses? Can those people say they joined the authorities to stop a madman from killing the sheriff and his girlfriend?"

Marlee's eyes widened. "Are you serious? You've done all that?"

"You sound surprised."

"I am," she stated with a nod. Her bourbon-colored eyes darted away for a heartbeat. "You did all of that for your friends?"

Cooper nodded slowly. "And I know they'd do the same for me."

"You're telling me you can sit here and honestly tell me that none of your friends have been involved in anything illegal?"

He jerked back as if hit. "Damn straight, I can. Danny Oldman, the sheriff, made sure we kept our noses clean and did so all the way back to when he was a sheriff's deputy. Ryan Wells, the chief of police, is also a friend. You don't have friends like that if you're engaged in anything illegal."

"Some might claim that having those kinds of friends that you can ask to look the other way is exactly what you want."

Cooper leaned back and put an arm along the back of the booth. He had the feeling that Marlee was after something specific, and he wished she'd get there. "I'm a straight shooter, Marlee. If you have a question, just ask it. I don't do well with beating around the bush. And by the things you're saying, you know the question you want to ask."

She slowly sat back, though her hands still rested on the table. She clasped them together and drew in a deep breath. "I don't want to ask it."

"I think you need to. For both our sakes." Their food arrived, though neither looked at the waitress. Cooper's gut clenched. All this time, he'd held out hope that she might find him attractive, but he was beginning to suspect that she had an agenda.

"You really want me to ask it?"

He gave a single nod. "Yes, ma'am."

Marlee licked her lips. "Is there a chance that Brice and Naomi paid someone to kidnap a baby for them?"

The question hung in the air between them. Cooper was shocked to his very bones that Marlee would even think such a thing. But it was the way she worded it—as if she knew Brice and Naomi personally.

That wall around Marlee? It was put up out of fear. She erected it to keep people like him from learning anything about her.

Anger boiled within Cooper, but he kept his temper in check. He leaned forward, his voice low as he said, "I've been sitting here, charming you, making sure not to ask questions I know you wouldn't answer and otherwise doing my damnedest to woo you. And all this time, you only wanted to find out about my friends. You should've asked instead of wasting our time." He slid out of the booth and drew out his wallet to toss down enough cash to pay for his meal. Then he grabbed his jacket. "The answer to your question is, no, they would never do anything so heinous. They're good people. You'd know that if you talked to them."

Cooper left the café, got into his truck, and drove off. He had no idea where he was going until he ended up headed straight for the Rockin' H. Cooper didn't want to talk to Brice or Caleb about this now. He needed to calm down first. Cooper altered his course and went to Jace's apartment instead.

He banged his fist on the door.

A second later, Jace opened it. His smile died as he took a step back to let Cooper enter. "What the hell happened?"

Cooper walked farther into the apartment and found Ryan Wells there. He nodded at Ryan, though he still hadn't said anything.

"Whoa," Ryan said as he quirked a brow from where he sat at the kitchen table. "When I saw you earlier, you were all smiles, talking about that redhead you met. Does this mean she turned you down?"

Jace frowned. "Wait. What? I thought I had dibs on the redhead."

"You can have her," Cooper stated and strode to the fridge to get a beer. But as he reached for one, he changed his mind and slammed the door. Then he turned and grabbed the bottle of bourbon.

"Ah, shit," Jace said. "It's bad if he's skipping beer and going straight for the bourbon."

Ryan was all serious as he said, "Coop, tell us what happened."

Cooper went to drink from the bottle but Jace took it from him and poured some into a glass. Cooper tossed that back before he yanked out a chair and sat at the table. "I ran into Marlee at the café. I thought it was innocent, but she was there to meet me."

"Why do you say that?" Jace asked as he leaned back against the counter, watching him.

Cooper shrugged. "Oh, because all she wanted to know was if Naomi and Brice paid someone to kidnap a baby for them."

"What?" Jace bellowed in outrage. "She's out of her mind!"

"What if she's not?" Ryan asked calmly.

Cooper swung his gaze to the chief. "What do you mean?"

"I know you've both heard about the string of murders and the babies that have been taken."

Jace made a face. "Yeah. Crazy assholes."

"Without a doubt," Ryan said. "However, recently, a week-old infant was abducted at a shopping mall in Dallas."

Rage still burned in Cooper, but not nearly as brightly. He held out his glass for Jace to fill again. After tossing back another swallow, Cooper looked at Ryan.

"What can you find out about Marlee?"

Chapter 8

She'd blown it. Marlee couldn't believe she'd been so fucking stupid as to blurt out the very thing she wanted to know. All because Cooper had drawn her in and made her think she could ask him anything.

"Stupid. So damn stupid," she reprimanded herself once she was back in her motel room.

She paced the small space, her mind going through the various options she had. Usually, she liked to scrutinize an area and the subjects to gather as much evidence as she could. Only then did she approach law enforcement with her proof and let them take it from there.

This job had been different from the very beginning. She thought it was because she had just come from her last case that hadn't ended well.

Being unable to locate a missing child always struck her particularly hard. Sometimes, she was able to uncover things the authorities missed, which helped to find the child. Other times . . . well, other times it didn't go so well.

In some cases, the child seemed to simply vanish. In those instances, she never gave up hope and never stopped looking. Those cases—and there were more than she wanted to admit—were filed at her home office. She often looked through them, seeing if she could find something new.

But the worst cases were the ones when she had to inform parents that their child was dead. Those weighed heavily on her. And that was what'd happened with her last job. She could still hear the mother's grief as she wailed her misery, her husband simply holding her, his tears falling silently down his face.

The scene was so reminiscent of her parents when she'd told them about Macey and the baby that it took her months to shake it off.

Marlee stopped in the middle of the room next to the bed. She looked at the pictures scattered across the duvet and on the wall. The one of Naomi and Brice Harper looking lovingly at each other struck her. Maybe it was because of the strange and unwanted feelings Cooper stirred within her, or perhaps it was his icy fury at the thought of his friends doing something unlawful. Still, Marlee knew she had to deviate from her usual *modus operandi*.

Now that Cooper knew what she was about, she only had two choices. She could go to the police and give them what little she had, or . . . she could go to the Harpers and talk to them.

It only took half a second to decide. She strode from her motel room to her rental. All the way to the Rockin' H Ranch, Marlee went over how she would approach the couple. She listed her qualifications, how she came to have her current assignment, and detailed what she needed. It was so good that she went over it a second and a third time.

But the minute she stood before their door, and it opened to reveal Naomi, everything Marlee had planned rushed out of her head.

"Hi," Naomi said with a small frown, her chestnut eyes filled with concern. "Can I help you?"

"Who is it, babe?" a deep voice asked from behind her. A moment later, Brice's tall frame came into view. His dark brown hair was trimmed neatly as he wrapped an arm around his wife. "Hi there," Brice said. "How can we help?"

Marlee's stomach tightened with anxiety. A part of her wanted to make up some excuse and run away, but she couldn't. She knew that. So, she steeled herself and swallowed. "I'm sorry to intrude and to come by so late. My name is Marlee Frampton. I'm a private investigator, and I was wondering if I could speak with the two of you."

Unease had Naomi's hand tightening on the door. Brice didn't so much as twitch. Marlee met the couple's stare and waited for them to make a decision.

Brice's voice was even as he said, "We got a call from the chief of police, Ryan Wells. Cooper told him about you. Ryan suspected you might stop by."

Naomi nodded to Brice. He then released his wife so she could move and open the door wider. "Please, come in," Naomi told Marlee.

As soon as she walked into the house, she felt its welcoming embrace. There was love here, and it gave off an energy that couldn't be dismissed. Marlee looked at the entry that was both simplistic and amazingly stylish. An elegant table with iron legs and a thick wooden top sat against the wall. Two stacks of books were piled on its surface, one on either side of a clear vase with a floral arrangement inside. A large, oval mirror hung on the wall above the table. Opposite the table was a large photograph of a pasture at sunset with horses grazing. It was so stunning that Marlee couldn't look away.

"That picture is . . . I can't even put it in words," she said.

Brice smiled. "Naomi has a gift, that's for sure."

"Thank you," Naomi told her.

Marlee glanced at the floor, embarrassed to have forgotten that Naomi was a photographer.

"Let's go into the living room," Naomi said and motioned to a doorway.

She led the way with Marlee following her. Brice brought up the rear. After being invited to sit in a chair, Marlee quickly took in the clean lines of the furniture and the neutral colors that gave her a feeling of peace.

"Would you like some coffee or tea?" Naomi asked.

Brice raised a brow. "Or something stronger? You look like you might need it."

Marlee smiled despite herself. "I'm not going to lie, a stiff drink sounds nice, but I think it's better if I refrain for now."

"Then why don't you tell us what brought you here?" Brice stated as he sat beside his wife on the sofa.

In an instant, she knew that Brice was on edge, but he was keeping it in check for Naomi. Marlee didn't blame them. She'd likely be acting similarly if the roles were reversed. That didn't make things any easier, however.

"I don't normally come to the family first," she began. "I have a set path I take on cases, and I rarely deviate from it. But this case isn't like any others."

Naomi glanced at Brice. "What case?"

Marlee leaned forward to brace her forearms on her legs and clasped her hands together. Her chin dropped to her chest, and she gave a small shake of her head before looking up again. "Long ago, I worked as a police officer for a small town in California. A case there led me to where I am now."

Brice leaned back, his pale blue eyes locked on her. "I have a friend who is a private investigator."

"Then you might understand that while most PIs take

on all sorts of cases, some of us specialize in specific areas."

Naomi fidgeted. "What kind of area do you specialize in?"

"Missing children."

The moment she said the words, the couple stiffened. Naomi's face paled with shock, while Brice looked as if he wanted to tear someone in two.

Brice asked, "Why are you here? Specifically."

"Because I believe the child you adopted is the same little boy who was cut from his mother a little over a week ago," she told them. She hadn't meant to be so graphic, but the sooner they realized how serious the issue was, the quicker they might be willing to help her.

Brice said nothing as he closed his eyes. Naomi held his hand as if it were the only thing keeping her grounded. Her frantic gaze searched Marlee's face. "We did everything we were supposed to do. You must be mistaken. We never would've been involved in anything so horrible. You don't know us, but let me assure you, we did everything by the book."

"I'm sure you did," Marlee told the couple as Brice lifted his lids and met her gaze. "However, some of the adoption agencies also do adoptions off the books. Meaning—"

"We know what you mean," Brice interrupted her. "What do you need from us to know if Nate is the missing baby or not?"

Marlee didn't let herself breathe a sigh of relief just yet. Brice asking what she wanted didn't mean the couple would cooperate. "A DNA sample for one. Since the infant I'm looking for never saw a hospital, they don't have any records. However, his father and two other siblings submitted their DNA for comparison."

Naomi wiped at a tear that ran down her face. "We

tried for so long to have a child. When we learned we couldn't, we weighed our options. Finally, we decided on adoption. Then we began researching all the different agencies. We went with the one with the best rating. You have to be mistaken."

"I hope I am," Marlee told them honestly. "I really do. If I am, I begin my search all over again."

Naomi sniffed, anger filling her face. "If you aren't, then you'll take Nate away from us."

"To return to his rightful family," Brice told her and wrapped an arm around his wife to draw her close. "You wouldn't want to do that to a child, would you, sweetheart? Keep him from his parents?" he asked in a soft voice.

Marlee's heartstrings tugged. Not just for the couple, but also at the idea that she'd probably never have anyone to talk to her in such a manner. She had set out on her path without looking back or regret. Like her mother said, she had a destiny. And she was going to follow it.

Naomi turned toward Brice, resting her head on his shoulder. Marlee hoped they didn't push back. She had evidence to bring to the authorities, but it wasn't as much as she usually did. With the fact that the Harpers knew the sheriff and the chief of police, there was a chance the authorities wouldn't help her. In which case, Marlee would just continue to gather evidence.

"I have this, if it helps." She pulled a file from her purse and set it on the coffee table. It held a copy of all the evidence she'd gathered so far. Including everything on the Family First Adoption Agency.

Brice stared at the file for a long moment before he leaned forward and spun it around. Then, after a deep breath, he opened it. Naomi was the first to reach for a page and begin sifting through it.

Marlee sat silently, watching as the couple went through

page after page. A few items in there didn't have proof, just Marlee's gut feelings. Anyone without investigation experience didn't often understand those hunches. She could only pray that Brice and Naomi would.

It felt like years passed before Brice handed the last paper to Naomi, and she put them together and returned them to the file. The couple then looked at each other, their hands locked together. Once more, Marlee realized that she would likely never have someone she could turn to like that. It set off an ache inside her that she hadn't felt before.

"We'll help," Naomi said as she turned her head to Marlee. She wiped at her eyes again. "The agency gave us hospital records. Do you need those?"

Marlee nodded, relief surging through her. "That would be helpful, yes."

"What do we need to do?" Brice asked.

Marlee really hoped that Nate wasn't the child she was looking for. She had spoken to other couples like this, and they were all devastated. But there was something different about this couple. "Can you bring Nate to the hospital tomorrow? We can set up a time to meet. I have the forms needed so the hospital can conduct their tests and get the samples we need."

"We can do that." Naomi was once more back in control of her emotions. "Now that you've told us these things happen, I want to have everything in the folder we got from the agency confirmed."

Marlee got to her feet, feeling worse than she normally did at these meetings. "I am sorry. My job is to get the children back to their families. Trust me when I say that one of the hardest parts is taking a child from people like you."

At that moment, a cry sounded through the baby monitor. Naomi jumped up and made her way to the stairs. Brice stood and said, "I'll see you out."

They were both silent as they walked to the door. Marlee paused once she opened it and then looked back at Brice. "No matter how this goes, please believe me when I say I'm sorry."

"I can see it in your eyes." Brice blew out a breath. "How long have you been surveilling Naomi and me?"

There was no need to lie now. The truth of her arrival in Clearview was now known. "About a week. When the baby was kidnapped, I started keeping tabs on any male infants going up for adoption in the area. I then began investigating you, your ranch, and your family."

"What about the agency?" he asked. "I looked into them myself. Thoroughly. Even the evidence you gave us to look at doesn't say much."

Marlee looked away. "Maybe now isn't a good time to talk about that."

"When *is* a good time?" he demanded. "I think I have a right to ask these questions."

Marlee shut the door to keep the cold out and met his gaze. "You absolutely do. I said that because you won't like what I have to tell you."

"I haven't liked much of what you've said since you arrived. What makes this any different?"

She deserved that. Marlee didn't take it personally, though. "The government watches adoption agencies, but like all things, if someone wants to do something nefarious, they can. Thousands of children and babies are kidnapped every day in the US alone. Most of them are never found again or even realize they have been taken from their families. Some are located, but I only bring back bodies to those families."

"How many do you return to their families alive?" Brice asked in a soft voice.

"Not nearly enough."

He sat there for a moment in silence before he asked, "Can you meet us at ten in the morning?"

She nodded. "Absolutely."

As Marlee walked from the house, Brice said, "Perhaps next time, try not to use someone's friend to get answers. You should've come to us first."

Her steps halted as she thought about Cooper and the way he'd smiled at her. Then she recalled how cold his expression had gotten when she asked about his friends. Marlee looked over her shoulder at Brice. "I was completely out of line going to Cooper. I've never done anything like that before. I just thought . . . I've been doing this for long enough to know better than to do what I did. That's why I came here tonight, Mr. Harper. I'm trying to sort through the mess I've made of things."

He nodded slowly. "Be careful out there. The roads ice up quickly in weather like this."

And with that, he shut the door.

Chapter 9

Banging on his door woke Cooper. He pushed up on his arms and looked at his phone beside the bed to find that it was just after five in the morning. He twisted to get out of bed and grabbed his head as it throbbed in time to the pounding on his door.

"All right, all right!" he shouted angrily. "I'm coming. Just stop knocking."

He couldn't remember getting home last night, which meant that he had drunk more than usual. Cooper wasn't concerned, though. He knew his friends had gotten him home safely.

As he opened the door, he found Jace leaning against the doorjamb, dangling Cooper's keys on his finger. Jace's grin broadened as he raked his gaze down Cooper. "I didn't strip you to your undies when I tucked you into bed last night."

Cooper glanced down at himself to find only a pair of black boxer briefs covering his body. He turned around with a groan. "You're early."

"I tried to get you to sleep at my place last night, but you demanded I bring you home," Jace replied as he walked into the house and shut the door behind him harder than necessary.

Cooper winced, but he didn't say anything. He shuffled his way to the kitchen and pulled out some orange juice, drinking it straight from the carton.

"Hair of the dog, my friend." Jace tossed the keys on the counter and shook his head. "You know from experience, the only thing that'll dull that ache in your head is a swig of alcohol."

After Cooper finished the OJ, he reached for the bourbon in his pantry and poured a shot. He drank it and then replaced the bottle before he turned to Jace. "Tell me I didn't do anything stupid."

"You mean besides talking about Marlee all night?" Jace twisted his lips and shook his head. "Nope."

"Wonderful." Cooper pivoted and went to the bathroom to grab some ibuprofen. He took two and shut the door. "Going to take a quick shower," he called.

He heard Jace's laughter as he turned on the water. This wasn't the first time he'd been hungover. He and Jace traded places every couple of months with who was laughing at who the next morning. If only he hadn't bumped into Marlee the night before. Maybe he wouldn't be in this predicament.

By the time Cooper stepped out of the shower, he felt much better. He dressed and walked back out to Jace, who had cooked bacon and made some toast. He handed a piece to Cooper, and he didn't hesitate to eat.

"You were pretty upset last night," Jace said as he joined him at the table.

Cooper shrugged. "Damn straight, I was. Can you believe anyone would think that about Brice and Naomi?"

"Was that really what upset you?"

Cooper froze with a piece of toast halfway to his mouth. "Yeah."

"I'm not so sure."

"I think I would know what I'm pissed about."

Jace shrugged. "Not always. You forget I've known you for nearly our entire lives. You were angry about Brice and Naomi, yes. But deep down, what really upset you was that you thought Marlee wasn't interested in you. That she just wanted to get information about our friends."

"You're wrong."

"I'm not, but you can't see it now. You will, though," Jace stated and shoved a piece of bacon into his mouth.

Cooper shook his head and went back to eating. He didn't want to get into an argument right now with his head still throbbing. They ate in silence for several minutes. Jace bobbed his head as if listening to music, and Cooper kept thinking about what his friend had said about Marlee. He didn't want it to be true, but dammit if it wasn't.

"I'd like to do some digging into who Marlee is," Cooper said. "If she's nosing around us, then I want to make sure she's legit."

"She is."

When Jace didn't elaborate, Cooper stared at him. "You want to tell me what you know?"

"Sure. Just as soon as you ask nicely."

Cooper looked at the ceiling and slowly blew out a breath. He had a cool temperament, but Jace knew how to push all his buttons. Though Cooper knew how to rile him just as easily. That's what happened with friends who had known each other for as long as they had.

"Please tell me what you found out about Marlee," Cooper asked.

Jace grinned. "See? That was easy."

Cooper rose and took their empty plates to the sink to rinse them. "Thanks for breakfast."

"What are friends for?" Jace asked with a shrug. "Now,

to get to your question, you really intrigued both me and Ryan last night. The more you drank, the more you talked about Marlee. So, Ryan looked her up. Turns out, Marlee Frampton is a PI. She was once a cop in California."

"She was a cop?" Cooper asked with a frown.

Jace folded his arms across his chest. "Look, I'm going to tell you that I completely agree with how you reacted yesterday. I'd have done worse, I'm sure."

"But?"

"You've had some dealings with PIs."

Cooper blew out a breath. "You're speaking of Cash."

"Yep. He's able to get the tough jobs done."

"I know. What does he have to do with Marlee?"

Jace dropped his arms to his sides and shifted his feet. "Marlee isn't just any PI, Coop. She specializes in kidnapped children."

"Okay," he said slowly, letting that sink in. "Wouldn't there be easier money in other things like finding cheating spouses and such?"

"No doubt. But Marlee got involved because of an incident in her past. Her sister was eight months pregnant when she was murdered, the babe cut out of her and taken."

"Ah, shit." Cooper couldn't imagine having to deal with such a loss.

Jace ran a hand down his face. "As a cop, Marlee did all that she could. The Feds took over when another pregnant woman was killed, and her baby stolen in another state. Unfortunately, they didn't get anywhere."

"Marlee decided to find the answers herself," Cooper finished.

"It didn't take long for Ryan to find out that Marlee is good at what she does. Very good. She brings closure to families one way or another."

"And her sister's case? Was it solved?"

Jace shook his head. "No."

"How long ago was that?"

"Ten years."

Cooper shrugged. "I know what we'd do if this was one of our friends."

"We'd jump in with both feet," Jace said with a grin.

"You game?"

"Just try and stop me."

Cooper laughed. "Let's go find Marlee and see if we can lend a hand."

"Actually," Jace called before Cooper reached for his coat, "I've got another idea."

"What's that?"

"Marlee is looking for a kidnapped baby. While I get why she's focusing on Brice and Naomi, they can't be the only ones with a newly adopted child in the area."

Cooper frowned because he couldn't agree with or refute the statement. "We might be biting off more than we can chew."

"Maybe. But you and I both know Brice and Naomi would never have gotten involved with an agency that sells babies on the black market."

"No, I know they wouldn't. At least, not knowingly."

"You think the agency might have slipped a baby in?" Jace frowned as he wrinkled his nose. "Naw. Not with how thorough Brice and Naomi were in their research. Besides, the agency did a background check on them."

Cooper had forgotten about that. "So, they knew Brice and Naomi were well-off and had connections to the East Ranch."

"No way the adoption agency would've pulled a fast one on them."

Cooper shrugged. "Though, who better to give such a child to than a couple like them?"

Jace sighed loudly. "I know why Marlee does this job, but damn. I don't know how she handles it."

Cooper did. She put up walls. Not because she was afraid of people, but because she had suffered a tragedy the likes of which few understood. Her way of dealing with things was to find the missing children.

"I know that look," Jace said. "You've got an idea."

A slow smile pulled at Cooper's lips. "I do."

"You sure? You don't think Marlee might get upset?"

"If her end goal is to reunite the stolen kids with their families, I don't think she'll mind."

Jace thought about that a moment. "Maybe so. You want to bring Danny and Ryan in on this?"

"Danny's wedding to Skylar is approaching. I don't want to add anything to his plate. We'll keep Ryan in the loop, but let's do this just between us."

"Then you need to catch up on some news."

Cooper's brows snapped together. "What are you talking about?"

"Yesterday morning, your mom and I were talking about the last woman who was killed and her baby stolen."

Cooper couldn't believe he'd forgotten that. "That was where? Houston?"

"Dallas."

He cleared his throat. "Look in the drawer to your left. There's a map of Texas."

While Jace got that, Cooper found a blue marker. They spread out the map on the table as they both looked at it.

"Yep. That's Texas," Jace stated. "She's awfully big."

Cooper rolled his eyes. "You said I needed to catch up on the news, so catch me up. Let's mark where these murders and kidnappings have taken place."

"Ah. To see if they have a favorite place."

"Yep."

Cooper leaned over the table and marked Dallas as Jace read the news brief from the day before. Over the next hour, they had more than a dozen spots marked at

Dallas, Austin, San Antonio, and Houston, with some sprinkled between all the cities going back over a decade.

There had to be a relationship between them, but Cooper couldn't see it. He straightened to stretch his back, then froze as he caught the pattern.

"What are you doing? I've got another one," Jace said.

Cooper pointed to Clearview, which was situated nearly right in the middle of all the cities.

"That can't be right," Jace said.

Cooper tossed down the marker. "This is going to take a lot more digging than we realized."

"And the cases keep going further and further back. Coop, what the hell have we stumbled onto?"

"I don't know, but I think we're about to find out."

Chapter 10

Caffeine was her addiction. It wasn't a healthy one, but Marlee knew there were worse ones. In the early morning hours, she pulled her baseball cap low over her face and walked into the donut shop. She got a croissant with ham, egg, and cheese and a large coffee. Her penchant for sweets was satisfied when the owner dropped two donut holes into the bag. That saved Marlee from not only giving in to the need for a full-sized donut, but also the calories that went along with it.

She smiled in gratitude when he handed her the coffee. She used to take it with lots of cream and sugar, but too many stakeouts had driven her to learn to like it black. Her eyes closed as she let the hot, caffeinated liquid slide down her throat. It would take more than one sip to get her moving, but the first taste was like manna from the gods.

By the time she was on her third sip, her order was ready. Marlee paid and hurried back out through the cold to jump into her car. She longed for the temperate climate of California. The cold was really affecting her here. But that wasn't all that had put her off-kilter in a way she hadn't been since her sister's death.

Marlee started the car and let the heat begin to fill the vehicle before she reached inside the bag for her food. Her fingers brushed the glazed donut hole first. She usually waited to eat them last, but this morning, she needed the sugar along with the caffeine.

As she munched on it and unwrapped her croissant sandwich, a truck pulled up next to her. She ignored it. In a town full of nothing but SUVs and large work trucks, she had gotten used to being dwarfed in her tiny rental. The smell of the delicious breakfast sandwich made her stomach rumble in anticipation. She had stumbled upon the little donut shop on the outskirts of town early on, simply because she needed coffee. But it quickly became a favorite.

She happily ate her breakfast and drank her coffee while listening to the radio. Her love of eighties music was often joked about, but she didn't care. Hair bands and power ballads were her things. She ignored passersby and focused on her meal. Marlee didn't allow herself to think about the case, the Harpers, and especially not Cooper. These few minutes in the mornings were all hers to clear her mind and mentally get herself where she needed to be.

When she happened to look out her windshield, her gaze locked with forest green eyes. Cooper stood before her car with his cowboy hat on, and his hands tucked into the pockets of his coat. He nodded. For a heartbeat, Marlee wasn't sure what to do, so she lifted her hand in a little wave. To her shock, Cooper walked to the passenger side of her car.

Marlee unlocked it and watched as he folded his large frame into the rental. His knees hit the dashboard until he slid the seat back as far as it could go. She finished chewing, her gaze on him as he stared forward. She wasn't sure if he would berate her, threaten her, or what. And for some reason, she had allowed him inside the car to do whatever he wanted.

"I heard you went to see Naomi and Brice last night," Cooper said, still not looking in her direction.

Marlee lifted the coffee cup to her lips and took a drink before saying, "I did."

"Do you really think Nate is the stolen infant you're looking for?"

"If I didn't believe there was a chance, I wouldn't be here," she told him.

He blew out a breath and dropped his chin to his chest. "Fair enough."

"I was wrong to approach you last night. It's not something I usually do, but I want to get this case solved."

His gaze lifted to the windshield. "I can understand that. I just wish you would've told me."

"I did that once. It was my second case. I thought I'd get somewhere faster if I just told those I was investigating what I was about. The moment I did, they vanished with the child. I never found them again."

Cooper closed his eyes for a moment. "I'm talking to you like you know me, but you don't. Not really. You couldn't possibly know how I'd react if you came to me with the truth."

"No," she said with a shake of her head. "I might do background checks and surveil everyone for a time to get the gist of someone's character, but I can't really know them."

"How do you do it?" he asked, his head swinging to her.

She shrugged and looked away for a heartbeat when his gaze met hers. "Everyone is good at something. I'm good at this."

"What if you're wrong about Brice and Naomi?"

"There's always that possibility. I look at the facts and follow the evidence. Am I always right? No. Am I usually?" She paused and nodded. "Yes."

Cooper turned his head to face forward. "I can help you. So can my friends. You know how close we all are. Otherwise, you wouldn't have approached me last night. Let us help you find the real infant because I know in my gut that it isn't Brice and Naomi's."

"Did you not hear what I told you about my second case?" she asked in disbelief.

He frowned as he looked her way. "Of course."

"Yet you're asking me to do the very thing I swore never to do again."

"I'm not asking you to."

She blinked, taken aback. "That's exactly what you're doing. There's a very real chance that Nate, while loved dearly by Naomi and Brice, is indeed the baby I'm tracking. Why would I bring you in on my investigation so you can prevent me from learning the truth?"

"Or," he said firmly, "you can look at it another way. You'll find out soon if Nate is the baby you're looking for—which I know he isn't. Once that happens, you have no reason *not* to trust me or my friends."

Well, when he put it like that, she didn't. Marlee sighed and shook her head as she looked forward. "Do you know anything about PIs?"

"A friend from my military days became a PI. He's very good at what he does. Highly sought after and paid well."

Marlee laughed dryly. "Good for him. I likely take on twice as many cases as he does, and I won't even talk about the money. These families are devastated, and many are low-income so they have very little—if anything—they can use to pay."

"You do these pro-bono?"

"Sometimes." She glanced at him. "I saw a lot of things when I was a cop. Things most people can't comprehend. But child abduction cases were the worst for me."

Cooper's lips twitched as he shifted in his seat and looked her way again. "I saw my fair share of things when I was in the Air Force. I can relate. What you're doing is admirable. I want to help. Not just to clear my friends' names, but because I don't like the things I've been learning about how frequently children are taken."

"There are more than you know. Women who can't have children, when IVF hasn't worked. Or, for whatever reason, have been turned down for adoption. They will do anything to get a baby. I've seen it firsthand."

He nodded slowly and rubbed his hands up and down his thighs. "I'm glad you went to Brice and Naomi. They're good people, and while they might not like what's going on, they'll do the right thing."

"I hope so."

"Here," he said and handed her a piece of paper. "It has my cell phone number on it. Call anytime."

She wanted to believe he was interested in helping her. Still, past experience had taught her that people in his position only wanted to help their loved ones—even if that meant committing a crime.

"You won't use it," Cooper said with a wry smile. "But you have it anyway."

Without another word, he got out and closed the door behind him. Marlee turned her head to watch him, amazed to find that he'd parked right next to her. He didn't tarry. Instead, he drove away as soon as he was done with her. She thought about Cooper's visit as she finished her breakfast, washed it down with the remaining coffee, and ate the last donut hole.

Only then did Marlee allow her mind to drift to the

case. There had been no additional reported kidnappings the previous night, which she deemed a win. That didn't mean it hadn't happened. The kidnappers took from all walks of life—the rich, the needy, the poor, the homeless, and most especially those in the country illegally.

Marlee dialed the friend she had in the FBI and put it on speaker as she put her car in reverse and then headed to the hospital.

"Marlee," Stephanie said when she answered the phone.

Stephanie Smith had been Marlee's first contact in the FBI after her sister's murder. She and Stephanie had remained in contact through it all and had established a friendship. Marlee didn't take advantage of that fact, however. She was always careful about how she asked Stephanie for information.

"Hey," Marlee said with a genuine smile on her face. "It feels like forever since we last spoke."

"A week. Tell me how you are, girl."

"The usual."

Stephanie grunted. "That good, huh?"

"Livin' the life, girlfriend."

The two shared a laugh. Then Stephanie said, "You're calling about the recent murders and infant kidnappings."

"Yeah."

"I figured you might. I pulled some data on them as soon as we got notice."

Marlee breathed a sigh of relief. "Steph, you're the best."

"Don't thank me yet."

"Why?" Marlee asked, suddenly wary. Whenever Stephanie said that, it meant bad news was coming.

Stephanie's voice lowered, and it sounded as if she covered her mouth with her hand. "I think I found another woman who was killed with her infant cut from her.

A man was seen near the mother, obviously distraught and trying to revive her. By the time the cops came, he was long gone."

"You sure he wasn't the perp?"

"Based on reports from witnesses, it sounds like they're illegals."

Marlee flattened her lips. "They're terrified of being deported, so they won't go to the cops. Shit."

"It gets worse."

"How can it get worse?"

"They found three more murdered women, all pregnant. One of the babies didn't make it and was left with the women. The three females and the infant were found in an abandoned building in Houston."

Marlee's stomach churned with the news. "Let me guess, all illegals?"

"Yep. There could be more. We just have no idea because those in this country illegally won't come to us."

Marlee pulled into the hospital lot and found a parking spot. She closed her eyes and shook her head. "Thank you."

"I can get in a lot of trouble for giving you this."

"I know. I won't be stupid. I know what to do."

"Do you?" Stephanie asked, her voice harsh. "You're out there on your own. No one should be without a partner in this. Especially you."

It was a reminder of the time she had been attacked by a member of the family she was investigating. "I won't make that mistake again."

"Marlee, you're only one woman. Sure, you've solved cases, but how much longer do you think that can happen going out on your own as you are?"

"Well, you can always quit the FBI and join me." It was a running joke they'd had for years.

Stephanie chuckled, her voice lightening. "Then who would you get all your information from?"

"Good point. I'll check in soon."

"You better," Stephanie threatened.

Chapter 11

If Marlee was surprised to find Cooper at the hospital with Brice and Naomi, she didn't show it. Not that Cooper thought she would. She was nothing if not professional. He wanted so badly to ask her about her sister, but that was something only she could share. If she wanted to talk about it, she would.

And why would she discuss it with someone she barely knew? Someone she still deemed working against her? She wouldn't. He wished he didn't know about it. He wished Jace hadn't told him, but he knew why his friend had. It helped him understand Marlee a little better, as well as gave him insight into what drove her.

Because each of them had something that guided them.

"Damn," Jace whispered as he leaned over to Cooper. "She is stunning."

Marlee's bourbon eyes briefly landed on Cooper, and she flashed him a slight smile—the only thing she did to acknowledge him.

"Yikes," Jace said and flicked his hand as if he'd burned his fingers. There was a smile on his face when he looked at Cooper. "I think I've got a shot with her now."

Cooper was surprised by the fury that rose within him. He bit back his reply to his best friend, the order to stay away from Marlee, but just barely. Instead, he walked away, trying to figure out why he had reacted so violently to a jest.

"Everything all right?"

Cooper turned his head to find Clayton standing beside him. Though fifteen years his senior, Clayton could probably still kick his ass. Clayton had been a Navy SEAL and was damn good at his job. He was an even better rancher.

"Yeah," Cooper replied and found his gaze redrawn to Marlee, who was now speaking with a doctor, Naomi, and Brice.

Clayton made a sound in the back of his throat. "I've known you and Jace for as long as I've known Caleb and Brice. And you know I think of all of you as my younger brothers."

"I know. Jace and I feel the same about all of you."

"Good. So, hear me when I say that while I've seen all of you bicker and fight among yourselves, I've never seen anger like you just had on your face toward Jace. I know you aren't okay."

Cooper ran a hand down his face and turned to Clayton. "Honestly, I don't know what the hell is wrong with me."

"What did Jace say?"

"Just that he had a shot with Marlee."

Clayton suddenly smiled. "It appears you've got a thing for her."

"I barely know her."

"It sometimes takes even less." Clayton turned his head to his wife of eighteen years. "I still remember the first time I saw Abby. When she walked into the interrogation room with Danny at the sheriff's station, all I could think about was how gorgeous she was. I didn't want to talk about Brice being arrested for cattle theft. I just wanted to ask her to dinner."

Cooper watched love fill Clayton's pale green eyes. "I don't think you ever told me that."

Clayton shrugged and returned his gaze to Cooper. "Sometimes, it merely takes a look. Sometimes it takes a meeting, and sometimes it takes longer. But it all ends up the same—with people finding each other."

"I'm not looking for anything. Hell, I don't even know what I want to do with my life."

"Do you have any idea what you do for all of us, Coop? You're there to help out at my ranch, the Rockin' H, your mom's salon, and with Jace without having to be asked. You instinctively know when an extra hand is needed. I won't even go into the many things you've done to help both Danny and Ryan. You might not have a job you clock into every day, but you do have a job. I just wish paying you wasn't an act of God."

Cooper chuckled. "I help my friends. Getting paid for it just seems wrong."

"Have you thought about why you know when you're needed somewhere?"

He thought about it for a moment then shrugged. "No."

"It's because you read people, and you're damned good at it. You also assess situations and see the weak links. That's when you fill those holes."

Cooper crossed his arms over his chest. He appreciated Clayton's words, but he still felt as though he had yet to find the thing that would put him on the right course for the rest of his life. Though he wasn't dissatisfied with his current state of affairs.

"Now," Clayton said, "when it comes to Marlee, you need to think about what's really bugging you."

Cooper frowned as he dropped his arms to his sides. "What do you mean?"

"Are you still pissed because she made sure to be at the café last night to *accidentally* run into you? Are you irritated that she's looking into your friends and the fact they might have gotten themselves into a sticky situation without meaning to? Or are you so tightly wound because you like her, and you don't think she's interested in you?"

"Before I answer that, are you angry at all about this?" Cooper asked and waved his hand around.

Clayton shot him a dry look. "You know I am. But I also realize that if Family First gave Brice and Naomi a kidnapped child, they're not going to know what hit them. We're going to come down on the adoption agency like a hammer. In the meantime, we're going to make sure the child is returned to his rightful family by helping Marlee do her job. This isn't her fault."

"I know it isn't."

"Do you?" Clayton asked as he quirked a brow.

Cooper nodded his head. "I do. I may not act like it, but I do. As for your earlier questions, I think my ego's bruised from her using me. And, if I'm completely honest, I don't think she's interested."

"I don't need to tell you to give her some space. I also talked to Jace earlier. He told me what you and he are doing. Don't crowd Marlee, but I don't think it will take her long to realize that you're helping her. Give her time to trust you. She doesn't have a reason to yet."

"That's what I intended." Cooper squeezed the bridge of his nose. "Did you talk to Ryan?"

"I spoke with Danny. He told me about Marlee's past after learning about her from Ryan. I don't think she's going to like that we've done a background check on her."

Cooper glanced at Marlee to see her still talking to Naomi. Their body language said the tension was gone, though the worry still shone on Naomi's face. "Marlee knows. She's a PI. She'll realize we've checked up on her, especially with us knowing Danny and Ryan."

Marlee started their way, but she halted before reaching them. Clayton slapped Cooper on the back as he nodded at Marlee and headed off. She made her way to Cooper's side, her smile hesitant as if she wasn't sure what to say.

"You were right," she said. "Naomi and Brice just want to help."

Cooper grinned. "How long until the hospital is finished with Nate?"

"Another few minutes, and then Brice and Naomi can take him home."

"You worried they're going to bolt?"

She shoved her hands into the back pockets of her jeans. "That's always a worry. But I hope their close ties to family and friends and how they handled things here means they won't."

"If Nate is the child you're looking for, they'll be crushed, but they won't run. What we'll do to the adoption agency is something else entirely."

"I wish all jobs were this easy." She gave a shake of her auburn curls. "So many start off saying they want to help, but they never really do. Some have waited years to adopt a child."

"You've seen some ugly situations. Does that make you not want children?"

She blinked and scrunched up her nose. "I think I gave up the idea of a private life the moment I started down this path. I don't even have my own place because I'm never there. All of my things are at my parents' house. How can I have a relationship or even children when I'm always on the road for some case or another? I fly all over the country."

"Not internationally?"

"There were a couple of cases where I had to leave the country, but they went cold after that."

He glanced down at the floor. "That might not happen if you had a team."

"A team?" she asked, her brows knitted together.

Cooper nodded as he leaned against the wall. "Since I've not seen anyone with you, I gather you do this on your own. Think of how many additional cases you could solve, or solve faster, if you had more people working for you."

"You're the second person today who's said something like that." She chuckled and tucked her hair behind her ear. "I think I'd just lose focus on the cases because I'd be worried about those working for me doing their jobs properly."

"You'd have to hire good people."

Her bourbon eyes cut to him, and he saw a teasing light there. "You applying for the position?"

"Maybe." The word was out of his mouth before he realized it.

Both of them were so shocked at his reply that they stood in silence for a few moments. Then Marlee said, "I've thought about having a partner, but this line of work takes a special kind of dedication. Most who work just one of these cases never do it again. Even the authorities that get child kidnapping cases all inwardly cringe because they know the statistics. And those are generally older children. It's even worse for infants and toddlers."

Cooper wasn't sure how to reply to that. Thankfully, he didn't have to because a nurse came out of the back with Nate in her arms and handed him off to Naomi. She promptly put him into the carrier as Brice finished signing the papers.

When Marlee walked to the couple, Cooper went with

her. He nodded to Brice and peered inside the carrier to find Nate sleeping soundly while sucking on a pacifier.

"Thank you again for doing this," Marlee told the couple.

Naomi smiled, though it was tight. "How long are the tests going to take?"

Marlee shrugged. "I've no idea. Sometimes it's a day. Sometimes up to four."

"So we could only have one more day with him," Naomi told Brice.

Brice wrapped an arm around her. "Let's go home, love."

Cooper moved out of the way to let the couple pass. Clayton and Abby fell in step behind them, leaving Jace and Cooper with Marlee.

Jace held out his hand to her. "I know you know who I am, but we've not been properly introduced."

Marlee chuckled and clasped his palm. "I'm Marlee. Nice to meet you."

"Likewise." He released her hand and gave her a nod before he glanced at Cooper and followed the others.

Marlee watched him before her gaze slid to Cooper. "I really hope your friends don't run. I can see by their faces that they want Nate."

"They won't run. And if they do, I'll track them down myself."

She didn't smile. Her lips parted like she was going to say something, then she seemed to change her mind. She shot him a tight smile and started toward the exit.

Talking with her, seeing what was happening to his friends made Cooper want to get to the bottom of whatever was happening more than ever.

And nobody could stop him.

Chapter 12

"She's here."

The deep voice on the other end of the line made Stella go cold with anger—and a little bit of dread. Marlee Frampton was a thorn in her side that she hadn't been able to dislodge in over a decade.

"Do you want me to take care of her?" Chuck asked.

Stella gripped her cell phone tighter and leaned back in the office chair. "Leave her alone."

"Why?" he demanded, anger making his voice go even deeper. "She's gotten close to us more times than I like to admit. The fact that she's sniffing around here tells me we need to get out. Now."

"No."

"Why the fuck not?"

Stella looked out the window of her rented home to the pasture beyond. The house was out of the way and difficult to find. Just the kind of place for her. "I don't owe you any kind of explanation. You work for me, Chuck. And if you want to quit, then by all means, do it."

"I'm only trying to protect things," he replied gruffly.

"Killing Marlee would bring more attention to us.

We've been able to use our friends to keep a step or two ahead of her. We'll keep doing that for as long as we have to."

Chuck blew out a breath. "I can make sure she gets another lead somewhere and then do it."

"No, and I'm not going to tell you again."

"Why are you protecting her?"

"I'm not protecting her," Stella answered tightly. "I'm protecting *us*."

Chuck made a sound in the back of his throat. "Nope. You're protecting her. I could've killed her multiple times already. Instances that never would've led anyone to us because our friends would've made sure of it."

"I'm not having this conversation again. I've told you my decision, and I expect you to follow my orders as you always have."

"You're going to look back one day and realize that you should've heeded me on this," Chuck said and hung up the phone.

Stella tossed her cell on the desk and leaned back, slipping her fingers into her short blond hair. She stared at the ceiling for a few moments before she lowered her arms and sat up straight. She might have acted nonchalantly with Chuck, but the truth was, she was worried. Very worried.

Marlee had no idea how close she had come to destroying everything Stella had built for over two decades. And it was true, she could've had Marlee killed many times over. She wished she could get it done, but she just couldn't. It would destroy Diane. After what'd happened to Diane and her husband after Macey was killed, Stella couldn't bring more harm to the family.

But if it came down to her survival or Marlee's, Stella wouldn't hesitate to do what had to be done.

After pulling open the top left drawer of her desk, she

removed a wooden box about eight inches long and four inches deep. She flipped the lid to reveal an expensive pen set. Stella didn't look twice at the Montblanc pen as she lifted out the tray to reveal a hidden compartment beneath, the space holding a burner phone.

She reached for it and turned it on. The phone was only used in emergencies, but this was definitely an emergency. She selected the only saved number and brought the cell to her ear as it began to ring.

There was no answer, but that wasn't unusual. She waited for the voicemail to start. "It's me," she said. "My little problem is closer than ever. The operation here has been very successful, but I think it's time I find a new location before she gets lucky and finds us."

After she ended the call, Stella shut off the phone and placed it in the box before she put everything back where it had been. The next location had already been picked, and a team had been sent to set up the area in case they had to leave Texas suddenly. The entire reason Stella had begun to pick out the next territory well in advance and set up a team to get things ready was because of Marlee.

The intrepid cop-turned-PI had nearly cornered Stella three years earlier. That was the closest Marlee had ever come and was the closest Stella would allow anyone to get. Too much was at stake.

Stella got to her feet and walked around the bedroom she'd turned into her office. It was small, but she didn't need much space. She had learned to keep her business tidy, and with everything in the cloud nowadays, everything she had was highly encrypted and stored electronically. It made her life much easier.

Pure luck had led her to this path to begin with. She'd been young, broke, and homeless at seventeen. Living on the streets had been the hardest thing she'd ever done, but she'd found a friend, another runaway who understood that life on the streets was rough. However, sometimes, living at the home you ran away from was even harder.

She and Jenny had become close. A couple of months later, Jenny told Stella exactly why she had run away from her family—her father had raped her since the age of six. At sixteen, she found out that she was pregnant and told him not to touch her again. That's when he started hitting her. Jenny managed to get away and jumped out a window. All she'd had on was a pair of shorts and a shirt but being barefoot didn't stop her. Eventually, she found her way to Los Angeles, and that's where she met Stella.

Stella had no idea what to do for someone who was pregnant. She had gotten good at stealing food, but soon, that wasn't enough to feed them since Jenny couldn't move as fast as she used to. Stella honed her skills as a pickpocket, and that's how she kept food in Jenny's belly for her and the baby. When the weather turned, Stella sometimes managed to get enough money to rent a room for the night.

She smiled as she remembered how Jenny used to stand beneath the shower, washing herself and her hair dozens of times before she finished. Stella's smile vanished as she closed her eyes. Jenny began to complain of her back hurting. Stella knew that Jenny needed a doctor, but it took some convincing to make Jenny see it, as well.

The day Stella was going to bring Jenny to the clinic, she went into labor in the room they had rented. She tried to get Jenny to her feet so they could go to the hospital. She knew in her gut that something was really wrong, but every time she touched Jenny, the girl screamed in pain. Finally, all Stella could do was hold Jenny's hand and do whatever she could to deliver the baby.

There was so much blood. Stella had never seen so much before in her life. She had been shocked by it, but then suddenly, there was this little baby wiggling in her arms and screaming at the top of its lungs. Out of all that pain, a new life had been born.

She laughed and held the baby up for Jenny to see her son. Only Jenny was dead. Amid her tears, Stella managed to cut the umbilical cord and wrap the baby in a blanket. She wanted to stay with her friend, but if she alerted anyone to what had happened, the cops would come—and they always asked too many questions.

Stella looked down at the baby. She had no idea what to do with him, but she wasn't going to let him go into the foster system like she had. She was determined to take care of him. The problem was, stealing money or running any cons with a crying baby was impossible. He wouldn't stop screaming.

The resolve she had to take care of him quickly turned to resentment because she couldn't leave him alone to get the things he needed, but she also couldn't bring him with her. She realized that he was starving, and she had nothing to give him. It wasn't until his cries turned to whimpers and he began to look ashen that she realized that he was dying.

Stella walked all night to the orphanage. She hadn't wanted to put him in the system, but she didn't want him to die either. She owed Jenny that much, at least. But as Stella walked around the back of the building, a man stepped from around a shed and stopped her.

"What are you about, girl?" he demanded in a sharp tone.

She held up the infant, who was no longer moving. "My friend had this baby, but she died."

"You think we'll give you food or clothing for him?" The man snorted in laughter. "That won't happen."

"I—" Stella started.

But the man moved a step closer and lowered his voice. "Is the babe still alive?"

Stella put her hand beneath his nose and felt his breath. "Yes."

"I know someone looking for a little boy for themselves. How about I offer you five hundred dollars for him?"

She'd never held that much money before. "Five hundred?"

"All right, eight hundred. He'll be fed and clothed and will belong to a good family."

Stella glanced down at the child. She'd planned to leave him at the orphanage, but if she could find him a family and get money to live off of, they both benefited. And wouldn't that have made Jenny happy?

She held the baby closer. "I want a thousand."

The man smiled slowly and drew out a stack of bills to count out the money. He held it out to her. "Here's your payment. Give me the baby, and you can be on your way."

There was a brief moment of hesitation, but the idea of not having to steal money for food for a while was too great a temptation. Stella jerked the cash out of the man's hand and shoved the baby at him. And she never looked back. After that, it was easy to find women on the streets who'd birthed babies they didn't want. Stella went back to that old man six more times, earning herself a little more each time and giving some of it to the mothers who'd sold their babies.

It wasn't long before Stella wanted even more money. Surprisingly, it wasn't too difficult to find people willing to pay tens of thousands of dollars for babies. Soon, demand exceeded supply, and Stella had to find other ways to get the children. That's when she met Chuck. He'd been a doctor in the military but had been kicked out for murdering someone. It made it impossible for him to practice again. Yet he was exactly what Stella needed.

She found the pregnant women, he followed them for

weeks and learned their habits. Then, he cornered them, knocked them unconscious, and cut them open to remove the babies. Once the infants were safely delivered, he sliced the mothers' necks so they bled out.

It wasn't optimal. In fact, it was the worst way to get the babies, but sometimes, Stella had to do whatever it took.

And it just might be time to remove Marlee from the equation.

Chapter 13

Marlee blinked and read the paper in her hand.

"The Harpers just left," the nurse said. "They're very pleased."

Marlee could only nod since she couldn't form words. She swallowed and reread the paper. Irritation began to grow and fester because, somewhere, somehow, she had messed up. But where? She had been so sure that Nate was the missing baby. But she'd gotten it wrong. So very wrong.

Her arm lowered to her side with the paper clutched in her hand. She walked numbly from the hospital to her car and got inside. Then she just sat while trying to evaluate the various emotions colliding within her like a stormy sea.

She was angry that she had overlooked something that had led her to the Harpers and little Nate. Though she also discovered relief among the emotions because she now got to tell Naomi and Brice that everything with Nate's adoption had been done properly.

Then there was the annoyance because she wanted to

end this job and get back to her parents. Along with that came regret, since she wouldn't be able to tell a grieving father that she had found his missing son.

Marlee tossed the paper onto the seat beside her and placed her hands on the steering wheel. Then she closed her eyes and tried to get a handle on the turmoil within her. She was so glad she hadn't mentioned to her mother that she was trying to come home early. However, now she had to start her investigation all over again. But first, she needed to pay the Harpers a visit. She owed them that, at least.

The hairs on the back of her neck suddenly rose. Marlee slowly opened her eyes and looked around without moving her head. She used the rearview mirror as well as the side mirrors, but like before, she found nothing. Still, a feeling like that didn't occur without reason. Not to her. Someone was watching her.

Adrenaline kicked in, but she held herself back. This wasn't the time to confront whoever it was, though she was getting tired of her watcher. Or was it all in her head? After all, despite the times she'd felt someone watching her, nothing had happened.

Marlee blew out a breath and started the car. She pulled out of the parking spot to drive through the lot. As she did, she let her gaze move over the many vehicles to see if anyone or anything caught her eye. The fact that so many people were getting in and out of automobiles made it difficult to tell who the culprit might be.

She finally gave up and drove away. Though her mind wanted to go over the details of her job to find out where she had gone wrong, she didn't allow herself that. At least, not yet. She needed a small break. She decided to drive to the Harpers'. They had gotten the results, as well, but she still wanted to talk to them. When she returned to her motel room, *then* she could look at the various reports, pictures, and all the other evidence she had and start fresh.

When she arrived at the house, Marlee saw Caleb's truck parked next to his brother's. She stopped her rental behind them and grabbed the paper before getting out. The front door of the house opened as she approached. Naomi stood with a smile on her face.

Marlee returned the smile. "Mind if I come in?"

"Not at all," Naomi replied as she opened the door wider.

Marlee walked inside as Naomi led her to the kitchen, where Brice and Caleb were seated. Naomi glanced at the baby monitor, the screen on it showing Nate sleeping peacefully. The little tyke had no idea what was going on around him. It was a good thing because while most kids forgot such turmoil, for some, it became imprinted on them forever.

Brice gave her a nod. "Did the hospital tell you?"

"They did," she said. "Congratulations. I'm very sorry I caused such worry."

Naomi walked to Brice as he got to his feet and wrapped an arm around her. Despite the hell they'd gone through over the last couple of days, there didn't seem to be any animosity directed at her.

"You were just doing your job," Naomi said.

Marlee forced a smile and turned to leave, but Caleb stepped in her way.

"What does this mean for you?" he asked.

She shrugged, her lips twisting. "It means I have to start my case over. I know it may not look like it to you, but I don't usually get these things wrong. There are instances, of course, but more times than not, my investigation leads me to the right person."

"I don't doubt that." Caleb glanced at his brother and sister-in-law. "Your investigation brought you here, though. I'd feel a lot better if you told me it was simply Brice and Naomi and not something more."

Marlee hesitated, feeling three pairs of eyes on her. "Something went wrong in my investigation. I need to figure out what that was. I'm going to start from the beginning and work through it again. It might take me out of Clearview—which it probably will."

"Is there anything we can do to help? I don't like the idea of babies being stolen from their families," Brice said.

Marlee shrugged. "It happens more than you know. Trust me, you don't want to know the statistics."

"I think I do," Caleb told her.

If they wanted it, she would give it. "A child goes missing every forty seconds in the US. Of those, over fifteen hundred are kidnapped. However, I think the number is actually higher."

Naomi's brows drew together. "Why?"

"Think of all the illegal immigrants in our country. Do you honestly believe all of them report when one of their children is taken or disappears?"

"No," Caleb said with a shake of his head. "Damn. I had no idea."

"I'm truly sorry I put all of you through this, but my job is to find the missing and return them to their families."

Brice held up a hand. "Thank you, but you don't owe us an apology. You did what you had to do. I wish you well in your hunt for the missing infant."

"Thanks."

Caleb walked her to the door and quietly let her out. Marlee got into her car and was just backing up to turn around when Cooper's truck pulled up. He rolled down his window, so she did, as well. She didn't want to be happy to see him, but something about him brought some calm to the storm of her life.

"Hey," he said with a smile as he pulled up alongside her. "I didn't expect to see you here."

"I just came to say congratulations."

His face lit up, then the expression died. "I'm happy for my friends, thrilled they get to keep their son, of course. But that means you're still searching."

"That's pretty much all I do."

"Do you ever get any time off?"

"I take what I can, when I can."

"How about tonight?"

She was so shocked by his question that she could only stare at him.

Cooper held up his hands and grinned. "You have to eat, right? It's already the afternoon. No sense in getting on the road now. Start fresh in the morning. If you're leaving."

"I'm not leaving tonight."

"Good." His smile widened. "Then let me buy you dinner."

"I should be the one buying you dinner after what I did."

He shook his head, his gaze never leaving hers. "My treat. Please."

"All right," she said, feeling as giddy as a schoolgirl headed on her first date. Which, sadly, was pretty much what this was since she couldn't remember the last time she had agreed to anything like this.

Cooper flashed her a sexy smile. "You've made my day. How does seven sound?"

"Perfect."

"There's a good steakhouse, but if you're vegetarian—"

"I like meat," she hurried to say. Then she giggled at how dirty that sounded.

By the look in Cooper's eyes, he had heard the double entendre, as well. "Shall I pick you up?"

At this, she hesitated.

"No worries," he said. "We can meet."

"Actually, I think I'd like you to drive. I'm staying at the local motel, room 110."

He wrinkled his nose. "That's not in the greatest part of town."

"Unfortunately, a lot of where I go isn't in the best parts of towns. I'm used to it. I used to be a cop."

"Right." He paused as if debating something internally, then he winked at her. "I'll see you at seven."

"Seven," she agreed and waved at him.

As she drove away, she couldn't stop smiling. Even after their not-so-great first two encounters, he still wanted to be around her. At least now, she knew it wasn't to get information from her regarding his friends. No, she believed he genuinely liked her. And when was the last time that had happened?

"Ugh. Don't even think about it," she told herself.

As she pulled onto the road, she turned up the music when a song came on that she liked. For just a few minutes, she wasn't a PI searching the country for kidnapped and missing babies. She was just a woman who had been asked on a date by a very handsome, very charming man that she wanted to kiss.

The mere thought of that had her thinking about sex, which of course, made her think of the last time she'd had a lover.

"Just stop," she chided herself. "I'm in a good mood. If I keep going down this thought path, I'm going to ruin everything for tonight."

The moment she got to the motel, she bolted the door and jumped into the shower. It was time she actually made an effort with her appearance.

And she might need all the time she could get.

Chapter 14

"Well?" Caleb asked when Cooper walked into the house.

Cooper looked between Caleb, Brice, and Naomi and shrugged. "Well, what?"

"We know you," Brice said. "More importantly, we've all seen how you look at Marlee."

"I think I should take offense," Cooper said.

Naomi was beaming when she said, "Don't. What Caleb and Brice are trying to say—badly—is that they know you're going to help Marlee."

Cooper shrugged in an effort to not say anything. He hadn't intended to tell any of them what he and Jace were up to. Then again, the four of them rarely kept secrets from one another.

"You might as well give it up and tell us everything," Caleb said with a grin. "By the way, where's Jace?"

Cooper sighed loudly. "Did y'all ever stop to think that maybe I wanted to keep you out of it because of Nate?"

"No," the three answered in unison.

Naomi finished stirring the soup and looked his way. "Whether Marlee came today to take Nate from us or to give us the news she did, I'd still want to help her. Because what she's doing makes a difference. Nate might not have come from my body, but I love him as if he did. If anyone took him, I'd be devastated."

Brice brought Naomi's hand to his lips and kissed her knuckles. "My wife's right. So, go ahead and tell us what you've got."

"Not as much as you think." Cooper shrugged as he leaned against the counter. "Jace and I have been marking locations on a map where pregnant women were killed and their babies taken."

Caleb crossed his arms over his chest. "And? What have you learned?"

"That our county is in the middle of it all," Cooper stated.

Brice ran a hand down his face as he shook his head. "Damn. I'd heard a few news stories, but that's it."

"Some cases don't make the news." Cooper shrugged. "Jace and I are still trying to get a handle on it. That's what we were doing last night. We got a new map, but before we began marking it, we wanted to find all the news stories we could."

Naomi started to cut up some carrots. "Is this just in Texas?"

"That's what we began with, but we're thinking it'll need to be extended to the entire country."

Caleb shook his head. "Not just America. Worldwide."

"We don't have the resources for that," Brice said. "Hell, I'm not sure we'll be much help for Texas."

Cooper removed his Stetson and slapped it against his leg. "I feel the same, but something brought Marlee here. She might have gotten it wrong with Nate, but what if the location is right? The simple fact that these kidnappings and killings are happening all around us makes me wonder what's in this county. And if there is something here with us, why haven't any of us seen it?"

"Because we don't want to," Naomi replied.

Brice lowered his gaze to the floor. "When we began looking into adoption, there were so many agencies to choose from. So many children waiting to find homes. And that's only here in the US. Even more children are adopted overseas and brought here. The sheer amount of paperwork we had to do just to be considered is mind-blowing. They did background checks on us multiple times. I didn't once think the place might not be legitimate."

"You had no reason to. The process was long and arduous, and you two waited months for Nate," Caleb said. "You always hear of black-market things on the news and television, but no one ever thinks it's happening near them. Marlee mentioned that some of the babies cut from their mother's wombs might be illegal immigrants."

Cooper set his hat on the counter. "That means whatever statistics are out there, we need to raise them."

"No, double them," Naomi said.

Brice looked at his wife and nodded. "Damn. This is an epidemic that few even know about. What little is on the news isn't enough."

"What is ever enough?" Cooper countered. "No matter how much you tell people, how much you warn them to be wary, at least half of them will discount it."

Caleb made a sound in the back of his throat. "I don't care. Everyone needs to know about this danger."

"Is there a chance I'll get into a wreck the next time I'm in a car?" Naomi nodded her head. "That risk is there every time any of us gets in a vehicle. If one of you are riding, the horse could step in a hole and break its leg, throwing you in the process. You could die. A woman can die in childbirth. Yes, it's horrendous that pregnant women are being killed for their babies, but it's not like this has only just begun. It's been going on for decades, no doubt."

Caleb scratched his chin. "Even if we want to help, I don't think Marlee will welcome it."

"Maybe. Maybe not," Cooper said with a shrug. "I plan on talking to her about it tonight."

It was the wrong thing to say because suddenly, all three were very interested in the fact that Cooper was seeing Marlee later. They bombarded him with questions, but he refused to answer. Thankfully, little Nate woke and gave him a reprieve. Brice hurried from the room to check on his son.

Naomi dumped the carrots into the pot and stirred the contents before putting the lid on and looking at Cooper. "Marlee handled our situation well. I don't really know her, but she seems nice. I applaud her for the work she's doing. I'm not sure if I could do it. If you can help her in any way, then do it. And let us know if we can help, as well."

Cooper grabbed his hat and put it on his head. "Will do."

"What about Cash?" Caleb asked as he followed Cooper outside. "Could he help?"

Cooper twisted his lips. "I contacted him. He's in deep on a case and is unavailable to help right now. He said he'd try to get here as quickly as he could. Marlee seems competent. I just think she needs some help."

"She's used to working alone. Some prefer it that way."

"True, but that kind of life takes a toll on a person. I won't push her, but I'm going to let her know that we can help. I got the feeling she really wanted to wrap this case up. Now, she has to start again."

Caleb slapped Cooper on the back. "Good luck tonight. It's obvious you've got it bad for her. Maybe don't talk about work this evening. Perhaps make it about the two of you."

Cooper's balls tightened just thinking about him and Marlee in his bed. "Yeah. The two of us."

Chapter 15

This was the first time Marlee wished she had packed nicer clothes. The fact that she contemplated going shopping just so she'd have something decent to wear told her how excited she was about the date.

A date. A freaking date. She couldn't believe it. Not to mention, she was going to dinner with one of the sexiest men she'd ever encountered. What was it about Cooper Owens in those Wrangler jeans and that Stetson hat? Combine that with his heart-stopping smile and eyes that drew her in, and she couldn't stop her attraction if she tried.

And she really, really didn't want to try.

She hadn't felt anything like this in a long time. For an instant, she hadn't known what the feeling was, but her body had. Then, her mind had caught on. It was that moment when the attraction hit, and the one who caught your attention became the only thing you could think about. Yeah, she remembered that all too well. And she had missed it.

She smoothed her hand over the gray sweater she'd

worn a few nights back when she lay in wait for him at the café. This time, she left her hair down, the curls doing their thing as they always did. She had stopped trying to make them behave. If there was a lot of humidity, they curled. If the weather was drier, the curls weren't nearly as tight, and even sometimes fell into more of a wave.

Marlee didn't have any makeup, but she did find some lip gloss in her purse—no doubt put there by her mother. Marlee added it to her lips for a bit of shine and just a hint of color. She looked at herself in the mirror and contemplated changing just as a knock sounded at the door.

Her eyes jerked to the nightstand and the clock that read seven p.m. on the dot. Her heart lurched as she turned to the door. Nerves made her hands tremble and her knees weak.

"Who is it?" she called.

"Cooper."

She unlocked the door and opened it to find him filling the doorway. "Hi," she said.

He tipped his hat at her. "Hi. You look beautiful."

"Thank you." A blush crept up her cheeks. It had been years since anyone had made her blush. She took in his black jeans and boots and saw the dark green shirt beneath his jacket. "You look very handsome."

If it was possible, his smile got even sexier. "Thank you."

Her room was filled with papers from the investigation, so she put on her coat and grabbed her purse. "Shall we go?"

He waited for her to close the door, then they walked to his truck. To her surprise, he opened her door for her and waited until she was inside before he closed it and walked around to the driver's side.

Once he was behind the wheel, she said, "I thought people only did that in the movies."

Cooper chuckled. "Many still do it around here. My momma told me if I didn't remember anything else she taught me, I was at least going to know how to treat a woman."

"I really think I like your mom."

"Oh, she's going to love you." He started the engine.

Marlee chuckled. "Why do you say that?"

"You're independent, have your own business, are strong-minded, and you don't put up with anything."

"I don't think anyone has ever spoken about me like that before."

"I bet they have. You just didn't hear them."

She looked out the windshield. "I guess I never considered myself in such a way. I just found a path and took it."

"Do you regret your decision?"

"Not at all. I don't like when I can't solve a case. And I regret not seeing my parents more, but they're very understanding. Unfortunately, they're not in the best of health." Marlee wondered why she had told Cooper that. She rarely shared anything about her private life, and especially not things about her parents.

But with him, she found she wanted to talk. To share things.

He wore a frown when he glanced her way. "I'm sorry to hear that."

"I'd planned to go home for a few months after this case. I really thought I was going to be leaving for California tomorrow."

"Do your parents need you?"

"A nurse lives with them. My father suffered a stroke about ten years ago. He can't use his left arm and he can't talk. My mom just went into the hospital for pneumonia. But I spoke to her. She sounded good."

He nodded slowly. "But life can be taken away in a blink."

Marlee looked down at her hands. She knew he was speaking of his father, but her mind was on Macey.

"My father was the picture of health," Cooper said into the silence. "He always made sure we were safe, that he was safe. He worked at the sawmill, and one day, an accident happened. It changed our lives forever. Since the fault lay with the company, they paid out a lot of money to my mom. She hated that money for a long time."

"Because she would've rather had your father with her."

Cooper shot her a smile. "That's exactly what she used to say."

"I'm sorry about your dad. I can't imagine growing up like that."

"It was hard, though I think it was harder on Mom. Jace and his family were there for us, though. I don't know what we would've done without them."

Marlee leaned her head back against the seat. "It's good that you and your mom had someone to lean on. It looks like things turned out well for you."

"You should know," he said with a chuckle. "You looked into us."

She wrinkled her nose as she lifted her head and smiled. "I'm sorry. I know it must be awkward to realize a stranger dug into your life."

"A little," he replied with a shrug. "Tell me what you thought about me."

Her eyes widened as she looked at him. "No one has ever asked that of me."

"Good."

His smile was infectious. Marlee found her lips turning up at the corners. "Okay. Well, I was impressed by the fact you joined the military. I wasn't able to get a lot of information about your time in the Air Force, but what I did learn was that you were a highly decorated airman. I might have been a little jealous of the fact that you were an honors student in school with a 4.0 GPA in college that resulted in a business degree."

"I studied my ass off," he said with a laugh.

"Mmmm. I probably should've done that."

They laughed.

She looked out the window at the oncoming lights. "What I found was that you're a good guy. You've done things for your friends and family that others might not have. To top it off, you're gorgeous."

"Gorgeous, huh?" he asked as his forest green eyes met her stare as they stopped at a light. "I'm glad you think so because I can honestly say I've never encountered anyone as stunningly beautiful as you."

For the second time that night, Marlee blushed.

Chapter 16

Cooper couldn't remember ever being so nervous. As they reached the restaurant, he walked Marlee to the entrance. He loved that a blush continued staining her cheeks whenever she looked his way. The cop-turned-PI seemed as if nothing could faze her, and yet his compliments had done just that. It made him want to continue lavishing her with such words to keep her blushing.

As they were led to their table, Cooper held out her chair and waited for her to sit before taking his own seat.

"You keep doing things like that, and I'm going to start expecting all men to treat me that way," she said with a smile.

He shrugged. "Shouldn't all men treat women with respect?"

"Absolutely."

"However, I know some women don't like having doors opened for them." He shrugged. "It just wasn't how I was raised."

They shared a smile. He gazed deep into her bourbon-colored eyes and found himself drowning there. He wanted to know all there was about her, every detail. She had no idea how appealing she was to him or how much he . . . craved her.

She bit her lower lip, and he held back a moan. His blood had been on fire from the first moment he saw her. Now, every time they were together, he wanted her more. He hadn't even had a taste of her yet, and he was already addicted to her. How bad would it be once he finally had her?

"What are you thinking?" she asked. "You look deep in thought."

"I was thinking about how beautiful your eyes are. They're the color of my favorite drink."

She quirked an auburn brow. "Oh? What would that be?"

"Bourbon."

That made her chuckle. "And here I thought they were just plain brown."

"There's nothing plain about you."

The conversation was put on hold as they ordered, but as soon as they were alone again, Marlee asked, "From what I learned when investigating you, and from what others around here told me, you're quite a catch. How is it you aren't married?"

"I could ask the same of you," he said with a grin.

Marlee pulled a face. "That's easy. My job keeps me single."

"Fair enough." He thought about it for a moment and twisted his lips. "I don't really know why I've not settled down. After seeing my friends find their wives, I realized that it would happen to me when and if it happened. That I couldn't go looking for it."

"Good answer." Marlee rested her forearms on the table, leaning toward him. "This may sound out of line, but I really hope you asked me out to get to know me, not to talk about the case."

"In my opinion, the case with Brice and Naomi is finished. I'm here with you tonight because I'm interested in you. But I'm not going to lie, I'd love to talk to you more about what you do."

She shrugged. "Sure. But not tonight. Tonight, I'd like to pretend I'm just a woman on a date."

"I think we can accomplish that."

They traded small talk for the next twenty minutes with Cooper speaking about his time in the rodeo and calf roping. She had a million questions, and he was content to answer all of them. When their food arrived, Marlee seemed more relaxed than he had ever seen her. She was smiling easily, laughing often, with her eyes twinkling as she listened raptly to what he had to say.

"I've been doing all the talking," he said. "Tell me about you."

She shrugged and cut into her steak. "There really isn't much to tell."

"I beg to differ. You were a police officer before you became a PI. Why did you become a cop?"

"I honestly have no idea. No one in my family had ever been part of the police force. I just felt drawn to it." She paused and took a bite, then sighed blissfully. "This is the best steak I've ever had."

Cooper laughed, nodding. "No one can cook steak like we do in Texas."

After she swallowed, she said, "My parents weren't thrilled with my decision to become a cop because they were worried about my safety, but my sister supported me fully."

Now that she had mentioned her sister, Cooper didn't feel odd asking more about it. "A sister?"

"My twin." Marlee's smile was slow, a deep sadness coming over her face. "Her name was Macey. I was older by two minutes."

"Were you two close?"

"Oh, yeah. Twins usually are." She set down her fork. "You know, don't you?"

Cooper didn't pretend not to understand what she was asking. "I do."

"Thank you for not asking about it."

"I'm sorry. I know that doesn't mean much, but I really am sorry about what happened to her."

Marlee picked up her fork and began eating again. They returned to small talk, and he let it happen. Obviously, she wasn't ready to tell him more about her sister, or maybe since he knew the facts, she didn't think she needed to elaborate. Either way, he wasn't going to push her.

It wasn't until they walked from the restaurant that Marlee said, "My goal is to find the person who killed my sister and took her baby."

"I'd do the same in your shoes."

"I was on duty when it happened. We lived together. Macey's pregnancy had been an accident, but it never entered her mind to do anything but raise the baby herself. She would've been an amazing mom, and I planned to be right there to help her the entire time."

Cooper reached over and took her hand, their walk to his truck slow.

Marlee glanced his way and then smiled. "My parents were so excited about welcoming their first grandchild. And I couldn't wait to become an aunt. We spent months getting the baby's room ready with my parents chipping in to help. Those months were glorious, which is odd for someone having a child out of wedlock." Her smile faded. "The day Macey died, I went shopping to pick out a Halloween costume for my unborn niece. It was for the next year, but I'd seen it and just had to buy it. It was a surprise for Macey, and I rushed home to show her. The moment I walked in the house and didn't see her, I knew something was wrong."

Cooper squeezed her hand as they reached his truck. He didn't open the door for her. She stood staring out across the street, but he knew she didn't see the passing cars or the businesses, she was in the past.

"I ran upstairs, shouting her name. I called her cell phone again and again. Then I called the station. My sergeant told me that my partner was coming to the house. I knew then that something had happened." Marlee paused and then turned to him. "She wasn't that far away. They took her when she went for a walk. In the middle of the day. They dumped her less than five minutes from our house. When my partner drove me to her, there were police cars everywhere. I remember the flashing lights, the yellow tape. I remember my partner talking to me, but I couldn't hear what he said because all I could see was the white sheet covering a body."

Cooper pulled her against him and just held her. He closed his eyes, picturing everything in his head.

"They knocked her unconscious," Marlee's voice cut through the silence. "Once they had the baby, they sliced her throat. Her phone was just out of reach. It looked as if she'd tried to get to it, but she bled out before she could. They left her to die on the street."

The sound of Marlee's voice shaking caused fury to erupt within Cooper. While he might have known her sister was murdered, he hadn't known these details. The kinds of things that sent a person reeling. The kind of stuff that changed the course of a person's life.

The kinds of details that destroyed people.

But not Marlee. It had put her on a new path, one that helped so many others who were in the same position that she and her parents had been in. Cooper rubbed his hands up and down her back. She held on to him tightly, her fingers digging into the material of his jacket at his back. He doubted that she had told very many people what she'd shared with him tonight, and he felt honored that she had opened up to him.

Marlee sniffed and pulled out of his arms. She looked into his eyes. "I had to tell my parents. I couldn't let anyone else do it. My father had a stroke that night. I know it was caused by what happened. I took a leave of absence to take care of my parents and to handle the funeral. Then I began looking for the assholes who did that to Macey. Except I was met with dead end after dead end after dead end. When the FBI was brought in, I thought maybe something might actually happen with the case, but it soon stalled out there, as well. That's when I decided that if I didn't want Macey to end up a cold case, I had to do something. I quit the force and became a private investigator."

"How long until you had your first case?"

"A week." She shrugged and huddled into her jacket as a defense against the cold. "I've been working ever since. It has its rewards, but more times than not, I deliver no news to the family. Or worse, bad news."

"News is news, whatever kind it is, I'd think. Everyone needs some kind of closure."

She nodded. "That's true."

"Come on," he said. "How about some coffee to warm us up?"

"Sounds perfect."

They got into the truck and were pulling out when his phone rang through his Bluetooth. He recognized his neighbor's number and answered. "Hey, Ted."

"Evenin', Coop. I'm hoping you're near the house because I was alerted that Big Tom is out again. Dumbass nephew can't seem to learn to close the damn gate. We're in Fort Worth for the weekend and can't get back in time."

Cooper smiled as he glanced at Marlee. "Don't worry about it. I'll take care of it."

"Thanks, Cooper. I owe you."

He disconnected the call as Marlee said, "Big Tom?"

"It's Ted's bull. He's quite the ladies' man, and if he can get into another pasture with more cows, he's going to do it. Mind if we make a stop?"

"Not at all. I'm curious to meet Big Tom."

Cooper laughed and turned the truck around.

Chapter 17

Whatever Marlee might have thought she'd see when they arrived, it was not the massive bull standing beside the road, munching on grass as if he didn't have a care in the world. When the truck's headlights touched the animal, she saw the deep burgundy color of his coat. He swung his head in their direction, then went back to eating, uncaring that someone was there.

"Is he dangerous?" Marlee asked, the hairs on the back of her neck standing up.

"Any animal can be dangerous, especially ones that size. However, Big Tom is pretty much a gentle giant until you get him around ladies in need."

Marlee busted out laughing.

Cooper chuckled and shrugged. "It's true. I've seen him plow through a fence before."

That sobered her quickly. She looked out the truck's windows into the inky night. There wasn't a single light anywhere to show them what was out there, other than the sliver of the moon and the truck's headlights. "Are you sure about this?"

"I've been around cattle and horses my entire life. I

was riding a horse before I could even walk. I know what I'm doing," Cooper assured her. "Especially with Big Tom. This isn't the first time I've had to put him back in his pasture."

Marlee eyed the huge animal. "If you're sure."

"There's no need for you to get out. Stay right here. You'll be fine. I'll be back before you know it."

She saw his grin in the dim lights of the dashboard. She smiled back, unable to stop herself. Something about Cooper made her feel safe. As if nothing could harm her. It was the first time she'd ever felt anything like it, and she wasn't really sure how to handle such an emotion.

Part of her wanted to run straight for him as if she was sure he'd catch her—figuratively, of course. But the rational part of her, the bit that had seen untold cruelty and savagery as a cop and a private investigator, warned her.

Cooper paused in getting out. "It'll be fine. I promise. Big Tom won't hurt me."

"It'll be easier with two people, won't it?"

He shrugged, his lips twisting. "It would, but I've done it on my own before."

"I'll help," she stated. "Though this is the first time I've been around cows of any kind."

A slow smile spread over Cooper's face. "Then Big Tom is a great introduction. Come on."

Now that she'd said it, Marlee couldn't back out. After all the perps she'd chased—both on foot and by car—and brought down, she shouldn't be afraid of an animal. Then again, she had never been so close to a bull before. He could toss her fifty feet with a swing of his massive head. Any sane person would be more than a little cautious.

"Come on," she whispered to herself after Cooper was out of the truck. "You can do this."

Marlee quietly got out. She didn't slam the truck door

as Cooper had. Instead, she softly pushed it, not latching it completely. Her gaze moved to Cooper to find him talking softly to the bull as he walked up. Marlee pressed her lips together when she heard Cooper talking about how it wasn't Big Tom's fault that he got out, and that Cooper would've done the same thing in his position.

She gradually made her way around the front of the truck. The bull lifted his head and looked right at her. Marlee froze, wondering if she could get on top of the truck in time. Yet Big Tom ignored her and turned to move a few steps to Cooper. To her shock, the bull halted before Cooper and bowed his head. That's when Cooper rubbed the bull, scratching behind his ears. All the while, Big Tom made deep grunting noises as if he thoroughly enjoyed the attention.

In fact, Marlee was sure she'd make similar noises if Cooper's hands were on her.

At that moment, Cooper looked at her, a big smile on his face. "I can't say this for all bulls, but Big Tom really is gentle. Want to pet him?"

"Sure."

Cooper held out his free hand to her. Marlee didn't hesitate to walk to him and take it, though her gaze did dart to Big Tom to see how he'd react. Her body cut in front of the headlights, blocking out the light for a fraction of a second. The moment her hand connected with Cooper's, warmth spread through her.

"He's like any male," Cooper said in a low, husky voice. "Big Tom wants to know he's loved."

Marlee couldn't help but smile. "Is that so?"

"Absolutely. He might like me petting him, but he'll know the difference as soon as you touch him."

Marlee jerked her head to Cooper and frowned. "Because he can smell me?"

"He smelled you the moment you got out of the truck.

It's because women touch animals differently than men. My dad told me that once. I didn't believe him until he proved it with my mother. And I'm going to prove it to you now."

"All right." Marlee was more than ready to pet the bull.

Cooper moved a little behind her, pressing against her back. She felt his hard body and had to remind herself to keep her attention on the bull, not the very handsome, very arousing cowboy behind her.

"See my hand? See how I'm stroking the top of his head?" Cooper asked her.

She nodded. "Yes."

"You're going to do the same thing. Ready?"

Marlee swallowed. "Yes."

"He's all yours."

Cooper moved his hand, and Marlee put hers in its place. She was shocked at how soft Big Tom's fur was. It wasn't as dense as a dog's or cat's, but still silken. With her hand moving in the same manner as Cooper's had, the bull stayed still for a heartbeat. Then he raised his head a little to look at her with his soulful black eyes. He blew out a breath and nodded his head, bumping her hand.

"He wants more," Cooper said, a smile in his voice.

Marlee laughed and continued petting Big Tom, but it wasn't enough. The bull then pressed his head against her body. When he did, she began to tilt backward, but Cooper kept her upright.

"See?" Cooper said. "I told you Big Tom would know the difference."

She could only smile in amazement as she stared at the bull. "But he was making those noises with you. He isn't making them with me."

"He knows me, and I know what he likes. But he likes you much more than he does me."

Marlee shook her head as the bull gently butted his

head against her again, seeking more of her touch. "I can't believe this."

"Don't do this with all bulls," Cooper cautioned. "I know some who would just as soon trample you as have you get near them. But then there are those like Big Tom. The softies."

Marlee was soon petting the bull with both hands. "He is. I think I adore him."

"Which usually happens." Cooper chuckled and gave the bull a light shove when he pushed more weight into Marlee. The bull took the hint and stepped back.

"He's so well mannered," Marlee stated in amazement.

"If you didn't tell him no, he'd likely have you on the ground. He has no idea how powerful he is. He needs reminding." Cooper gave Big Tom a pat. "Time to go back in your pasture."

Marlee wrinkled her nose. "Really? I was just getting used to this."

"Now that Tom knows you, he'll come greet you next time."

Her eyes widened. "I've got to see that."

"Then we'll plan on it."

She smiled as their eyes met. "Okay."

He gave a tip of his head and then, with a hand on Big Tom, started toward the open gate, leading him back into his pasture. Marlee watched the males and realized she'd never thought to be looking at a man walking a bull down the road. She meandered on the quiet dirt road, wondering how it would be to live in such a place.

Suddenly, the hairs on the back of her neck stood up again. She looked around, but the darkness hid everything. When they first arrived, she'd thought it might have been the unknown danger of the bull that had her senses heightened, but that wasn't the cause now. Every instinct she had told her that she was being watched.

Her eyes scanned the area. She wished the moon would shed more light, or that there were streetlights, but this was out in the country where people could still lift their gazes to see a multitude of stars. Whatever—or whoever—was out there was being shielded by the dark. But Marlee would find out who it was.

There was a sound behind her. She whirled around and saw a mass fill the area before she was unceremoniously jerked away. Marlee found herself pinned between the wooden fence and a hard body that she was coming to know well.

"Are you all right?" Cooper asked, his eyes filled with concern.

She nodded. "What was that?"

"A deer. It hadn't been headed toward you at first, but something clearly spooked it and it shifted course. You were so still, I'm not sure it realized you were there until you turned."

Marlee raised a brow. "Are you telling me I scared the deer?"

Cooper wrinkled his nose and nodded twice. "I'm afraid so."

She couldn't help but laugh now that the situation was over. Marlee didn't want to think about what might have happened had Cooper not been there. "Is Big Tom up?"

"He's safe in his pasture, unaware and unconcerned about the deer."

"And the deer?"

Cooper shrugged. "I think he'll be traumatized for a bit, but he'll recover."

She laughed, quite liking being in his arms. His body was nestled tightly against hers. He had pulled her in for protection, but now that the threat was over, he hadn't moved away. And she was glad he hadn't. It wasn't just his heat she enjoyed. It was the man himself.

"And me?" she asked.

He raked his gaze over her. "I think you're tougher than anyone I've ever met."

"I was nearly done in by a startled deer until you saved the day."

His eyes lowered to her mouth, and her heart thumped wildly. "Woman, do you have any idea what your smile does to me?"

She did now, and oh, how she liked how that felt. Marlee reached up and moved his hat back so she could see more of his face in the shadows. "And what does it do to you, cowboy?"

"Shall I show you?" he asked and lowered his head.

The moment their lips met, she sank into him. Nothing had ever felt so right, so . . . perfect, as if this moment had been set in motion eons ago.

Chapter 18

The kiss set Cooper's soul on fire. Desire surged within him until he burned with it. His arms tightened around Marlee as she sighed. He'd tried to take things slow, but there was no stopping the emotions he felt for her. They struck him at odd moments, propelling him toward her no matter how much he warned himself to be nonchalant.

But it was difficult to act like that when all he wanted was Marlee. It should've been enough that they had gone to dinner, but it wasn't. It should've been enough that they had a nice time, but it wasn't. It should've been enough that she had agreed to go with him to deal with the bull, but it wasn't. And it should've been enough that he held her in his arms.

Yet, that was the very thing that had desire raging within him now. He couldn't remember ever . . . craving . . . someone as he did Marlee. Touching her had been a thrill, but holding her? Well, that was another heart-stopping moment altogether. Having her against him heated his blood in ways that had never happened before. And when he looked into her beautiful bourbon-colored eyes . . . For all her heartache, for all the trauma she'd witnessed and endured, there was still so much hope there that it was nearly blinding.

She was the strongest, bravest woman he knew—and that was saying something with the resilient, courageous women he was around every day. There was so much he wanted to tell Marlee, but it all got lost in the passion that'd consumed him the moment he made the mistake of looking at her mouth.

The curve of her smile made his soul sing. The way she laughed was something he hadn't known he longed to hear. But the desire he saw in her eyes when she looked at him made him forget all about going slowly. It pushed him over the edge of reason, and he wasn't about to put on the brakes.

He deepened the kiss as her hands slid from his chest upward and linked around his neck. Her taste was heaven. There were no awkward moments, no bumped heads or miscommunication. And the longer he held her, the longer the kiss went on, the more he knew, without a doubt, that he'd found the one person in the billions around the world that was meant for him. It should startle him, or at the very least take him aback, but it didn't. How could it when everything felt so right?

All Cooper wanted to do was keep kissing her, but he knew it would lead to other things if he did. And while he had no problems having sex outdoors, it was cold, and he at least owed Marlee a fire. Reluctantly, he slowed the kiss and then ended it. Somehow, he was able to release her and step back.

Marlee's chest heaved as she touched her lips. "I've been wondering what your kiss would taste like."

That was the last thing she should've said. He reached for her at the same time she reached for him. Their mouths clashed again, their tongues dueling as the flames of desire grew. Cooper slid his hands under her coat and felt the way her body trembled when he touched her. He ground himself against her, unable to stop himself. She moaned and shifted her hands to his hips, holding him tightly against her as they moved against each other.

This time, she was the one who ended the kiss. Their eyes met as he stepped back, trying to get himself under control. He took a deep breath and adjusted his hat. If he didn't, he was going to reach for her again. And this time, he might not let her go.

"That was . . ." Marlee said, her voice trailing off.

Cooper nodded. "Yeah. For me, too."

She pushed away from the fence and moved toward him. He held up a hand, stopping her. "You should know that if we kiss again, I'm not going to stop."

"Thank God," she said.

He blinked, not expecting her to react in such a way. "When it comes to you, I have no willpower. I want you. It's as simple as that."

"That's good since I feel the same."

Cooper looked up at the stars, doing his best not to pull her against him.

Marlee drew in a breath and then slowly released it. "Usually, a response like mine gets the other party moving, not standing still."

Cooper chuckled. "You'd think that, right? Things are different with you. I feel . . . out of control."

"I like that."

He looked at her. "You barely know me. I barely know you."

"True. But I know I like how this feels. I don't want to think about anything else. For the first time in years, I'm going to think about myself and what I want. We can stand out here and talk about things because it is beautiful. Or we can go somewhere so I can rip off your clothes and see that fine body naked."

"Where the hell have you been all my life?" he asked in amazement.

She shrugged, her smile growing. "Apparently, waiting to find you."

"Come on," he said as he took her hand. "We're getting out of here and going back to my place where *I'll* be the one to rip off your clothes and see that fine body of yours."

Marlee laughed and quickened her steps to match his long strides. "That sounds like fun. I wonder if we can wait to get to your place."

"Hell. That's a good question."

With desire throbbing, they looked at each other and smiled. The moment was one he'd never forget. They finally reached the truck and released each other's hands to get into their respective seats. He jumped in first and glanced over at her as he started the engine. That's when he saw her looking around as if she were searching for something.

"The deer is gone," he teased.

She smiled as she glanced at him and buckled her seat belt. "Old habits."

He wanted to ask her more about that, but it would have to wait until later. Cooper continued down the road to his place, which was, thankfully, very close. At any other time, he might have wondered what she thought as they drove up the drive to the old farmhouse he'd bought to restore. Now, all he wanted was both of them in the house with his cock inside her.

The moment the truck was in park, her door was open. Cooper met her at the front of the vehicle, and they half-ran up the steps to the porch where he keyed in the combination and the door unlocked. No sooner were they inside than Marlee shut the door and pushed him against the wall.

His hat tumbled off as their lips met. He blindly reached over and locked the door before yanking off her coat. It hit the floor, and he turned her. With their lips still locked, they took turns removing one item of clothing at a time while navigating their way to his room.

When they reached the doorway, they were both naked. Cooper turned her and pressed her against the wall, running his hands down her slender build from the indent of her waist to the flare of her hips. His palms itched to feel the weight of her breasts. Slowly, he caressed back up until he cupped her breast. Her nipple pressed tightly into his palm, making him groan, and his balls tighten.

He tore his mouth from hers and kissed down her neck until he brought one nipple at a time to his mouth and swirled his tongue around it before suckling. Marlee's head dropped back, her eyes closed as her swollen lips parted with her sighs.

Cooper kissed between her breasts and lower while he rolled her nipples between his fingers. He dropped to his knees and slid his hands to her hips. There, he paused and looked up at her. After a moment, she lifted her head to meet his gaze. He gave her a smile and slipped his hand behind the knee of one leg. Slowly, he lifted it and draped it over his shoulder.

Her breath came faster now as she realized what he was going to do. He held her gaze as he moved his head toward her sex and licked her. Her moan—full of longing and a deep ache—nearly made him spill his seed right then.

Cooper took his time as he licked and laved her, learning her, tasting her essence. Her hands splayed on the wall, and her moans had turned to soft cries, but he wasn't finished with her. He waited until she was shaking with need before he slid a finger inside her and flicked his tongue over her clit.

Her breath hitched, and her body tightened right before she jerked with a climax. He continued teasing her until her body stopped moving. Then he lowered her leg, her foot on the floor, before he straightened.

"I forgot what that felt like," she murmured.

He cocked his head. "What?"

"Pleasure."

"Then you'll have as much of it as I can give you."

She smiled and leaned forward to flick her tongue across his nipple. "I'm going to hold you to that."

"Are you?" he asked with a smile. Then he bent and lifted her. She wrapped her legs around his waist. "I don't think you're going to have to hold me to anything because I can't get enough of you."

Her arms wound around him as she leaned forward and gave him a soft kiss. "I don't understand what's happening. And right now, I don't care. I just want to keep feeling this way."

"Then feel." He lifted her until her body was poised over his cock, then slowly, he lowered her.

Another orgasm built within Marlee. She had yet to run her hands over Cooper's fine body, but she'd gotten a good look at his muscular form from his broad shoulders, to his chiseled abs, and impressive arousal. His cock was at her entrance now, the blunt head pushing slowly into her. She wanted him all the way inside, deep, but he held the reins and took his time.

"I can feel you clenching around me," Cooper said tightly.

She nodded. "I can feel you inside me. My God, you feel so good."

Muscles along his jaw tensed as he lowered her inch by inch. Then, finally, he was fully inside. She smiled and tried to move her hips, but he held her still.

"It's not your turn yet," he told her with a grin.

She started to argue and then realized that she wasn't going to pass up such an opportunity. "Do with me what you will."

"Oh, I will, darlin'. I most certainly will."

The words had barely penetrated her mind before he pulled out of her slowly, only to thrust hard. She gasped at the pleasure that burst through her. He repeated the movement twice more, increasing his tempo each time. She clung to him, as her climax remained just out of reach.

Then he turned and walked through a door. The feel of him moving inside her as he moved left her moaning for more. She didn't get it though as he laid her on the bed and grasped her ankles. He began driving inside her with controlled movements. She clutched at the comforter, her body pulsing with a need that tightened with each movement.

Cooper's thrusts became faster, moving deeper, harder. She said his name, lost in the passion. Then he leaned over and teased her nipple. That was all it took to fling her toward another climax.

She screamed at the intense pleasure that left her body weak and pulsing for more. She reached for Cooper and only then realized he hadn't orgasmed yet. She held on to him as he put a hand on either side of her head and began to piston his hips faster and faster. Marlee looked up at him, their eyes meeting just as he peaked.

He jerked out of her, spilling his seed on her stomach as his body shuddered. He held her until the final vestiges of the climax waned. For long moments, they didn't move, didn't speak. She'd never been in such a situation, but she wanted to stay here forever.

"I should get something to clean you off with," Cooper whispered.

She shook her head. "Can we just stay like this? I'm quite content right now."

"Darlin', we can do whatever you want. So long as you stay with me tonight."

Marlee lifted her head to look at him. "You want me to stay?"

"I do. I want more of you, whether it's sex, holding you, or talking. I like you."

"I want to stay and do all those things and more."

He grinned and gave her a soft kiss. "Ah, woman, you've made me the happiest man on Earth."

Marlee snuggled against him and closed her eyes. "And you've made me the happiest woman on Earth."

Chapter 19

Marlee's warm body lying beside him made Cooper smile as he woke. An auburn curl tickled his chin, but he didn't move it. He slowly opened his eyes to see light filtering through the blinds. The night had gotten away from him. He'd intended to wake Marlee and make love to her again, but they had fallen asleep. And for some reason, he'd slept the sleep of the dead.

He heard the flap on the door and the soft jingle of Pesto's collar as the Doberman came into the room. Cooper motioned to Pesto with his free hand. The dog's dark eyes slid to Marlee as he extended his head and gently sniffed her hand. Satisfied, Pesto sat, his tongue hanging out of his mouth as he panted, waiting for Cooper to get out of bed.

Something caught Pesto's attention, and a low growl rumbled in his chest. Cooper didn't think anything of it since Pesto kept the wildlife away from the house. He put his finger to his lips to quiet the dog when Pesto turned his head back to Cooper. Then the dog stood, his little nub of a tail wagging as if silently asking if he could go back outside.

Cooper motioned him out, and seconds later, the dog flap sounded again. He'd come across Pesto quite by accident at the local animal shelter. With his schedule, the last thing he needed was something else to take care of, but Pesto had needed him, and as it turned out, Cooper needed the dog, as well. They'd been together for five years now, and Pesto was the best dog he'd ever had.

Cooper had fences up around his property, but Pesto never wandered off. He stayed near the house and had free rein to come and go from inside as he wished. But the dog was the best at keeping raccoons and other things away. Though Cooper had seen Pesto walking with a calico cat. And on one occasion when it had been cold out, he'd spotted the two curled up together. That's when Cooper began feeding the feline.

He yawned and held Marlee tighter. Neither had moved since they drifted off to sleep. He'd been shocked and pleased when she had agreed to stay. He couldn't explain it, but he had known that she needed to remain with him. Perhaps it was because he was so attracted to her. Whatever the reason, he wanted to have her around more.

But she would be leaving soon. He wasn't sure how that would work, but he wanted to try. Long-distance relationships failed more often than not, but he knew there was something special about Marlee. He shouldn't let that go without trying.

The fact that they just met and were getting to know each other was probably a concern for her. It wasn't for him. He'd dated enough women to know that what he'd found with Marlee was special. The kind of special that people searched for and never found. The kind of special that would make him give up everything just to be with her.

The kind of special he didn't think he'd find.

Marlee inhaled deeply and shifted her leg to rub

against his. He felt her smile right before she lifted her head from his chest and met his eyes.

"Good morning," he said.

She blinked and moved the hair out of her face. "Morning. How long have you been awake?"

"Not long."

"You should've moved me."

He frowned at her. "Why? I was comfortable. Besides, I enjoy having you in my arms."

Her smile grew as her eyes crinkled. "You like to cuddle?"

"I admit, I'm a cuddler. You?"

"I definitely am, but most men aren't."

Cooper rolled his eyes. "Then they're stupid."

"I could get used to this."

"The cuddling?"

"That and the fact you agree with me."

He chuckled and ran his hand up and down her back. "I'd like to think the times we might disagree, it would be done in a civilized manner. Though I've noticed you're quite stubborn."

"I am." She ducked her head and laughed. "Probably not one of my better traits."

"I don't know. I think it could be a good quality in some instances."

She stretched and moved so she could prop her chin on his chest and look at him. "I don't normally sleep through the night. I'm usually looking at evidence or searching for some lead."

"Everyone needs a break. My mom calls it self-care. I tend to agree with her. People get burned out. Why do you think companies require people to take vacation days? Because everyone needs downtime."

She shrugged. "I have to admit, you're right. The sleep did me a world of good."

"I like hearing that. Though it might also have something to do with the sex."

Her lips curled up in a grin. "The food, the sex, the comfortable bed, the cuddling. Yep. It was a recipe for an amazing night. You need to be careful. I may demand it again."

"I hope you do." And he was serious. She could demand it every night for the rest of his life, and he'd gladly give it to her.

"I want to." The smile was gone as she grew serious.

"Nothing's stopping you."

Her brows rose on her forehead. "There's my work."

"You can't help others until you take care of yourself. Take a few days here to go over the evidence that led you to Brice and Naomi. I can help if you'd like. Just . . . stay here. Let me spend more time with you."

Her gaze lowered as she blew out a breath. Then her bourbon-colored eyes met his again. "Then what? We go through this again? I'm going to have to leave eventually. It's what my work entails. All I do is travel."

"I don't know what's going to happen today or tomorrow. I understand what you're saying, but all I know is that I like how I feel when I'm with you. I want to enjoy more of that."

"I'd be lying if I said I didn't."

He ran a finger down the side of her cheek. "Then stay for a few days."

"You can't use that sexy voice while I'm lying naked next to you and not get the answer you want," she replied with a smile.

Elation swept through Cooper. "Now I know how to get you to say yes."

They shared a laugh. As it died away, they stared into each other's eyes. Just as Cooper leaned in to kiss her,

Pesto began barking. Marlee jerked, but Cooper shook his head. "It's fine. It's my dog."

"He sounds upset."

Pesto certainly did. Cooper knew that bark, and it was one that meant something, or *someone*, was on the property. He sat up as Marlee rolled away. He threw off the sheets and jumped to his feet as the sound of Pesto's barking moved farther away from the house. Cooper rushed into the living area and looked through the open windows and out back to see Pesto running after something as he barked even harder.

"Should we follow him?" Marlee asked from behind Cooper.

He watched Pesto until the dog finally stopped, though he continued barking a little longer. Pesto remained in that position, staring after whatever it was for a long moment before turning and trotting back to the house. Cooper let out a whistle, and the dog ran to him.

The moment Pesto came through the doggie door, he rushed to Cooper with his little nub wagging. Cooper rubbed his head and smiled down at the dog. "Did you get him, boy? Good boy. That's a good dog."

"He's beautiful."

The moment Pesto heard Marlee's voice, he forgot all about Cooper and went to her with his tongue lolling. Cooper shook his head at the dog. Not that he blamed Pesto. He'd want to be with Marlee, too. "His name is Pesto."

"Aren't you a handsome boy?" Marlee said as she let the dog smell her and then ran her hand over his head. She looked at Cooper. "I don't remember a dog last night."

"We weren't looking at much of anything but each other."

"Ah, no, we certainly weren't."

His gaze lowered to her nakedness as she went back to petting Pesto. Cooper couldn't believe he wished he was the dog in that moment to have Marlee's hands on him. He'd seen his fair share of pretty women in his life, but Marlee surpassed them all. From her wild curls to her heart-stopping eyes to her tenaciousness to her body that he couldn't wait to sink into once more, she was perfect for him.

"You're staring," she said without looking at him.

He felt his cock stirring. "You're naked, and you don't want me to look at your beautiful body?"

She licked her lips and straightened before turning to him. "Well, when you say it like that, no."

He groaned when she looked at his rod. The driving need he felt, the hunger for her was something he'd never encountered before. Cooper wanted to hold on to her tightly and never let go, but he knew he couldn't do that. All he could do was savor whatever time he had with her—for however long that was.

Something hit the window, and he realized it was raining. He walked to Marlee and took her hand. "How about a shower?"

"I am getting chilled."

"I've got a very large stall, big enough for two."

She laughed as she followed him, Pesto on her heels. "Is that right?"

"The bathroom was the first thing I remodeled when I got the house seven years ago."

He brought her back into the bedroom and then into the master bath that had a shower in white marble tiles surrounded by glass with two showerheads. Next to it was a tub that would also fit two, a long counter with two sinks, and two cabinets and entries into two separate closets.

Cooper stood back while Marlee looked at all of it. He

turned on the shower to heat the water. She returned from her tour of the closet and gaped at him.

"This is incredible. I can't wait to see the rest of the house. Did you do all the work yourself?"

He shrugged. "Some of it. Other things I hired people to do. I know my limits."

"You're one incredible man, Cooper Owens."

He stepped into the shower and pulled her with him. "Oh, I'm just getting started with you, Marlee Frampton. Just you wait."

Chapter 20

The hot water and Cooper's soapy hands on her body were enough to make Marlee promise to never leave Texas, much less the house. His hands moved over her slowly, teasing her swollen breasts and turgid nipples until she burned for him.

She braced her hands on the wall in front of her as he stood behind her, the water cascading over them from both sides. His arousal pressed against her, and her sex throbbed to have him inside once more. It didn't seem to matter that she had been pleasured twice the night before. Her body responded as if it might wither without his touch.

He pulled her in to press her back against his chest. She tipped her head to the side as he kissed her temple and then across her cheek, his fingers rolling her nipples. He hadn't even reached her sex yet, but she was sure that if he continued on his present course, he could make her orgasm.

"You're so damn beautiful," he whispered.

Marlee wanted to let him continue touching her, but

she turned in his arms and met his gaze instead. "You had last night. This morning is mine."

If it was possible, his green eyes darkened even more as his nostrils flared. "Given how I want you, it won't take me long."

Instead of answering, she smiled at him and rubbed her soapy breasts against his chest. Cooper let out a low moan. Marlee took her time as the water rinsed the last of the suds away and used that time to smooth her hands over his broad shoulders and arms thick with sinew. He had calluses on his hands, proving that he worked hard, which made her want him even more.

She tilted her head up to him as her hands moved around to his back and down to his trim waist before splaying over his tight ass. His gaze narrowed as he did the same to her, grinding his cock into her stomach.

"Woman," he said.

She loved how he said it as an endearment. Her blood heated even more. She began kissing his chest, following the water's path as it ran over him down to his nipples. He sucked in a quick breath when she swirled her finger around one of his tight buds. She bit back her smile when she felt his arousal jump in response.

Her kissing path took her down his tight abs until she was on her knees with his beautiful rod waiting. She wrapped her fingers around it and gently stroked up and down his length. Cooper moaned again and leaned forward to press his hands against the tile just as she had done.

He was thick and oh, so hard. Marlee brought her mouth to him and ran her tongue over the head of his arousal several times. Then, she parted her lips and wrapped them around him. He whispered her name, his voice thick with desire. Marlee slid her mouth up and down his length. His hand grabbed a fistful of her hair and held her as he moaned in pleasure. She couldn't remember a man ever responding to her so blatantly before, and it drove her to give him even more.

It turned her on, and she moved a hand between her legs to begin rubbing her clit. Suddenly, Cooper had her on her feet and facing the wall again. In one thrust he was buried inside her.

"Damn, woman, you drive me to the brink of need like no one ever has before," he murmured in her ear.

She leaned her head back and nodded. "I burn for you."

"Then let me ease us both."

Cooper began moving with deep, hard thrusts. He held her hips tightly as he propelled them toward ecstasy. Marlee steadied herself with her hands on the cool tile as she found herself careening toward orgasm. It came over her quickly, tossing her into an abyss of bliss.

"Marlee," Cooper said against her ear in a rough voice. "Ah, baby."

She reached back and touched him just as he climaxed. He pulled out of her again, but this time, she spun around and took him in hand, moving up and down his hard length to finish him. He pressed his forehead against hers as they stood there in the spray of water.

A long while later, he lifted his head and cupped her face with his hands. "We really need to get some condoms. It's getting harder and harder not to come inside you."

"I know one place we're going today then," she said with a smile.

He wrapped an arm around her and kissed her deeply. It wasn't the fiery kisses from the night before, but something deeper, something even stronger. She felt his emotions in the kiss, even though she didn't understand them all. But that didn't matter. He showed her how he felt in ways no one ever had. And she did the same in return.

There was no reason to hide anything. Cooper had been open about everything, which gave her the same freedom. They had this day and maybe the next. Who knew after that? Marlee didn't want to think that far ahead. All she wanted was to take this time that had been given to her and enjoy every last millisecond of it.

The kiss ended, and she pressed her face against his chest as they held each other tightly. If she had to make a decision in that instant, she knew she'd never leave Cooper. Yes, everything was new, but the feelings between them, the way he made her feel, it was all exhilarating. She knew with unwavering certainty that she could be happy with him.

Then she thought of Macey. She'd made a promise to her sister and their parents. Marlee couldn't stop now.

"Don't pull away," Cooper said.

She shook her head. "I'm not. I'm holding on to you."

"Your body might be, but your mind is drifting."

She didn't know how he knew. Marlee looked up at him and smiled. "I'm not used to taking much time for myself. I feel guilty."

"Because people are in need?"

"And I've still not found my sister's daughter."

"Marlee . . . you know you may never find her," he said gently.

Marlee glanced to the side. "I know, but I have to keep looking."

"Even if it means harming yourself?"

"I'm not harming myself."

"Really?" he asked, brows raised. "I feel the stiffness in your shoulders from lack of rest. I can't imagine you eat very healthy on the road."

"I do the best I can. More places offer better food now." She didn't know why she felt defensive. Cooper was only pointing out the very things she'd already told herself.

"You just admitted not taking time for yourself, whether that's sleep or just resting. And what about your parents? What you do is beyond admirable, but they need you."

She looked down at his chest and nodded. "I know."

"Hey," he said and smoothed her hair back from her face. "You're doing great things. I'm simply saying you should take a break sometimes and take care of yourself."

"I'm doing that now."

His smile was slow. "I plan on continuing like this for as long as you let me."

The problem was, she feared she would never want him to stop.

"You can trust me," he told her. "I'm a good guy. I won't hurt you."

"I wouldn't be here with you now if I thought you would."

"Then let me help you. Or, if you don't want my help, then let me help you find someone you will allow to help you out. This thing you're doing is huge. It takes more than one person."

She blew out a frustrated breath. "I'll gladly take your help while I'm in town, but I've already told you, I tried having people on payroll before. It doesn't work."

"You had the wrong people. Imagine how much easier life could be with the right ones."

"It would be incredible," she admitted. "I could do more than one case at a time, and I wouldn't have to travel constantly."

Cooper's smile was blinding. "Exactly. I think you just need to find people as passionate about what you're doing as you are."

For so long, Marlee had rejected the notion of hiring anyone after the failed attempts she'd tried. But now, she thought it might not be a bad idea to give it another go.

She'd had years to learn where she needed the help and what she could do on her own.

"An assistant," she said. "I'd love an assistant who could field the calls and know which cases were for me or for someone else."

Cooper kissed the tip of her nose. "Keep thinking along those lines."

Now that her mind was there, Marlee couldn't stop it. And she didn't want to.

Chapter 21

He'd had the chance to kill Marlee, but Chuck hadn't done it. Regardless of what Stella thought, the Frampton woman was a nuisance that needed to be removed. He should've done it a few years ago, but he'd listened to Stella. Now, look at what that had gotten them.

Marlee had the uncanny ability to figure out where they were located and find her way there. The fact that she kept sticking her nose in their business and getting closer and closer to them proved his point. If Marlee wasn't taken out of the picture, he and Stella would find themselves behind bars—and that wasn't something he would allow.

Chuck sat in his truck and glared in the direction of the house. He hadn't expected the dog. Damn thing had nearly bitten him. He'd left his handgun in the truck, deciding on a knife as his weapon of choice. If he'd had the gun, he would've killed the dog the moment it first spotted him.

Frankly, Chuck was surprised that Marlee and Cooper hadn't come running out of the house. Then again, they'd been all over each other the night before when they put the bull back in the pasture. More than likely, they had still been having sex. That would've allowed him to kill them easily since their attention was on anything but him.

Too bad the dog had brought attention to him.

Chuck wasn't giving up on ridding the world of the nosey Marlee Frampton once and for all. He didn't care if she was alone or with someone. She was going to die. He hadn't clawed himself out of the gutter, only to have his cushy life taken away from him.

Age slowed him. Stella didn't realize it yet, but she would soon. He had maybe another three years before he would be replaced. In that time, he planned to gather as much money as he could, and nothing sold as well as a child. People did anything for babies, which was ridiculous, considering there were so many in the foster system. But for reasons he didn't understand, those kids were tainted to some.

He'd grown up in the system, and he'd turned out all right. He didn't see the issue. Then again, if someone wanted to pay him for a baby, he'd get them a baby. It was as simple as that. And with Stella lining up the clients, all he had to do was find the pregnant women. That was the easy part. Those women were everywhere.

He didn't discriminate either. If he found a woman and the situation allowed him to get her alone and the baby out alive, he did it. Everyone had a job. That was his. He didn't like it or dislike it. What he did like was the money. For the last ten years, he'd lived comfortably. He had things he never thought he'd be able to get.

Marlee Frampton threatened all of that. She had to go. The government had taught him how to kill in the military. He was using those skills, and he would continue doing so until his bank account showed the number he wanted. Then he'd retire, though he'd still have some kind of hand in Stella's business. After all, finding good people to work with was hard.

Chuck glanced at his phone when it buzzed. He spotted Stella's name and answered it. "Yeah?"

"How soon do you think you can get me another baby?"

He shrugged. "Give me until tomorrow."

"Can you do it sooner? I've got someone willing to pay a hefty sum."

Chuck let out a whistle. "Why the rush?"

"Why do any of them come to us instead of a legit adoption agency?"

"True. Give me twelve hours."

"You've got eight. These people have a flight leaving the country tonight."

Chuck sat up straighter in his seat. "I'm on it."

He ended the call and tossed the phone onto the seat beside him as he started the engine. His gaze went to Cooper Owens' house.

"Looks like the two of you get a reprieve. Enjoy your day, because I'll be back."

Chapter 22

While Cooper made breakfast, the handle on the door twisted. Marlee stiffened on the stool at the island, her gaze jerking to the source of the noise. Before Cooper could make a move, he heard the number being punched in and then the door unlocked. Suddenly, Jace stood there, his gaze moving from Cooper to Marlee.

"Ah . . . I think I'm interrupting," Jace said.

Marlee instantly eased and shook her head. "You're fine."

Jace looked to Cooper, who motioned him inside with his head. "It's pretty common for Jace to show up anytime he thinks there might be food."

"That's not true," Jace said with a roll of his eyes as he stepped into the house and closed the door behind him. Then he paused and smiled. "Actually, it is."

Marlee chuckled and leaned on the island. "Do you not have food at your place?"

"Oh, yeah. I keep everything stocked, but I'm a growing boy and must eat," Jace replied.

Cooper made a sound in the back of his throat. "You do realize your mother quit saying that to you when you were sixteen and you were eating her out of house and home, right?"

"I like to eat," Jace said with a shrug.

Cooper went back to cooking with a shake of his head. Some things about Jace never changed. But a great many things had. Those things, the bad ones, Jace had shared about only once. It had been one of the lowest times of Jace's life, but Cooper, as well as Brice and Caleb, had been there for him. For a while, they all thought that Jace was getting better.

But Cooper knew differently. Jace pretended. He smiled and put on a show that things were fine, but they weren't. Far from it, actually. Cooper kept a close eye on his friend in case Jace fell down that rabbit hole and couldn't get out of it. He would always look out for Jace.

Cooper's gaze briefly landed on Marlee to find her watching him. She gave him a soft smile, and he realized that she knew about Jace's past. He kept forgetting that she had done a deep-dive on all of them—something he would have done, as well.

"So," Jace said to Marlee as he took one of the stools at the bar and poured copious amounts of sugar into his coffee. "What do you think of Cooper's fixer-upper?"

She sat up and looked around at the crown molding that had gone up about a month ago and was waiting on paint. "I think Cooper pays attention to details. He's taken this farmhouse into a new century, yet somehow managed to keep most of the charm. Like the real wood floors in the thin slats and the crown molding. It harkens back to a time when people took a lot of time and care with woodworking."

Cooper smiled. He'd known that Marlee had an eye for details, but he hadn't realized how much she saw.

Jace took a drink of his coffee and set down the mug. "The fact that he's had this house for seven years and still hasn't finished with the renovations tells you the time he takes. You sound like you know a lot about woodworking."

"My dad did some small things as a hobby. He always pointed things out to me growing up," Marlee said.

Cooper slid the omelet onto a plate and handed it to Marlee, along with some sausage and toast. "I have no skill with woodworking, but I know what I want."

"And he makes sure he gets it," Jace said with a smile as he rose and grabbed a piece of sausage to eat.

Marlee shrugged, her lips twisting. "I'm the same way. If I pay for something, then I'm going to make sure I get what I paid for."

"I just love talking about remodeling," Jace said with an exaggerated sigh. "But there's something else I'd like to talk about."

"Not now." Cooper knew Jace wanted to discuss the missing child that Marlee was searching for, but Cooper wanted to give her a little more time to relax.

Marlee smiled at Cooper before she tucked an auburn curl behind her ear and looked at Jace. "Your friend is trying to give me some downtime, but what Cooper doesn't know is that I've not stopped thinking about any of it. So, please. Tell me whatever it is you have."

Cooper turned back to the stove and the omelet he was making for himself. At least Marlee looked more relaxed than she had the day before. She was smiling easier, as well. Maybe the time with him had done her some good.

Arms came around him as Marlee pressed against his back. "Thank you for breakfast. The omelet is delicious. And thank you for taking care of me. It's not something I'm used to."

He put his arm over hers and turned his head to look at her. "It's been my pleasure."

"I think I might gag," Jace mumbled sarcastically. "Yep. I gagged. You two need to just get a room."

Marlee released Cooper and said, "We had a room. We actually had an entire house, then you showed up."

Jace busted out laughing. "Damn, Marlee. You fit in well."

"She certainly does," Cooper said with a smile as he looked at her.

She shot him a wink and returned to the stool to dig into her breakfast. By the time Cooper had finished cooking his omelet and turned to the island, Jace had a map of the United States laid out. Marlee held her plate to give him room.

"Holy hell," Cooper mumbled when he saw all the marks Jace had made.

Jace made a face. "I've been busy." His hazel eyes swung to Marlee. "Yesterday, Cooper and I began marking the locations around Texas where the infants were kidnapped, and the women were murdered. Turns out, they're all around us."

"Us, meaning Clearview?" Marlee asked as she looked between them.

Cooper nodded as he swallowed his food. "Yeah. It was very curious to me. At first, I didn't think much of it since we're pretty central to all the major cities in Texas, then I thought about you coming to our little town."

"That's right. Your evidence led you here. You just had the wrong people," Jace added.

Marlee set her fork on the plate and crossed one leg over the other. "I always follow the evidence."

"Then you came to the right place," Jace told her.

Cooper nodded as he finished off his omelet. "What evidence led you to Brice and Naomi, if you don't mind me asking?"

"It was the adoption agency, really. Let's just say they

aren't totally on the up and up, but there hasn't been anything definitive that I could bring to the authorities. The age of the infant your friends were looking to adopt got my attention initially since I was sure that Nate was the baby I was searching for."

"Makes sense," Cooper said. "Then again, I have no idea how many children you were looking at."

Marlee blew out a breath. "More than you can fathom. It makes my job even more difficult, and while I rely on my instincts and training, it's more about the evidence. I know another investigator who works in the Dallas area. His infant grandson was kidnapped, and his daughter was killed. I asked him to watch Brice and Naomi. After they left the adoption office, John went inside to take a look around. He said he saw the same security guard who worked at the agency he believed took his grandchild. He left right away, but he's sure the guy recognized him."

Jace's brows drew together. "Why would the security guard recognize John?"

"Because John went after the company with everything he had. Eventually, they shut down, but he's always been convinced they just moved and changed names."

Cooper set aside his plate, nodding. "He believes he found the place then. That's good for him, I suppose. But how does that help you?"

"It didn't, but it's information I can use. Now that I know for sure that Nate isn't the child I'm searching for, I have to go back over my evidence because I went wrong somewhere," she said.

Jace sat back and rested a hand on his thigh while his other splayed on the island. "What if you didn't?"

Marlee frowned as she swiveled her head to face him. "You think the tests at the hospital lied and that Nate is the baby I'm looking for?"

"No," Jace said with a shake of his head. "I think your

evidence led you to the wrong people, not the wrong area."

Cooper lifted his hands, palms out. "Hold up. Jace. Are you saying that we need to look into every male infant around the same age as Nate and test them?"

"It wouldn't work," Marlee said before Jace could respond. "Whoever has the child would find out what was going on and run off. That's why I need to approach things carefully."

Jace rolled his eyes. "Guys, give me some credit. Of course, I don't want us to bring in every male infant in the area. What we can do, though, is find out what children have been registered at doctors' offices compared to those at the hospitals. No doubt there will be some discrepancies. Then, we can look into those."

Cooper looked at Marlee to find her considering Jace's plan. It was a good one, that was for sure.

"I've never done anything like that before," Marlee said with hesitation. "Usually, that kind of information has to be obtained through the hospitals and doctors via the authorities. And that isn't something they usually give someone like me."

Jace flashed her a smile that usually made women swoon. "Good thing you know us then since we're friends with both the sheriff and the chief of police."

"I can't let you do this," Marlee said with a shake of her head.

Cooper laid his hand atop hers, drawing her attention. "You aren't *letting* us do anything. We're doing this to help you since this involved our friends. Trust me, both Danny and Ryan want to help. And . . . there might be someone else I can bring in."

"Cash," Jace said.

Marlee bit her lip and turned her gaze to Cooper. "The other investigator you told me about?"

He nodded. "I don't want to step on your toes, bu—"

"Step," she interrupted him. "I'd rather a child be found and returned to its family than worry about who's getting credit for it."

Jace stood and made his way over to the counter for another cup of coffee. "You've got to stop this, Marlee. Not only do I like you, but I'm respecting the hell out of you now. Keep it up, and we may never let you leave."

It was said as a joke, but since Cooper and Marlee had briefly spoken about the future earlier, it made him look her way to find her staring at him. He saw something odd in her gaze, an emotion he didn't quite recognize. This wasn't the time to ask about it, so he let it go.

"All right. Let's see what your friends the sheriff and chief say," she told them. "Now, show me this map."

Jace finished fixing his coffee and hurried back to the island. "This is what I put together in twelve hours yesterday."

Cooper gazed at all the different-colored markings. "Twelve hours?"

"I pulled up all the reports of kidnapped infants and pregnant women who had been killed," Jace said, his voice filled with shock. "Look at all of them."

"I am." How could Cooper look at anything else? The dots were everywhere, in every state. It boggled his mind.

Marlee finished her food. "I did one of those after my sister was killed. It's what propelled me to do what I do now."

"How can this continue to happen without the police catching anyone?" Jace demanded to know.

Marlee shrugged. "How do so many murders of any kind happen that are never solved? It is what it is."

Cooper took her plate and set it atop his. "I'm having a hard time accepting that. I don't like the idea of murder, but this is different. These are pregnant women who have their children ripped from them and are left to die. There should be something about this that hits the Feds' radar."

"It has," Marlee told them. "I have a contact there. We met during my sister's case. I wish I could tell you they are making headway, but they aren't."

Jace shook his head. "With all the equipment, manpower, and surveillance we have now, there has to be *something*."

"It's the same question I ask myself weekly, and there's never any change."

Cooper folded his arms over his chest. "Then let's make sure there is some."

"Now that's what I'm talking about," Jace said with a grin.

Chapter 23

Marlee stared with sickening dread at the explosion of marks on the map. So, so many more had been added in the ten years since she had done a similar one. She had hoped that by trying to locate the missing children, she could make a dent in all the chaos, but she didn't think that was possible.

No matter how you looked at it, babies were thought of as a commodity, and people with an agenda were going to exploit that. Never mind all those in foster care or those in orphanages. For reasons she couldn't even begin to fathom, so many ignored the babies and children in desperate need of homes and love. Instead, those same people wanted infants to raise as their own, babies who hadn't seen the horrendous depths humanity could sink to.

Those people paid untold sums of money on the black market for babies. They didn't ask where the infants came from, because they didn't care. All that mattered was that they got what they wanted—a baby they could call theirs.

Macey's daughter was somewhere out in the world. Marlee knew in the depths of her soul that her niece was alive. If not, Marlee would've found the body by now because she had left no stone unturned. At least in the States. She hadn't looked abroad, but she wanted to. She'd always wanted to.

That cost money, however. Funds she'd been trying to raise for ten years. Every time she got a little bit saved, something came up, be it part of a job or with her parents. At this rate, she'd never be able to search the world for her niece.

Cooper's words from that morning came back to her. The idea of having people working for her was something she wanted. Instead of hiring the first person she thought was a decent fit so she could hand off some work, she needed to approach it differently. First, they needed to have the kind of dedication to the job that she had. That was the biggie. If they didn't, then it simply wouldn't work.

She blinked and noticed that Jace and Cooper were staring at her. She'd been so engrossed in her thoughts that she hadn't paid attention to them. "I'm sorry. I was lost in thought for a moment."

"We can hold off," Cooper suggested.

She shook her head and smiled at him. "I can handle it. I should've been doing this all along. That first year when more and more marks went on the map, and I didn't make any headway, it was . . ." She paused, looking for the right word.

"Daunting," Jace offered.

Cooper then said, "Discouraging."

"Both," she replied. "I wanted to make a difference. Instead, more and more women were being killed, their babies taken. So, I stopped tracking then. It allowed me to focus on the cases at hand instead of all the ones out there suffering as my family did."

Cooper ran a hand up and down her arm from across the space of the island. "That was probably a smart thing to do. Did you keep track of the cases you solved?"

"Oh, yes." She smiled, thinking of the board her parents had created at the house. "I let my parents know, and they kept track of them, sending me pictures to help bolster me." Marlee shook her head as she thought about that board. "For so long, I thought they did it for themselves. It wasn't until a few years ago that I discovered they'd done it for me because they thought I needed to see how many I'd helped."

Jace asked, "And *did* it help?"

"It did. I'm so glad my parents did it. They even kept a record of the cases I solved, even if I wasn't able to deliver a child back to their loved ones alive." Marlee took a deep breath and looked at Cooper. "However, I think it's time to bring out the map again and track it. Especially if I'm going to hire people."

Cooper's smile was slow and so damn sexy that she wanted to go to him and kiss him. "Think what you could accomplish if you trained others in how you work. You could solve double the cases. Hell, triple."

"That's why I'm considering it. That, as well as the fact that I can't keep running myself into the ground like I have been." It was a big wakeup call. One she should've heard years ago but had ignored.

Jace rubbed his hands together. "So. Back to the map. You'll see I used different colors. The purple ones are for locations where infants were kidnapped. I kept it to infants so we could see a correlation. The green ones are for pregnant women killed and the babies taken. The orange ones are pregnant women killed where the infants didn't survive."

"There are so damn many of them," Cooper murmured.

Marlee's gaze was glued to her little town in California. There were four green dots there. One of them was for Macey. While she mourned her twin as well as her niece, Marlee inhaled deeply and let her gaze move over the map. Every state had dots of all three colors. Still, there were a few states with more than any other—Texas, California, New York, Florida, Louisiana, and Nevada.

Jace pointed to each of them. "What makes these so special? Texas, I get. It's vast with a lot of wide-open spaces."

Marlee considered it for a moment. "There's some correlation we're missing, but I don't know what it is. I know that while there are a lot of marks on that map, I'd guess we're missing at least half."

"Illegal immigrants," Cooper said.

Marlee nodded. "They won't tell the police anything. And if we don't know about them, we can't guess where they are."

"Which means we can't come up with anything to work with without all the data," Jace said and ran a hand down his face. "This could be why the Feds haven't done anything."

Marlee shrugged, thinking of Stephanie. "Like I said, I made a friend in the FBI. I'd like to think she's been honest with me, but I can't be certain. For all I know, they aren't doing anything. I don't think that's true, but I only have her word to go on."

"Where does that leave us, then?" Cooper asked.

Marlee tapped her finger on the map as her mind raced through the different scenarios. She slid off the stool. "My evidence. It's like the two of you said, it's what got me here. There's a reason for that. While I'd like to end the kidnapping of children and the killing of pregnant women, right now, I want to find the assholes who brought me here."

"I'm willing to help," Cooper replied.

Jace cracked his knuckles. "Try and stop me."

Marlee winked at Cooper and went to get her shoes

on. She didn't care that she was in the same clothes she'd worn the night before. She was with someone she liked a great deal. That in itself was something new to her. For the most part, Marlee enjoyed being by herself. Few people understood her. Once they found out what she did for a living, they distanced themselves. As if it were too morbid or something. She didn't know or care why they did it.

That wasn't the case with Cooper or any of his friends, though. They wanted to help, and it wasn't just because they wished to protect Brice and Naomi. It was because they genuinely cared. Which made her like Cooper even more.

The thing was, she *really* liked him. If she allowed herself, she knew that she could fall for him. That excited her for sure because she'd finally found someone she was attracted to, who treated her amazingly and kissed like he would die without her.

Then there was the fact that she wasn't working alone. The one thing she'd done for most of the last ten years was the very thing she didn't want to do any longer. She knew a lot of that had to do with Cooper and their attraction, but she didn't care. All this time, she'd shouldered the load of her work herself, and she'd done all right. Nothing spectacular. She'd solved cases and managed to bring back a few babies to their families. But the toll had been severe.

Now that Cooper—as well as Jace—was taking some of the load from her, she realized how weighty it had been. With it gone, she wondered how she would ever shoulder it on her own again.

"Hey," Cooper said as he walked into the bedroom after her and closed the door. "You can tell us to back off, you know."

"I know. I'm actually looking forward to the help. I

was just thinking about that, by the way. You two are looking at the same data as I am, but you're seeing it differently. That is an asset I've been without—probably to the detriment of some of my cases."

Cooper shook his head as he approached her and pulled her into his arms. "Don't be too hard on yourself, especially with things from the past. It's done and over. You can't change it. All you can do is be in the here and now and change the things before you."

"I want to change them. You've helped me see that. And, yes, I do regret taking so long to come to this realization. But now that I have, I'm going to make a change. Right after I finish this case," she said with a flash of a smile.

His forest green eyes studied her for a moment. "You're beautiful."

Warmth spread through her at his words. "And you're gorgeous."

"I mean it, Marlee. You amaze me. The strength and courage it took for you to leave your job to become a private investigator is something few would do. That took drive."

She laid her hands on his chest and shook her head before looking at him. "Actually, it was grief and the need to get answers. I had skills from the police academy that I used to get certified as a PI, but anyone could've done what I did."

"You need to give yourself more credit. You've kicked ass."

"Well, I'd like to kick some more. And I'd like for you and Jace and whoever else wants to help to join me."

Outside the door, Jace said, "I was hoping you'd say that."

Marlee and Cooper laughed before Cooper leaned down and gave her a long, languid kiss. When he lifted his head, he met her gaze. "I'm going to steal as many kisses as I can."

"I expect nothing less."

"And I'm going to taste that sweet body of yours again."

Her nipples hardened at his roughened voice. "I'll demand it."

"Woman," he said and rubbed his thickening cock against her. "That's what you do to me."

"It's a good thing because you do the same to me."

"You shouldn't tell me such things. I'll throw you on the bed and strip you bare."

She rose up on her toes and whispered, "You shouldn't say such things unless you plan to carry them out."

"Guys!" Jace hollered from the kitchen. "You got quiet. Please tell me you aren't, you know . . . having sexy time. I'm waiting on you."

Cooper grunted and pressed his forehead to hers. "He's like a child."

Marlee laughed. This time when her mind went to her niece, it wasn't filled with as much pain as the last time.

Chapter 24

This wasn't how Cooper had planned to spend the day with Marlee, but he wasn't upset about it. The fact that he was with her was good enough for him. Her gaze sought him out as they walked to the motel room she'd rented. He reached for her hand, and she smiled as she linked her fingers with his.

Jace walked behind them. Cooper glanced back at his friend and found Jace's gaze on the ground, a peculiar expression on his face. Cooper didn't get a chance to ask him about it because they reached Marlee's door. She used the key to get in and walked inside.

Cooper had gotten a quick glimpse of the room when he'd picked her up the night before, but his eyes had been more on her. Now, he got to see it all. The walls were covered with pictures of Brice, Naomi, and the rest of their group. There were pictures of the adoption agency in Dallas, of an older woman in her late fifties walking out of the office with her head turned to the side, and another of that same woman talking to a man with a baseball hat, who had his back to the camera. There were more pictures on the second bed and even some on the floor.

Jace let out a low whistle as he shut the door behind him. "Damn."

"I like to see things set out," Marlee explained. "Stuff can get lost in the shuffle in a file."

Cooper spotted a picture of him and glanced at Marlee. "Makes sense. Tell us what all you have."

She took a deep breath and went to the wall nearest her. "The first half of this wall is dedicated to the family of the missing infant. Including copies of a few of the crime scene photos."

"Damn," Jace said again when he looked closer at a picture of a body covered with a white sheet, blood pooled all around it. "That's a lot of blood."

"That's what they do," Marlee said. "What they do is brutal. And slow."

Cooper walked to Marlee and retook her hand. He gave it a squeeze, letting her know that he was there to help in whatever capacity she allowed.

She gave him a nod before pointing to the next section, which was significantly smaller. "I also began making a note of who investigated the crimes to see if I could connect them."

"You think they could be working with someone?" Jace asked as his head snapped to her.

Marlee shrugged. "At this point, I'll consider anything. I'm ruling nothing out. Including the authorities working with each other to keep things quiet or working with the criminals."

"I agree, it's a possibility," Cooper said.

Jace shrugged. "And these photos?"

"That's everyone that I've found who is connected to the adoption agency in some form or fashion," she explained.

Cooper let his gaze move slowly over the various pictures. Below each one was a name and their role with the company. "I suppose you already looked into these people?"

"Yes. It's ongoing, however."

He nodded slowly. "Anything useful with any of them?"

"A couple." Marlee walked to the wall and pointed to a middle-aged woman and a younger woman. "These two."

Jace eyed both of them. "What about them?"

"On two separate occasions when pregnant women were killed and their babies stolen, both of these women were out of the office."

Cooper thought about that for a moment. "Separately? Or together?"

"Together," Marlee said. "I could've overlooked one incident as someone calling in. But twice?" she asked, her brows raised.

Jace snorted. "That would make me do a double take, as well. How far away were the pregnant women killed?"

Marlee walked to the bed and sat as she pulled open a notebook. It took her a few minutes of flipping through the pages before she said, "One was eighty miles away, another was nearly two hundred miles away."

"Easy driving distance," Jace said as he looked at Cooper.

Cooper blew out a breath. "That it is. Have you found other timetables with them or other employees at this agency?"

"I've been looking, but I've not found anything yet," Marlee replied. "I had to focus on where I thought I could gain the most intel."

Cooper rubbed his hand over his chin. "Understandable. Let's come back to this because I've got a feeling there's something there."

"I do, as well. I've just not been able to devote the time and resources to it as I'd like." Marlee turned to another wall. "This is, well . . . all of you. Whenever I'm looking into a family, I expand out as far as I can with friends and family. Most times, there isn't anything there. But there have been occasions where something connects, and it gives me what I need."

Jace shrugged and shot her a grin. "I'd do the same in your shoes. But I'm curious what you found on everyone. There has to be some secret Cooper has that I don't know about. I mean, I have known him since we were five, so I'm pretty sure I know everything. Still, any chance I can see the file?" he joked.

"Not happening," Marlee said with a laugh.

Cooper shook his head while grinning at his best friend. "I tried to keep a secret from you once. You remember how that turned out?"

Jace busted out laughing to the point where he bent over, his eyes squeezed shut.

Cooper turned his attention to Marlee. "From the moment Jace and I met, we just clicked. We were inseparable, really. Thankfully, our parents let us hang out all the time. We shared everything. People began thinking we were brothers, not friends. Because we were always together."

"We shared everything except girls, of course," Jace said, his smile wide.

Cooper rolled his eyes. "When we got older and started taking an interest in girls, I was able to talk to them, but not Jace. He'd get all tongue-tied and spew nonsense."

"It was horrible," Jace said, pulling a face. "It was like I was speaking in tongues. The words were in my head, but I couldn't get them out of my mouth. And the girls would laugh, which made it worse."

Marlee looked between them, her interest evident.

Cooper drew in a deep breath and released it. "Then, one day, Jace saw Katrina Thompson and fell head over heels. She was the new girl in school, and very pretty.

Katrina and I had English together, and she sat right beside me. We flirted, and I asked for her phone number. When I met up with Jace for lunch to tell him, he started talking first. He went on and on about how he'd finally found a girl he knew he could talk to."

Marlee's eyes widened. "Oh, no."

"Oh, yes," Jace said with a grin. "And do you know what Cooper did? Instead of telling me he already had her number, he told me to go talk to her."

"Awww," Marlee said as she looked at him. "That was sweet."

Cooper shrugged. "I wanted to help my best friend."

Marlee frowned as she cut her eyes to Jace. "That's the story? That's all? What's so funny about that?"

"Well," Jace said, drawing out the word.

Cooper pointed a finger at him. "My story. I get to tell it."

Jace held up his hands, conceding as Marlee laughed.

"As I was saying," Cooper said, smiling at Jace, "you see, I thought I was doing a good deed. For the first time, I didn't tell him about a girl I liked. I had no idea that it would backfire on me so spectacularly."

"What? What happened?" Marlee pressed when he didn't immediately continue.

Cooper chuckled. "Jace, feeling confident as hell, went right up to Katrina the next day. He talked to her with words, even some complete sentences."

"I practiced those lines all night," Jace said, nodding. "I was smooth, articulate, and wooed her like she'd never been wooed before."

Cooper could barely hold in his laughter. "All the other girls around Katrina stopped and took notice of Jace. A few of them even had drool running down their mouths."

Marlee playfully hit him. "They did not."

"Oh, they did," Jace stated emphatically.

Cooper shrugged. "Every female there—including any teacher that was nearby—became instantly smitten with Jace. Every female, that is, except Katrina."

"Here I am, pouring my heart out to this girl," Jace said, smiling, "and all the while, she's looking at me as if I've grown horns. When I finished and proceeded to tell her how much I was in love with her, she thanked me politely and walked straight to Cooper."

Cooper threw up his hands. "I had no idea she'd do that."

"The one time you kept a secret, and it changed my life for the better." Jace shook his head as he looked at Cooper. "From that day on, I never had a problem talking to women."

Cooper snorted. "From that day on, women were all over you. You've never lacked for female companionship."

"Nope. I sure haven't," Jace replied with a half-grin.

Marlee laughed. "You two are something else, that's for sure."

The story had alleviated some of the heaviness of their situation, at least for a moment. But it was time to get back to work. Cooper faced the last wall. "What is all of this?"

"Pictures of people I have yet to identify or even know if they're connected to the adoption agency, the authorities, or the murderers and kidnappers," Marlee told them. "I keep them there in case I see them in another picture to connect them somehow."

Jace moved to the large section of the wall that looked like one of the boards that authorities put together on crime shows, showing how everyone was connected, the timeline of events, and any missing parts. "This is a lot of information."

"More than you know. I couldn't put it all up there because there simply isn't room. I did the major dates of things, like when my client's wife was murdered, and her son cut from her and—"

"I've got a question," Cooper interrupted her. "What made you believe that the child you were searching for was the one Brice and Naomi adopted."

Marlee turned and grabbed a stack of papers from the bed. "Precisely twelve hours after the baby was kidnapped, three calls went out from the adoption agency. One was for a little girl, two were for boys. The first call went to a couple in Fort Worth. They had suffered several miscarriages and tried IVF multiple times before turning to adoption. They wanted a child and didn't care what race or sex it was. The baby boy they were called about was of Asian descent, which didn't match the child I was looking for. So, my attention turned to the only other call that night."

"The one to Brice and Naomi," Jace said.

Marlee nodded. "Exactly."

"What is so important about that time? Why not the earlier calls? Or the next day?" Cooper asked.

Marlee flattened her lips as her expression fell. "Just like people want to adopt puppies and kittens instead of older dogs and cats, the same goes for children. Newborns are highly sought after. Those of us in this line of work have learned that twelve hours is the sweet spot. Could it be earlier or later? Yes, of course. But the timing of those calls caught my attention. I also believe they placed several calls at once to throw off anyone who might be investigating them."

"What if they didn't make a call at all?" Jace asked.

Marlee's face went blank, her lips parting as if she hadn't thought of that.

Cooper nodded. "If two of the three calls were for newborn males, and we know that neither of them was the right infant, then . . ."

"Then I messed up," Marlee said. She sank heavily onto the bed. "I must have missed something."

Cooper put a hand on her shoulder and rubbed it. "Don't beat yourself up about it. It happens."

"No, it shouldn't," she told him. Her anger wasn't at him but directed at herself. "I know better. I've done this for too damn long to make such a stupid mistake."

"Unless it wasn't a mistake," Jace replied. He looked from Marlee to Cooper. "What if those calls were done intentionally, just as you said? What if they wanted you to come here and look into Naomi and Brice?"

Cooper frowned as he tried to see where Jace was going. "I get the calls, but why would they care about Naomi and Brice? Why them?"

"Why, exactly?" Jace said. "Remember the map? Remember what was situated nearly in the middle of everything?"

"Holy shit," Cooper murmured.

Marlee frowned. "What are you two talking about?"

Cooper looked at her. "Earlier, when I told you that Jace and I looked at a map of Texas and began marking where the babies had been kidnapped and the women killed, there was a central location—us. Right here in this town."

For several moments, Marlee didn't speak, she just blinked as she stared at Cooper. "The timing of those calls was on purpose. I know that in my bones. And the more I hear you and Jace speak, the more I think that someone sent me here, knowing the newborn I was looking for wasn't the one your friends adopted. They could be throwing me off the trail, but they could've done that with another couple. No, I was sent here on purpose. And if that's the case, then there's something here I need to find."

"Like those doing the kidnapping and selling the babies," Cooper replied. "It makes sense. Nothing has happened here, but there have been attacks all around us."

Jace leaned back against a wall and crossed his arms over his chest. "There's only one thing to do in times like these. We go hunting."

Chapter 25

The longer Stella sat in her office and thought of all the things that had gone wrong for her over the last decade, she couldn't deny that the main cause was Marlee Frampton. The fact that she had known the Framptons shouldn't make a difference. But it did.

She'd never intended for Macey to be harmed. Chuck had been told to stay away from the Frampton twins, but he hadn't been the one to kill Macey and take the baby. That had been another employee, Martin—an ex-military friend of Chuck's—that she had hired that very day. He was supposed to sit back and watch how things were done before he got his assignment. He'd been driving around to gather information on pregnant women and saw Macey walking. He'd taken the opportunity that presented itself and grabbed her.

Stella leaned back in her office chair and looked at the ceiling. In all her years, she'd had very few that she had called friends. Her relationship to the Framptons had been by accident, really. She'd rented the house next to theirs when she first got back on her feet. None of her business had been conducted there, so no one knew anything. She left for work every day, just like everyone else. Except the Framptons wouldn't leave her alone. Diane spoke to her first. The matriarch of the family had been kind, bringing over fresh-cut flowers. Macey and Marlee had been young children at the time.

Stella kept her distance from the family, but every time Diane saw her, she'd wave. And Stella would wave back. After a year of that, they began chatting a little. Small talk, really. But it was something Stella hadn't had since Jenny died. She enjoyed seeing the family and how kind they were to her.

She stayed in that house for another five years before she moved to another state. By that time, Diane had her number and called her regularly to make sure she was all right. Despite knowing how dangerous it was, how it increased the possibility of being found out, Stella not only took Diane's calls, she also made her own.

Another five years passed before Stella returned to California and the small town of Shell Ridge. She told herself it was ripe with pickings to keep her ever-growing business running, but that was only part of it. She wanted to be near Diane again. As soon as Stella moved back, she and Diane met for lunch and made it a weekly occurrence.

Diane—and the entire family, really—became a friend again.

So, when Macey was murdered, and her baby was stolen, Stella hadn't known what to do. She had briefly considered ordering Chuck to return the newborn to the family. Yet, she didn't. Martin's skill and speed had been incredible. He had taken Macey during the day, and no one had seen him. Chuck rarely worked during the day, and while she hated that Macey had been killed, she *was* running a business.

Stella forced herself to pay her respects to the family

as they grieved. Diane didn't seem to even be aware that she stopped by on several occasions. Her visits tapered off until she finally stopped going altogether. She no longer lived beside them, so no one knew where she was at any given time. After about six months, she moved away again, but not before giving Diane a call. Just as Stella expected, Diane hadn't been around to answer the phone. Stella left a message and told Diane to call her whenever she could.

It took another eight months, but the phone rang. Stella almost hadn't answered it. She'd really hoped that Diane would never call her again. They chatted for a few minutes where Stella learned of Diane's husband's stroke and how Marlee had been doing her own investigating on the side. That made Stella nervous because she knew how good Marlee was at her job.

The fact that Marlee was a police officer had been something Stella had kept a sharp eye on. Because Marlee could ruin everything for her if she looked closely enough. But Marlee hadn't. Or at least she hadn't until her sister was killed. Then, Marlee had become relentless, looking into everyone who might have had a connection to Macey, and anyone Marlee deemed relevant.

It was no surprise when Marlee got in touch with Stella. The phone conversation had lasted no more than ten minutes. Still, in that time, Stella became aware that Marlee was weighing every word Stella said—and would continue to do so long after they hung up.

From that moment on, Stella had looked over her shoulder. Marlee had gotten close, but never close enough to take her down. How many more times would Stella get away, though? The business was still doing well. Well enough that she had enemies. No matter what type of business someone had, there would always be competitors. A few of hers had tried to take her down, but Stella was nothing if not determined. She had clawed her way out of the gutter, and she was never going back. Death was preferable to living on the streets, starving and fending off others. So, she'd done whatever had to be done to keep her enemies away—even if that meant killing.

Stella had gained a reputation as someone who got the job done. She had never failed to procure a newborn for someone willing to pay for it. The one thing that kept her from being betrayed was that she kept her business small. Only a handful of people worked for her, and when she needed new hires, she lured them away from her competitors with money. Those who had never been in the business weren't even considered anymore. There were too many ways they could be undercover Feds. No, she kept to people she knew who had been working for a while and had proven themselves.

It was one of the reasons she did so well. She didn't trust anyone, and she listened to her instincts. And right now, they were telling her to get out of Texas. Except if she did, it might bring more attention to her than if she stayed put. She'd tested those waters twice, choosing a different option each time.

The time she ran, Marlee had missed her by thirty minutes. The time she stayed, Marlee hadn't gotten near her. Now that Stella had the same choice again, she wasn't sure which one to choose. If it were up to Chuck, he'd kill Marlee and be done with it. He thought that was the answer to everything, but it wasn't. The fact that Marlee was spending time with Cooper Owens, who had ties to not only the Harpers but also the Easts, made Stella uneasy.

She knew firsthand what could be done when someone had money to spend to get—or track down—what they wanted. Chuck would likely argue that Marlee hadn't had time to develop strong enough ties with any of them. And he was probably right. But Stella also knew how quickly attraction could bind two people, and if that attraction began to shift to love? Well, all bets were off.

"What do I do?" she asked herself.

Just then, her phone rang. To her surprise, she saw Diane's name. It had been a month since they had last spoken. Stella wondered if Diane could know that Stella was thinking about her daughter. She lifted her phone, debating whether to answer it when it suddenly stopped ringing.

Stella let out a relieved breath and set her cell back on the desk. Her gaze snagged on her planner that showed her appointments for the next week. She had some very wealthy people flying in to meet with her. It was one of the reasons she had set up in the middle of Texas because it was easy to get to Houston or Dallas to meet with those individuals. If she changed things now, they would take their business elsewhere because they'd be scared off. Not that she'd blame them. She wouldn't agree to another meeting either if she were in their shoes.

That didn't even take into consideration the client she was meeting in just a few hours. Chuck had yet to arrive with the newborn, but he would. He'd never let her down. The house she was in was far from others, but that wasn't uncommon in this area. While most people kept to themselves, everyone noticed everything. It was one of the reasons she waited until the dead of night to leave the house to conduct her business.

Stella scratched her cheek near her eye, the pad of a finger brushing against a wrinkle. No matter how much money she had to buy products of all kinds, her body still aged. Granted, she looked younger than most women her age, but that's not what she saw when she looked in the mirror.

She rolled her eyes and got out of her chair to walk the small house. She had more wealth than most, but she didn't live lavishly. She couldn't bring that kind of attention to herself when she rented homes. Though she did have a couple of houses around the world that she got away to whenever she could. And it was definitely time for a vacation. Maybe even one longer than just a couple of weeks. A month, perhaps. She was just getting so tired of it all. And she never thought she'd say that.

"I could hang it up now," she told herself. "I haven't been caught, and I have enough money to sustain me for three lifetimes, even spending lavishly. So, why am I still doing it?"

Because she was damn good at it. She might not be on the cover of *Forbes* magazine or hailed as being the richest woman in America, but there was no denying that she was successful. She had built a company out of nothing, one that gave people what they wanted while keeping ten individuals on payroll and paying them very, very handsomely. They followed her rules, and because they did, none of them had ever been caught.

Why would she give all of that up now?

"Because I'm getting older. And because, eventually, I'll get caught."

That was the real reason. Stella had been a prisoner in her own home before she ran away. She'd been free, even if she was starving and homeless at the time. That freedom was something she knew she'd never give up. Ever.

What if she did hang it up and close the business after these final deals? What then? She had employees that would need work. While she left the country and began a new life, they would look for new jobs, which meant that the odds of them working for one of her enemies were good. No matter how good Stella had been to them through the years, the fact that she'd put them out of work would be all they cared about. It wouldn't be long before her old employees—and their new bosses—started talking.

If she thought she was looking over her shoulder now, it would only get worse if she left. Her enemies would use her retirement to frame her for not only her crimes but also theirs. And for all she knew, her employees would help them. She could either live free, or she could run. All the money in the world might keep her running for a long time, but eventually, she'd stop. At some point, she'd get tired. That meant she would only prolong the inevitable.

"There's no retirement for me," she said with a long sigh. "Ever."

The sound of a car door shutting drew her attention. She walked out of the office toward the back where the sound had come from. As she opened the door, Chuck stood there holding a baby carrier.

"You asked, I delivered," he said as he walked past her and put the carrier on the table.

Stella shut the door and walked to the table where she looked down at the newborn inside. "Everything go off without a hitch?"

"Always does. Even went by Doc's so he could check out the little princess. She's healthy and ready for her new family."

Stella looked into Chuck's face. They had been working together for years. She still remembered when there had been fewer lines on his skin and less gray in his hair. He stood tall, his body still on the slim side, though he didn't have as much muscle as he used to. He never wore anything but jeans and collared pullovers, with Polo being his favorite brand.

"Thanks."

His brown eyes narrowed on her. "You okay?"

"Just doing a lot of thinking."

"It's Marlee Frampton that's causing the stress." His lips were tight, a muscle jumping in his jaw.

Stella put her hand on his arm and smiled. They'd briefly been lovers, but both had realized it could interfere with their work, so they had mutually agreed to end things. Though as far as she knew, Chuck didn't have anyone. Then again, neither did she. Maybe she'd been wrong. Perhaps she should've kept him as a lover.

"Stella?" he asked with a frown.

"Just a long day. That's all. It has nothing to do with Marlee or anything else."

He searched her face for a long moment before he gave a nod. Stella lowered her hand and turned back to the infant. She took the carrier and brought it into the back room, where two Hispanic women were seated. They had been in Stella's employ for seven years, working as maids, cooks, and even nannies until the infants could get to their new families.

She handed the baby off to Maria, the older of the two women. "This one won't be with us but for a few hours."

Maria nodded. Her head of black hair was beginning to turn gray. Then she said, "I'll take good care of her, *señorita*."

Stella walked away, knowing that Maria would do just that. When Stella returned to the kitchen, Chuck was gone. She spun around and returned to her office to call the newborn's new parents. It was going to be a very nice payday shortly.

Chapter 26

It didn't matter how she looked at it, Marlee had screwed up. She'd made a rookie mistake, but now wasn't the time to think about that. Once she discovered why she was in the area, she would go over every decision she'd made from the moment she heard those phone calls from the adoption agency, and could figure out how to keep from being duped again.

"You're frowning."

She jerked her gaze to Cooper to find him staring out the window as they drove. Jace was behind them in his truck. "I'm not."

"You're frowning," he stated with a grin and briefly met her gaze. "That means you're thinking about how you believe you messed up."

"Because I did."

Cooper sighed. "I know you think that, but the way you were duped wasn't something you could've seen coming. And before you say that you should have, no one could've. No one."

She looked out the windshield and shifted in her seat. "I've wasted so much time looking into the Harpers and everyone connected to them. That was time I should've spent finding the infant."

"You thought you were doing just that. Look, if you want to beat yourself up about this, I can't stop you. But you know you'll be better if you focus on what we're doing now."

Marlee crossed her arms over her chest and cut him a look. "You're right, I need to stop thinking about everything I've done and look at what needs to happen going forward."

"That's my girl."

It was such an innocent saying, but it hit Marlee right in the chest. Her stomach clutched as if it were filled with butterflies trying to escape. She jerked her gaze away from Cooper and looked out the passenger window.

"We're going to find whoever this is," Cooper said.

"I sure hope so. I'd hate to think this was another wild goose chase. I'm not sure I'd know what to do if that happened."

Cooper chuckled. "I'm pretty sure you'd dust yourself off and find another piece of evidence."

She smiled. She couldn't help it. Then she looked at him. "Are you always so positive?"

"No," he said with a shake of his head before he glanced at her. "But in this situation, I am. You've got solid evidence, and your past experience says a lot. Add that into what Jace and I have found, and we're bound to succeed."

"Where are we?"

"There are a lot of smaller ranches in the area. People even lease their land for others to put animals on if they don't want to do it themselves. Since this location is the farthest away from town and the homes are separated by swaths of land, I think it's our best bet to locate who you're looking for."

She looked at the passing scenery and large pastures filled with cattle and horses as well as some sheep. "It would've taken me forever to find this."

"Not as long as you think it would've."

"You sure have a high opinion of me."

He lifted one shoulder before he slowed and turned off the road. "Like I said, your previous work says a lot."

Marlee swallowed as her mind drifted to her sister and niece. "Excuse me," she said and pulled out her phone to call her mom. There was no answer, so Marlee left a brief message. Then she called Pam.

"Hey there, Marlee," Pam said as she answered.

Marlee smiled. "Hey. I tried to call Mom, but there wasn't an answer. Is everything all right?"

"Oh, she's fine. So is your daddy. He wanted to see her, so I drove him up to visit. The TV was on, and a nurse is helping her shower."

Marlee glanced at Cooper to see him smiling at her. "I'm glad they're doing fine. Can you hold the phone to Dad for a moment?"

"Sure. He's doing good with his physical therapy, by the way. Still no words, but he keeps trying. He wrote down that he wanted to see your mom this morning. He didn't want to wait around for me to figure out what he was saying," Pam said with a laugh.

Marlee grinned. "I know they miss each other. Thank you for bringing him up there. I know it isn't easy."

"Honey, your parents are amazing, and so are you. Now, hold on and let me put the phone up to your daddy's ear." There was a brief pause, then Pam's voice could be heard at a distance as she said, "Talk now."

"Hi, Dad," Marlee said, putting a smile on her face. "I'm glad you got out of the house and are there with Mom. Make sure she gets better because I'm going to be home soon."

There was a grunt that almost sounded like a word, but Marlee couldn't be sure.

"I love you, Dad. I know how stubborn you can be, so listen to Pam while Mom is away, okay?"

This time, Marlee was sure she heard him say, "Love you."

"Did you hear that?" Pam asked through the phone. "He said 'love you!'"

Marlee was smiling widely now. "I heard it."

"All right. You get back to work and solve that case so you can come home."

"I will. Thank you again."

They hung up, and Marlee looked out the window.

"It must be hard for you," Cooper said after a bit.

She nodded. "Some days more than others. Pam is a lifesaver. She's expensive, but if I can't be there to watch over my parents, I wanted someone who cared about them to do it. Pam is amazing."

"Sounds like it. How are your parents?"

"After Dad had his stroke, it was tough. He's had some smaller ones over the years, as well. It doesn't matter that he can't talk. My mother says enough for two people. But, honestly, they've never needed words. They sit in silence, holding hands and looking at each other every now and again, sharing smiles that hold a multitude of secrets. It's as if that's all they need. Each other."

Cooper slowed as they approached a driveway. "Sounds like it. My parents were much the same way, but they talked. Sometimes, they would talk for hours at a time," he said with a small chuckle. "Their topics would be all over the place, but they easily moved from one subject to the other. It was fascinating to watch them."

"Your mom never remarried?"

Cooper turned onto the drive and slowly proceeded down the path for what seemed like a mile. "Never. She never dated, either. I tried to get her out there years ago, but she wanted nothing to do with it. She told me that no one would ever compare to my father, and it was pointless to waste her time as well as others' to know what she already knew—that Dad was it for her. He was the love of her life."

Marlee thought about that for a moment. "When I was a police officer, I saw a lot of people who swore they loved one another beat to a pulp or killed. It really colored my view of relationships, but then I saw my parents and realized that something real could be found. But I think it's more difficult than most people realize."

"I think you're right. Not to mention that I don't think many people even know what they want, yet they still marry. How can they do that if they don't know what they want?"

"Or if they don't like themselves," Marlee added. "You can't love someone else if you don't love yourself. My parents told me and Macey that for as long as I can remember. I used to think it made perfect sense. Then I went out into the world and realized that people need that drilled into them because they don't know it."

Cooper stopped the vehicle and put it in park. He shut off the engine and met her gaze with his forest green eyes. "You're right in every way. I think if people took the time to know themselves—their faults and strengths— they might be able to accept themselves as well as love themselves. Then they might determine what they want and need out of a relationship."

"That sounds entirely too easy," she said with a smile. "Plus, it makes sense."

"Which means, few will do it." They shared a laugh before he reached over and tugged on one of her curls. "I like you a lot, Marlee. I think you already know that, but I wanted to say it. I'm not helping out because I feel an obligation or because this involves my friends. I'd be right here with you regardless. Because I want to be with you."

She covered his hand with hers. "I'm glad you're here. Really glad. And if we're saying things, I'll tell you that I like you a lot, as well."

Cooper's mouth turned up in a sexy smile. His lips parted, but before he could talk, there was a knock on his window. When they looked, Jace stood there with one brow quirked.

"I think that means we need to get out," Marlee said.

Cooper nodded. "That it does."

As they exited, a blue Suburban pulled up. Marlee recognized it as belonging to Abby East.

"I asked Danny and Ryan for some help," Cooper told her.

She flashed him a smile. "Smart thinking."

The vehicle came to a stop behind Jace's truck, and four doors opened. Clayton East slid from behind the wheel with Danny getting out of the passenger seat. Caleb and Brice got out of the back. They shut the doors and made their way to Marlee, Cooper, and Jace.

"I didn't expect all of you," Cooper said.

Caleb gave him a flat look. "After all these years, he still doesn't know us."

Clayton laughed and nodded to Marlee before he said, "When one of you has been in trouble, when have the others *not* shown up to help?"

"Never," Danny stated from beside him, a wide smile on his face.

Jace crossed his arms over his chest. "Thanks for coming. Is Ryan held up?"

"Actually," Danny said, "he's doing a little surveillance of his own. Undercover, of course. We've both got teams who quickly put together a list of people who moved into the area going back two years."

Something niggled at the back of Marlee's mind. She couldn't figure out what it was, so she kept quiet. "How long is the list?"

"Not as short as I'd like," Brice stated.

Clayton's lips twisted. "It could be worse, but my concern is the length of time. Is two years long enough?"

"Long enough?" Caleb asked with a frown. "I think it's too long."

Marlee shoved her hair from her face as a breeze moved past her. "I probably would've gone back three years, but two is a good place to start."

"Why?" Caleb asked.

Jace then said, "Based on what Cooper and I found earlier, these people find a spot and stay. As I told y'all in my call, this area is in the middle of the major cities. It's prime hunting ground. Caleb could be right. They might have moved here recently, but my guess is that they've been here for a little while. At least a year, if not more."

Caleb pushed his hat back on his head and nodded. "That makes sense. I'm guessing we need to get started."

Danny slid a backpack Marlee hadn't noticed before off his shoulder and pulled out a tablet. He turned it on. As the screen filled, she saw there were two sections. One was a list of people, when they moved into the area, and their location. The other was a map with dots indicating what Marlee guessed were the locations in question.

She listened as Danny explained what the sheriff's office and the police department had put together in a joint effort. The list was significant, but it was also manageable with all of them splitting up to take sections one at a time.

Though this was her investigation, since the authorities had been called in—even as a favor for a friend—Marlee didn't try to run point. To her amazement, Danny looked at her and gave her a nod. "Tell us where you want us."

She was so surprised that she could only look at Cooper, who smiled at her. Marlee cleared her throat and pointed to the map. "I think the easiest thing would be to divide the areas up by locations so we're not crossing paths and wasting time."

"Agreed," Clayton said. "What are we looking for?"

Marlee blew out a breath as she thought about all the times she had managed to locate a child—dead or alive. "Despite my decade of doing this, I've never caught anyone who was involved. I've no idea who these people are. From all my training as a cop and the classes I took at the FBI to help profile cases, my guess is that they're flying under the radar. Meaning, they'll look just like you and me. Ordinary people you'd never suspect would hurt anyone."

"They make a lot of money, though," Jace said. "Won't they live in affluent areas?"

"I don't think so. Wealth draws attention," Marlee told him.

Danny nodded in agreement. "She's right. We'll take a look at all the houses, but I don't think it'll be in the wealthier neighborhoods."

Caleb dropped his arms. "Guys, I'm not trying to argue here, but if these people are how Marlee says, how will we know if we've found them?"

It was a valid question, one Marlee had been asking herself. "I don't have an answer. I'd hoped after ten years I could give you one, but I can't. Just make a note of everything about each of the residences."

"And take pictures," Cooper said. "Lots of pictures of everything."

Marlee smiled at him. "The more information we have,

the more we should be able to use to at least start marking people off the list."

Clayton divided everyone up into teams as Danny walked away to take a call. But he returned quickly.

"That was Ryan. He's on his way. I'll ride with him," Danny told them.

Clayton handed Danny the tablet after everyone knew their areas and said, "Let's get going. We've got a long day ahead of us."

As Marlee and Cooper walked to his truck, she saw Caleb climb in with Jace, and Brice return to the Suburban with Clayton. In minutes, they were headed out, going in different directions. All Marlee could think was that she really hoped something came of this. She'd never had such an amazing team helping her.

It had to be time for the bad guys to lose for once.

Chapter 27

"I've got a bad feeling about all of this," Danny stated.

Ryan Wells glanced at his friend and nodded as he drove to their section of the county to search. "Same for me. Ever since we discovered who Marlee is and why she's in town, I've known this wouldn't be good. What really burns my ass is that these people have been here, and we didn't know."

"Because they've been smart. They didn't commit any crimes that brought attention to them. So, what do you think the odds are that we'll catch them?"

"Before your wedding to Skylar?" Ryan asked as he glanced at Danny and shrugged. "Slim. I think it'll take our combined offices months to get any information and evidence to go after them."

Danny blew out a long breath. "I don't think we have that kind of time."

"They've been here this long, why would they leave if they didn't think we were on to them?"

"Marlee."

That one word was all Ryan needed to understand that Danny believed the criminals knew of Marlee's arrival.

In which case, they would either be looking to move on or retaliate. "The criminals have been here for some time. A year minimum. If I were them, I'd pack up and leave. All their hiding will have been for nothing if they go after Marlee now."

"If the agency in Dallas sent her here, then they want her to find something," Danny replied.

Ryan turned down a road and drove slowly through the residential area. "Since we know that Nate wasn't the newborn she was searching for, I have to agree. It appears as if someone sent her here. Too many variables had to line up just right for her to be here. That usually means that someone set it up."

"If only we knew more about this ring of baby snatchers. We might be able to piece together who the adoption agency sought to get rid of by sending Marlee after them. And if Marlee, who has been doing this for ten years, doesn't know, then I don't guess we will either."

Ryan pulled up next to a stop sign and waited for the car across the street to turn before he continued on. "We have very little to go on. That's nothing new for either of us, but we also aren't even sure what to look for. A needle in a pile of needles is what we have. Hence why I said we wouldn't have this done before your wedding."

Ryan spotted Danny's smile at the mention of the upcoming ceremony. Danny had been single not that long ago, but all that changed one December night when Skylar found her way back to her hometown and into Danny's arms.

"I still can't believe Skylar is mine," Danny said.

Ryan shrugged. "Yeah, none of us can either."

Danny laughed and shook his head. "Keep cracking jokes. I bet it won't be long before you have yourself a woman."

It was all Ryan could do to keep his grin in place. "Bite

your tongue. I've got enough on my plate. I don't need anyone in my life trying to change me or fix me or whatever it is that women want to do when they're dating a man."

"Not all women are like that."

Ryan issued a loud snort. "It could be throwing out your favorite shirt that they hate. It could be rearranging the pantry to suit how they like it. It could be forgetting to buy your favorite bacon or buying you a different cologne than you asked for. They always try to change a man."

"Maybe they're just trying to make things better."

"You're cute," Ryan said sarcastically. "But you're so in love with Skylar, you probably wouldn't care if she threw out all of your clothes and bought you new ones."

"I sure wouldn't. I've got other things to worry about. Like catching baby snatchers and murderers."

Ryan parked on the street and pointed to the house up ahead and to the right. "There's our first house."

"Looks normal."

They sat in silence as Danny took pictures of the building, the vehicles, and anything that might be important later. After about five minutes, the front door opened, and two boys ran outside with a soccer ball. They looked to be about seven and nine. A woman came to the door and shouted at them to be careful. She was smiling and wiping her hands on a kitchen towel before she closed the door and went back inside.

"What are the odds that a criminal who takes babies has kids of their own?" Danny asked.

Ryan watched the boys for a few minutes. "We both know of cases where serial killers had a family and children and otherwise lived normal lives except for their penchant for killing."

Danny lowered the camera and met Ryan's gaze. "Yeah."

Once Danny returned to snapping pictures of the kids, Ryan opened his computer and keyed in the address. "This house was bought seven months ago by Luis and Mandy Aguillar. They have two sons, Adam and Aaron. Luis is a welder by trade, and Mandy works as a cashier at the supermarket."

"Anything come up about either of them?" Danny asked, continuing to take pictures.

"Both clean as a whistle."

Danny sat back and looked at the paper with their next address. "You drive. I'll enter this one."

"It's going to be a long day," Ryan said as he pulled out and drove away.

"It's going to be a long day," Caleb said.

Jace glanced at their list of addresses. They had been to a handful already with nothing that seemed out of the ordinary to him, but Marlee might see something different. Besides the pictures Caleb was taking, Jace made notes about each place they visited, just in case. It would be a lot easier if they could use either Ryan's or Danny's computer to key in each address and pull up information on the people, seeing if they had records or not, but they didn't have that luxury. That would have to happen once they all met back up later.

"What do you think of Marlee?" Caleb asked.

Jace grinned. He'd been waiting on Caleb to ask about Cooper's new lover. "I think she's pretty and smart, but more importantly, Cooper likes her."

"That much is obvious," Caleb said with a grin as he turned his head to Jace. "Does he have it bad?"

"Oh, yeah. I've never seen Cooper act like this with a woman. Ever. I think he's falling for her." And that didn't bring Jace happiness as it should have.

Caleb's brows drew together. "Those words are meant to be joyous, but your expression says otherwise."

"She isn't from here. Her parents are in California. I can't see her staying."

"And you think Cooper will leave?"

Jace set down the pencil and closed the notebook since there was nothing else to write about this location. "He's not said anything, but you've not seen how they look at each other. It's the way you and Audrey look at each other. Or Clayton and Abby. Or—"

"I got it," Caleb said with a chuckle. But the smile died. "Even when the four of us joined the military in different branches, we always knew we'd return here. We have roots."

"Would you have stayed if Audrey's home was elsewhere?"

Caleb sighed and looked forward. "I honestly don't know. My family is here, but I'd have wanted to be with Audrey. A lot of people move away from family and only see them a few times a year. It's not the end of the world."

"I know. I just always thought we'd all stay here, and our children would be friends," Jace replied.

"No matter what, we'll remain friends, and our children will be friends. I promise you that."

Jace let the subject drop as he drove to the next house. It wasn't that he didn't want Cooper to be happy. What he didn't want was for his best friend to get hurt. And anyone who dared to give their heart away put themselves in that kind of predicament. Jace knew that all too well.

But he didn't need to ask Cooper how he felt about Marlee because Jace knew Cooper that well. Hell, he wasn't even sure if Cooper realized that he was already in love with Marlee. As for Marlee? Jace was positive that she was falling for Cooper, if she hadn't already. They were good for each other. Really good.

That was enough for Jace. He wasn't even jealous of the fact that their friendship had changed because Cooper found his woman. But if he were honest, everything had changed the day Brice fell for Naomi. They were no longer the Four Horsemen. It was a nickname that others used for them because the four of them were always together.

He would really miss things as they were, but he knew that the only thing guaranteed was change. He was used to that. Maybe, one day, he would even accept it.

"You're quiet. You good?" Caleb asked.

Jace slowed as he reached their next house. "Just focused on finding these assholes."

"Man, you're really into this."

Jace glanced at Caleb. "What's that supposed to mean?"

"Nothing," he said with a shrug. "I'm just pointing out how into finding these people you are."

"I'm always here for friends, and this is about helping old friends. As well as a new one."

"It's more than that."

Jace opened the notebook and began writing things down about the tan house with the black trim and shutters. He didn't like when his friends turned their attention on him. They saw things he'd rather them not see.

Caleb stared at him for a long time before saying, "I think it's that you like bringing down bad guys. I'm surprised you never wanted to be a cop."

"I like helping my friends, as I said. If that means I get to bring my military training along sometimes, that's even better," Jace said without looking at Caleb.

"How's work?"

Jace blew out a harsh breath and set his pen down to look at Caleb. "It's fine."

"You like teaching others to ride horses and wrestle steers?"

"It pays the bills."

"But is it what you really want to do?"

Jace made the anger that rose up inside him dissipate. It wasn't Caleb's fault that Jace wasn't happy. "It's a job. One I'm good at. Is it what I always saw myself doing? I don't know."

"What do you want?"

"I want you to stop worrying about me. And I want to find these assholes. I see someone. Get the camera."

Caleb chuckled, even as he lifted his phone and began taking pictures.

Chapter 28

Cooper studied the house and the woman who lived there. The section that he and Marlee had taken wasn't far from where they had all met up. If he were a criminal and looking to keep a low profile in a place where people wouldn't be watching his every move, it would be on the county's outskirts, as far from town as possible.

He took pictures as Marlee used her computer to do a quick background search on the woman living there. Cooper watched as the screen flashed, and the woman's driver's license popped up, along with her spotless record.

"Not even a speeding ticket," Marlee said.

Cooper grinned. "We should be happy that these people are clean. Gives me some faith in the human race that not everyone has priors."

"You're right," she said with a chuckle. "I didn't mean to make it sound as if I was disappointed with"—she paused to look at the name on the license—"Ms. Black. But with every person we look into and don't find anything—"

"You feel like capturing the bad guys gets further and further from your grasp," he finished for her. "In a lot of ways, I do, as well. But that just means we have to dig deeper. We still have several names and locations to check. And don't forget, there are three other groups out there looking."

She turned her face back to the house in the distance. Living out here also meant that they couldn't get as close to the residences as the others likely could. "But I agree with you. I have a feeling that whoever these people are, they're out here."

"Then we keep looking. However long it takes."

Her curls bounced as she turned her head back to him. "You seem rather suited to this kind of work."

"Probably because of my CCT training."

Her gaze narrowed as she cocked her head to the side. "Ah. A Combat Controller. I remember reading that about you. I had to go look it up. So, tell me if I have this right. You went into the Air Force, and they trained you as a CCT member, but because of that training, you were paired with other military branches?"

"That's right."

"Explain that to me, because it doesn't make any sense."

He grinned and took more pictures, glancing her way a few times. "Well, most of the difficult missions, the classified ones the public never knows about, are carried out by Combat Controllers. We're trained to operate in remote, hostile areas, paired with other special forces teams. We have a wide range of skills that include parachuting, snowmobiling, scuba, and several other things. We're also FAA-certified air traffic controllers, so we can establish air control and provide combat support all over the globe."

"Damn," she said, staring at him.

He lowered his phone. "I think one of my favorite parts was the SERE training."

"What is that?"

"It's three weeks where we're taught survival, resistance, evasion, and escape maneuvers. However, there's also the Special Tactics training. It's the longest segment, where we're taught advanced weapons and demolition techniques, as well as how to operate all-terrain vehicles."

Her grin widened. "Sounds like you really enjoyed it."

"I did."

"Then why come home?"

He thought about that for a moment and lifted one shoulder in a shrug. "For a long time, I was content with things. But as my tour was ending and my CO—my commanding officer—kept asking me to extend my time, I couldn't stop thinking about home. Jace, Caleb, Brice, and I all kept in touch as much as we could. Brice's tour ended first. He was already back here when I got word about Jace."

"You mean when he was captured and held as a prisoner of war?"

Cooper nodded slowly. "Jace doesn't talk about it. He acts like everything is fine, and some days I believe him. But other times, it's obvious he still carries that around."

"How long did they have him?"

"Two years. I extended my tour because of that. That's how I met Cash, my PI friend. He was also with CCT as part of another special forces team called in to free Jace and two more of our men, also POWs."

Marlee's face crumpled. "I didn't read that part in your military file."

"Because it was left out. The mission was classified."

"Ah. All the black ink I found on those papers. That was one of those missions."

Cooper ran a hand down his face. "I've known Jace for so long. No matter what, he'll always be able to come out ahead in any situation. He has the greatest attitude of anyone I know. Always positive, always lifting us up and telling us we can do whatever we want. I knew when we found him that he wasn't going to look the same. After all, it wasn't the first time I'd helped free our men from the enemy. But it was Jace. And the shell that I found that day was far from who he once was."

"He was a prisoner. I wasn't in the military, but I can guess what they did."

"They nearly broke him. One of the men captured with him is in a psychiatric ward now because they fucked with his head so much. The second was killed within the first week of their capture. The doctors who examined Jace said they couldn't believe that he'd held on for as long as he did. He has the scars to prove what happened to him."

Marlee reached over and touched Cooper's arm. "But it's the scars Jace hides that worry you the most."

"Yeah. As soon as Jace was located, I resigned my commission and accompanied him home. When we landed, his parents and my mom were there. But it took months before Jace could come home. He had so many injuries that it took time for the doctors to work on all of them. Some of his bones had to be rebroken so they could heal properly."

"I'm guessing the doctors used the time to evaluate him mentally?"

Cooper set aside his phone. "They did. Thankfully, Jace didn't pull away from the therapists. He found one he liked and had a couple of sessions a week with them. That went a long way to healing Jace. About a year after he came back, Caleb returned home. We had a big celebration, and the four of us began hanging out like we used to when we were in school. That's when Jace met a girl."

"Uh-oh. That doesn't sound good," Marlee said as she wrinkled her nose.

Cooper started the truck and turned around to head to their next location. "Let's just say that he fell hard for her. Real hard, and real fast. He was still dealing with a lot, and when the relationship began to fall apart, he didn't know what to do. Jace spiraled out of control pretty quick."

"But all of you were there for him."

"You bet your ass we were. We brought him back from the brink, but he's never been the same."

Marlee looked out the window. "That's so sad. Jace seems like a good guy, and from what I discovered about him when I was investigating you, he's a good guy on paper, as well."

"He's strong-willed, and he has us."

"Then he's very lucky."

Cooper smiled as he glanced at her. He found it so easy to talk to her. The kind of natural that didn't come along every day.

She went back to looking at the computer and entering the information for the next location. When he came to a four-way stop and looked in both directions, he happened to see a frown forming on Marlee's brow.

"Everything okay?" he asked as he turned to the left.

"This next place looks interesting. It's been rented by someone with a fake name."

Cooper sat up. "Looks like we might have found our quarry."

"How close can you get us?"

"Not as close as you'll want." Despite wanting to gun the truck to get there faster, he kept their speed regulated, though both of them were quiet as they drove.

He looked over when he heard Marlee's fingers punching keys on the laptop. She glanced up and saw him, flashing him a quick smile.

"I'm trying to see if I can dig up this woman's real name. No one comes out here with a fake name if they aren't hiding something," Marlee said.

Finally, they reached the house. It was set a ways off the road like most in the area. Unfortunately, Cooper couldn't park the car there since it was too exposed.

"We have no cover," Marlee pointed out.

Cooper shook his head and kept driving. "We're going to have to come back when night falls. If we attempt anything right now, we'll be spotted, and she could take off."

"Agreed," Marlee said, though her lips were tight.

He took one more look at the house in the rearview mirror. It was white with a dark green front door. One car was parked beneath the carport, but there was no sign of movement. Cooper turned his attention to the next address. For the next several hours, they crossed off every other location on the list, yet it still wasn't dark.

Cooper called the others so they could meet up again. This time, they headed to the East Ranch, where Naomi, Audrey, her sister Maddy, and Abby had been cooking all afternoon. Cooper was used to the welcome they got, but Marlee took it all in stride. She cast him a glance before she went with the other women to coo over Nate and catch up.

Jace handed Cooper a beer. "How'd it go?"

"Did you find anything interesting?" Cooper asked.

"Nothing. You?"

"Maybe."

Jace's hazel eyes brightened. "Really? That's good to hear."

"What's good to hear?" Brice asked as he walked up.

"Cooper and Marlee might have found something," Jace told him.

That instantly quieted the girls. Cooper looked into the kitchen and met Marlee's gaze.

Clayton, Danny, and Ryan walked out of Clayton's office toward the kitchen. Clayton gave Abby a kiss before saying, "I don't think this is going to wait until after dinner."

"I certainly don't want to wait," Ryan said, his green gaze pinning Cooper. "What did you find?"

Marlee spoke then. "One of the locations is being rented by a woman with a fake name. I attempted to locate her real name, but I've not found anything yet."

"We didn't get a chance to do any surveillance because we had nowhere to hide," Cooper told them. "Marlee and I figured we'd go back after dark."

Clayton's brows shot up. "That certainly sounds like something that needs to be looked into. My list with Brice was a bust. Everything looked normal, but I still think we should take a closer look into all of those to see if anything comes back interesting."

"Sounds like a solid plan," Caleb stated.

Danny said, "I've got a computer, and so does Ryan. Apparently, even Marlee has some access. That means only two groups need the names checked."

"Got them right here," Jace said as he handed the sheet to Ryan, who pulled out his computer and set it on the island.

Brice yanked a folded sheet of paper from his back pocket. "Here's ours."

Danny took it and motioned for Marlee to come with him. Cooper stood with the others and watched the three of them work. It seemed so easy the way Marlee fit in with everyone. Surely, that would make her want to stay.

The moment Cooper thought that, he remembered her parents. There was no way she would stay here with her parents out in California. And moving them? Why would she? It would be easier for him to move.

Whoa. Hold up, Cooper thought to himself. He was getting way ahead of things. He needed to pump the brakes a little.

The thing was, he didn't want to. He wanted to be with Marlee. And he believed that she wanted to be with him. That was enough, wasn't it? But he knew it wasn't. There had to be more. If only he had more time with her. He couldn't wish for them to not find the criminals, because they needed to be stopped. Yet, the quicker that happened, the sooner she would be out of his life.

"You should tell her," Jace said.

Cooper started and looked at his friend. "What are you talking about?"

"You love Marlee. You should tell her."

Caleb nodded. "Jace isn't wrong."

"Not at all," Brice added.

Clayton winked at Abby. "Don't wait around for the right time if you care about her. Plus, we know she plans on leaving. If you think there's something between the two of you, then you should share that with her."

Cooper knew that his friends were giving him sound advice, and he wanted her to know how he felt. He just hoped he didn't run her off in the process.

Chapter 29

The night was quiet and still. Mist billowed out around her as Marlee breathed. She huddled in her coat as the temperatures continued to drop. Ever since they had parked about a mile from the house and walked the rest of the way, there had been no movement. She and Cooper weren't the only ones there, either.

Danny and Ryan had refused to allow them to go alone. In fact, Clayton, Brice, Caleb, Ryan, Jace, and Danny were there. Each team was set up in a different area. For her and Cooper, they were toward the front right of the house.

"What are you thinking?" he whispered.

Marlee shrugged. "There are lights on inside, which makes me believe someone is in there. But they could also have the lights on a timer to make people believe someone is home."

"That's what my mom does."

Marlee sniffed and bit her lip. "I really wish Danny or Ryan could've uncovered this woman's real name. Especially since she's the only one we're looking into now."

In some ways, she was happy that there wasn't another name they had to dig into deeper. At the same time, the fact that everything rested on this individual, who was clearly hiding something, could make things even harder.

"We have nothing to go on here," Cooper stated in a low whisper. "Only the fact that her name is fake. Unless we can get some answers, we could be sitting out here for days."

Marlee wouldn't mind more time with Cooper, but she knew that action needed to be taken. She rose to her feet and started toward the door. Cooper grabbed her hand to stop her. She looked at him and smiled. "You said we needed answers. How about we go talk to her?"

"I'm not sure that's a good idea."

"I spent too much time going down the wrong path for this job. I don't want to do it again. Besides, I'm good at picking up on when people lie. If she's who we're looking for, we'll know."

Cooper blew out a breath and stood. "Well, you've got a point. Let's go."

"Let me do this on my own. She'll be more likely to talk if there's just another woman. I can handle this," she told him. "Besides, you and the others are watching my back."

He linked his fingers with hers and pulled her near. "Damn straight, we are. Be careful."

She gave him a quick kiss and walked away as he ducked back down behind some bushes. None of the others stood up to question her. No doubt, Cooper texted them to let them know what was going on.

Marlee went up the two steps to the porch. As she approached, the light came on outside the door. A moment later, a dog began barking inside, the sound deep and throaty. Marlee knocked and waited. There were no sounds of anyone walking toward the door, but the dog's barking grew louder as he or she approached. Then, suddenly, the dog was silenced.

After a moment, a female voice asked, "Who is it?"

"Hi. My name is Marlee. My vehicle broke down a mile or so back. I ran out of the house in a hurry and forgot my cell phone. I was wondering if I could use a phone to call my boyfriend for help," she said through the door.

There was a hesitation on the other side.

Marlee then said, "I don't have to come inside. You can just hand it to me through a crack in the door. I promise I won't be long. It's dark, and I don't like being out here on my own. People are crazy nowadays."

The sound of a lock turning made Marlee smile. That smile vanished when she heard four other locks being thrown. Then the door opened a crack so Marlee could see the woman. Her face was thin, her straight blond hair pulled back in a ponytail, a deep purple robe enveloping her body.

"Hi," Marlee said, waving. "Thank you so much for talking to me."

"I can't let you in."

Marlee took a step back. "I understand. I mean no harm."

"People always say that."

Something about the woman's tone combined with the various locks and the dog made Marlee take a second look at things. The dog, a big black and white one, stood beside his mistress, his gaze never leaving Marlee as if he were waiting for her to make a mistake so he could attack.

"I'm new around here," Marlee said. "I moved because of a guy, and I'm still trying to find my way around things. I'm from California and used to cities. Things here are so wide-open."

The woman suddenly tossed out a phone. "Be quick."

"Thanks," Marlee said after she caught it. She dialed her own number, thankful that her phone was on silent. Then, she left a quick message and handed the phone back to the woman. "I appreci—"

The door slammed in Marlee's face, the locks sliding back into place in quick succession. There was a very good chance this woman could be part of the criminal ring, but that's not what Marlee's gut told her. Marlee had a feeling she was hiding. The alias—and not one that took a lot to uncover as fake—the locks, the dog, and the fact that the woman never left the house and seemed paranoid told her everything.

Marlee turned and walked down the road back toward the truck. She knew the woman was watching, so she didn't stop next to Cooper. As she passed their hiding spot, she glanced over to find him gone. When she reached the truck, she found him waiting for her.

"Well?" he asked.

She shrugged her shoulders. "She could be the one, but my gut is telling me that she's hiding. It was too easy to discover her fake name."

"But not easy enough to uncover her real one."

"That is a good point. A really good point. Most times, name changes done to escape an ex are done well enough to get the person a new life, but not so well done as say, witness protection. It takes a PI or the authorities to uncover those real names. Yet, none of us were able to do that today."

Cooper pulled her against him and wound his arms around her. "What do you want to do? It's your call."

"We're in this together. All of us. I've made some mistakes on this one, and I'd rather not make any more. I want to get everyone's thoughts on this."

Cooper took out his phone and sent a text. "Consider it done. Caleb and Jace are going to get some pictures of the house. Ryan went into work, but everyone else will meet us back at the East Ranch."

They climbed into the truck and drove off. On the way, Marlee began thinking about Stephanie. She hated asking Stephanie for favors, but this was serious. Especially if Ryan and Danny couldn't find out the woman's real name. By the time Marlee and Cooper reached the ranch, she had made up her mind to call Stephanie in the morning if Ryan and Danny still couldn't get a name.

Cooper held the back door open for her to enter the house. Abby was coming down the stairs, pushing the sleeves of her light blue sweatshirt up to her elbows. She smiled at them and motioned for them to follow her into the kitchen after they'd hung up their coats on the hooks. Cooper then hung his hat and sat Marlee's backpack that held her computer on the floor.

"I've got coffee ready," Abby said.

Cooper grunted as he raked his hand through his dark brown locks. "Think we might need something stronger."

Abby turned and opened a cabinet, then pulled out a couple of bottles of liquor. "Pick your poison."

"I'll take mine added in the coffee," Marlee said as she walked around the island to get a mug.

Abby waved her away. "Sit, sit. I'll get whatever you need."

"You don't need to wait on us," Cooper told her.

Abby smiled at him. "Now, you know me better than that, Cooper Owens. This is my house, and y'all are my guests. Besides, both of you have been working this case really hard. Rest for a minute. I just got a text from Clayton. He and the others will be here in about five minutes."

Marlee blew out a breath and eagerly reached for the mug of coffee Abby handed her. She then added a shot of bourbon to it. The jolt of caffeine and liquor was the exact combination she needed.

After Abby gave Cooper his cup, she looked at Marlee. "This job takes a toll on you."

"It does," Marlee agreed. "However, I forget all about that when I'm able to give a family closure."

"I keep telling her she needs to hire others to help," Cooper said.

Marlee smiled at him and lowered the mug. "I have to admit, you're right. I've done this for too long on my own. Having you and the others helping has shown me what needs to change."

"That's good news," Abby said as she leaned back against the sink, holding her own cup of coffee, though hers didn't have any alcohol in it. "I'm gathering by the expressions on both your faces that tonight didn't go well."

Cooper lifted his brows briefly. "That's an understatement."

"I spoke with the woman inside the house. I wanted to see if I could determine if she was who we were after or not," Marlee said.

Abby waited a moment before she said, "And?"

Marlee took a drink of the coffee and shrugged. "I can't give a definitive answer. Part of me says that she's running from someone. The five locks on the doors, the guard dog, and the way she never left the house, or even opened the door all the way, points to all of that. But then I think about how no one has been able to uncover her real name."

"Not even Danny or Ryan?" Abby asked in surprise.

Cooper shook his head. "Nope."

"I see the conundrum," Abby replied.

Lights outside caught Marlee's attention through the large windows overlooking the barns out back. She turned her head and saw two vehicles pull up before the men made their way into the house. Clayton walked straight to

Abby to give her a kiss before he took off his coat and hat and hung them by the door.

"Tell us you got some good pictures," Cooper told them.

Jace held up the camera Danny had used earlier. "About to download them now. We walked all around the place, getting as close as we could without the dog barking."

"Let's get those pictures downloaded onto a computer," Caleb said.

Marlee jumped off the stool and went to her backpack. She pulled out her laptop and opened it. Jace plugged in the camera, and within seconds, the pictures were downloaded. Marlee crossed her fingers that they found something to put the woman in either the criminal category or the innocent one.

Chapter 30

The bitch was getting close. Chuck's fingers itched to have a weapon in hand so he could go after Marlee. Now that he was finished with Stella's most recent request, he could devote all the time he wanted to Marlee. Except, she hadn't been alone.

Chuck had been on his way to her motel to find her when he happened to see Cooper's truck turn down a road very near where Stella's house was located. That caught his attention quickly. Chuck had continued driving, but when he could, he turned around and followed Cooper. Chuck switched off his lights and rolled down his windows so he could listen as he slowly drove down the road. He even shut off the lights on his dashboard so nothing could be seen.

The wide-open pasture area made it easy for him to spot Cooper's truck. Chuck pulled over and quickly killed the engine. He watched as both doors of the vehicle opened, and two people stepped out. It was easy to spot Marlee's smaller frame and curly hair, even in the moonlight. Chuck waited until he saw them hide near a white house. It wasn't long before he saw a few more shapes take form, setting up a perimeter.

As much as he wanted to get closer and hear what they were saying, he didn't have to. Something about the house and its occupants had gotten Marlee's attention, and she had somehow been able to rope Cooper and his friends into helping her. It was no longer just a single woman trailing Stella and her crew. It was a group.

That put a whole new spin on things. If they looked deeply enough, they could find something about Stella's place that would make them take a closer look. Chuck wouldn't let that happen. He started his truck and turned around, keeping his lights off until he was a safe distance away.

Just when Chuck didn't think it could get any worse, his headlights caught another truck as it turned down the same road that he was on. The lights shone into the vehicle, and none other than Sheriff Danny Oldman could be seen behind the wheel. Chuck didn't have to wonder where the sheriff was headed—he was going to meet the others.

"Fuck. It just keeps getting worse."

Chuck reached for his phone and called Stella. She picked up on the second ring, her throaty voice coming across the line. "We've got a problem," he told her.

"What kind of problem?"

"The Marlee Frampton kind, except now, she isn't alone. She's got others helping her."

Stella was silent for a heartbeat. "Let me guess. The Harpers?"

"I didn't see them, but Cooper Owens is with her, and we know how tight that group is."

"And if the Harpers are involved, then I'm guessing the Easts are, as well."

Chuck sighed. "Probably. I saw the sheriff headed toward them in his personal vehicle."

"Headed toward them?" she repeated quickly. "What are you doing?"

"Driving away. They're not far from you. Two streets over. They've set up around a house to do surveillance. I saw the sheriff turn down the road as I was headed out."

"Was he alone?"

Chuck thought back. "There was someone with him, I know that much, but my attention was on him."

"Damn. This is disturbing."

"I think it's time we leave the area."

"I can't," Stella said. "I've got to meet a client tonight, and I have other appointments set up over the next few days that can't be canceled."

He rolled his eyes as he continued driving. "Then leave after that. But you can't stay here. It's only a matter of time before their attention is on you. But I can make it stop."

"I already told you not to touch Marlee."

"I know that's what you said," he replied tightly. "But I think you need to reconsider. Who cares that you were friends with her mom? That was a long time ago. Marlee is going to throw our asses in jail. Unless she isn't here to do that."

Stella's sigh was long and loud. "If you think killing her is the answer, then you aren't looking at the bigger picture. The authorities will double-down on their efforts. They'll look into everyone."

"The fact that they're looking at all should cause you to worry," Chuck stated.

Stella's voice was softer when she said, "It does. That, I can promise you. I've kept all of us out of jail for this long. Trust me on this, Chuck. Can you do that?"

"I've always trusted you."

"Good. Because I'm not going to put any of us in a position where we can be discovered by anyone, but especially not by Marlee Frampton," Stella assured him. "No matter how much it looks like we need to run, it's the last thing we should do. They'll be watching for that."

Chuck clamped his teeth together when he wanted to argue with her. The simple fact was that Stella had kept them all safe from the very beginning. Not once had anyone who worked for her been detained by the police. Because she was that good at knowing what to do. He had to remember that despite what he wanted to do.

"You're right," he admitted. "I just don't like Marlee around us so much. And how the hell did she know to come here in the first place?"

"That's certainly something I'll be looking into."

Chuck grinned because he knew that tone. "You know why she's in the area."

"It's a hunch."

"And your hunches are never wrong. Who is it?" he pressed.

The sound of Stella's chair being moved could be heard in the background. "The only one it could be is Penny Howard."

Chuck pulled into the motel lot and parked. He shut off the engine and snorted. "Of course it is. She got angry when the location moved from her agency to the one in Houston for the Mandels last month."

"Angry?" Stella repeated with a bark of laughter. "If I remember correctly, her exact words were, *'You'll pay for this.'* It wasn't my decision to move the adoption, and I told Penny that. I should've known that she would hold on to such anger. I paid her the commission she would've made had the deal gone through with her agency. That should've been enough. I was more than fair."

That she was. Chuck hadn't wanted her to give Penny the money, but Stella had said it was the right thing to do. She often did things like that. It was why so many wanted to work for her. She was fair. Always. Even to the detriment of herself sometimes.

"Shall I do a little digging?" Chuck asked.

"No need. I've got a friend doing it. Matter of fact, I should be getting a call shortly to confirm my suspicions."

Friend was her way of talking about her connections in the FBI. Chuck didn't like how Stella always took their word as gospel. Didn't she realize that they would eventually turn on her? Of course she did. Stella always thought ahead.

"You still with me, Chuck?"

"Yeah," he answered.

"You've been working really hard for me. You always have."

He shifted uncomfortably in his seat. "I'm just doing my job."

"The thing is, I want you here with me. Especially now that Marlee is in town."

Chuck narrowed his gaze out the window. "I figured the last thing you'd want is me near her."

"I know you'll heed my orders. If it comes down to us being caught, there's only one person I want with me. You. I know you'll be able to get us out. That being said, I need to show Penny and all the others working with us that I don't take kindly to what she's done. I've dispatched Martin to Dallas to await my orders once I hear from my friend."

Chuck closed his eyes. "You should've sent me to Dallas. Martin is good, but he's not as good as me."

"He knows what to do. And like I said, I'd rather have you here."

Chuck blew out a breath. "I'm here, Stella. I'm not going anywhere you don't send me."

"Thanks."

"Do you want me there tonight with the clients?"

Stella hesitated for a moment and then said, "Actually, I do. Meet me here at the house in two hours."

"Will do."

Chuck hung up the phone and looked at the door to Marlee's motel room. He'd planned to wait there for her all night until she returned, but that had all changed. He wasn't too disappointed, however. He'd been in love with Stella since the first time he saw her. It had torn him in two when she ended their affair, but he couldn't hold it against her. She was looking out for herself and her employees. They were a great team, even if she didn't allow him in her life. This was as close as he'd get. He'd known that for a long time.

Sometimes, she let him accompany her to client meetings, and other times, she didn't. He always asked. Any time he could spend alone with her were minutes he treasured. She was his boss as well as the woman who had stolen his black heart. He hadn't thought it possible to love anyone, but then Stella had come into his life and given him a reason to live.

She was everything to him. He protected her, and he'd continue to do that—giving up his life if necessary. That's how much she meant to him. He never told her any of that. It wouldn't do any good. Stella was a pragmatist. She didn't let sentiment get in the way of business. She kept a level head at all times. Which was one of the many reasons she was as good a businesswoman as she was.

Chuck got out of his truck and walked to the door. He used a device and unlocked it. He quickly stepped inside and took a look at all the pictures on the wall. Chuck slowly moved around the room, inspecting each photo with a critical eye. Marlee was good, he'd give her that. She had zeroed in on the adoption agency in Dallas. Frankly, he was surprised that she hadn't accumulated enough evidence to take them down, but now, he was glad.

If Penny had pushed Marlee in their direction, then the minute Penny and her business were shut down, she'd spill everything. There wouldn't be anyone in their line of work that wouldn't be named. Penny was the kind who looked out for herself.

It was a damn good thing Stella had sent Martin to Dallas to dispatch Penny. Chuck hadn't even considered the fact that Stella might be wrong about Penny because Stella was rarely wrong. And if she was, she wouldn't have Penny killed.

That was the one downfall with Stella. She didn't like to take a life unless she had no other option. Chuck had often told her to take out a person, but she always had a reason not to. So far, nothing had come back on Stella for those decisions, but someone had sent Marlee Frampton straight to their area.

When Chuck finished his circuit of the room, he realized that Marlee had nothing on Stella or any of them. There was a small victory in that, but how long could it last? Sooner or later, Marlee would have to be killed. Stella had to know that. But Chuck was willing to wait until the heat died down, and it wouldn't blow back on them.

He took one last look around the room before he walked out and got into his truck to drive to Stella's.

Chapter 31

"I just don't know," Danny said with a shake of his head.

Cooper sat at the other end of the table in the dining room, holding his mug that only had a shot of bourbon in it this time. His gaze swung to Marlee, who made a face as she shrugged.

"Exactly," Marlee said. "There's no definitive answer on this woman."

"And you really can't find her real name?" Abby asked.

Danny removed his hat to scratch his scalp before he returned the Stetson to his head. "I've done several searches and nothing. So has Ryan."

"There's one other avenue we haven't tried," Marlee said.

Jace laced his fingers behind his head. "We're all ears."

"I have a friend in the FBI. We got to know each other when she worked my sister's case. I've called Stephanie a few times when I've been in a bind. She's also given me intel on occasion," Marlee explained.

Caleb frowned and said, "Why haven't you already made the call?"

"Because you don't use contacts like that unless you have no other recourse," Cooper said.

Marlee smiled at him from down the table.

"Cooper's right," Clayton said. "However, if we want an answer, then Marlee has to make the call."

Brice leaned a shoulder against the wall of the dining room. "Out of all those names we checked, there wasn't one that gave us pause?"

"Not a one," Caleb answered.

Danny sat back in the chair and looked around the table. "Maybe we should look at those who moved three years ago. Or longer."

"For all we know, these people could be staying in a house that belongs to someone else," Clayton said with a shrug. "Hell, they may not even pay any of the bills themselves, which—"

"Means there's no record of them," Danny said over him. "Damn."

The little optimism that had been there at the start of the day was fast dwindling. Cooper saw it, but he wasn't sure how to change it.

"We're missing something," Marlee said. "I can feel it."

Caleb twisted his lips. "I can't imagine what it is but point us in the right direction. We'll find it."

"I agree with Marlee," Jace said as he rose and got himself another slice of cherry pie. "I may not have the evidence Marlee does, but there's no denying these bastards are here. In our town." He turned back to the group with the pie in hand. "I don't want them here."

Brice rolled his eyes. "None of us do. But we have nothing to go on now."

Cooper's mind was working, trying to solve the problem while the others talked, and he kept going back to their location that night. He'd thought it was a good location. Even now, he still knew it would be where he'd hide out.

His gaze snapped to Marlee to find her already looking at him. "We were in the right place."

"I think so," she said with a nod.

Danny frowned as he leaned his forearms on the table. "You mean tonight?"

"Not that particular house, but the area," Cooper said.

Caleb pinched off a piece of the pie crust from Jace's plate before Jace turned away so Caleb couldn't reach more. "It is very secluded in that area. Lots of acres between homes."

"And we didn't look at half of them," Marlee declared.

Cooper rubbed a hand over his mouth. "There are a lot of homes back there."

"It used to be one huge ranch back in the eighteen hundreds, but the surviving children of the owners sold it off in sections in the fifties. Some as small as ten-acre plots, but others as large as seventy and eighty," Clayton told them.

Brice scratched his temple before he dropped his arms and pushed away from the wall. "We can't go to every house and talk to them."

"Why not?" Caleb asked.

Cooper nodded. "We'd need a damn good reason, but we could."

"People open the door for kids selling candy," Jace said.

Abby laughed from the doorway of the kitchen. "Pretty sure that's only you. The Girl Scouts in the area go to your house first to sell cookies. That should tell you something."

Jace swallowed the last of the pie and shrugged. "I like cookies."

"You like everything," Brice told him with a grin.

Cooper sat forward and looked between Marlee and Danny. "What would need to happen for us to go to the houses?"

"You don't need my permission to do anything," Danny told him. "It isn't against the law to knock on someone's door. Now, what you do after that, or what you find, well, that's when it gets tricky."

Marlee met Danny's gaze. "Unless we don't do anything. Just like today, it was collecting intel. This will be, as well."

"I can't do it in the morning," Caleb said. "I've got to finish with the mare Doug gave me to train. He's coming tomorrow to pick her up."

Marlee smiled at him. "Thank you for the help today. Thank you to everyone. I'm used to doing things alone, but someone"—she paused and looked at Cooper—"told me I need to hire people. After today, I'm definitely going to do that. That being said, please don't feel like you have to help me. I appreciate anything you can do, but I don't expect anyone to work like I do."

"But we will," Jace said with a grin.

Caleb rose to his feet and pushed in his chair. "I'll check in with y'all after lunch and catch up then. For now, I'm getting home to my wife, who has been texting me nonstop for an update."

Caleb and Brice left while the others remained. Once it was quiet again, Danny asked, "What do you think you want to ask as your reason for knocking on these doors?"

"Whatever we say is going to be a lie," Marlee said. "Are you sure you want to know?"

Danny gave her a flat look. "There isn't a soul in this county who doesn't know how close I am with the Harpers and Easts, as well as Jace and Cooper. Anything that happens, people figure I'm in on it regardless."

"In other words," Clayton said, "Danny would rather be prepared than caught off-guard."

Marlee nodded and crossed one leg over the other. "Understood. Well, what I was thinking is that I know we'd cover more ground if we went alone, but I don't think we should."

"I'm in wholehearted agreement on that," Cooper said. He knew he wouldn't be able to concentrate if he was worried about Marlee.

Jace's and Clayton's smiles nearly made Cooper roll his eyes. He didn't care that it was obvious why he'd made that statement. Marlee knew he liked her. Hell, he'd told her as much. He just hadn't told her the rest. It had been a while since he'd told a woman that he loved her.

Marlee smiled at him for a moment. "We'll cover less ground, but it's safer. If we run across these people, I doubt they'll give themselves up easily. They murder pregnant women. They won't hesitate to do the same to us. Now, a good reason to go knocking on people's doors is because of an upcoming election. Anything going on?"

"Not for a bit," Danny answered.

"We can do a census for the county," Cooper offered.

Marlee's face brightened. "That's perfect. We're going to need clipboards, paper, and pencils."

"I think I've got all that here. Let me see," Abby said as she hurried away.

Danny nodded to Cooper. "That's a good idea, actually. Most people won't demand to know more information if someone comes to their door for a census."

"Can we pull up a map of the area with all the homes?" Marlee asked.

Clayton got to his feet. "I can do you one better." When he returned, he unrolled a map on the table. "My grandfather bought several plots of land when they went up for sale. He wanted to buy the entire ranch, but it didn't happen. He sold those pieces of property before I was born. But we never got rid of the map."

"I'm glad you didn't," Marlee said as she stood to get a better look at it.

Cooper also got to his feet so he could see. He'd dated a girl in high school who had lived back there. That's how he knew how secluded the houses were. "We need to mark off the houses we looked at today."

"On it," Marlee said as she got the paper from earlier with the addresses. Just as she was about to mark the map, she paused and looked at Clayton.

"Go on," he told her. "If this saves lives, you can do whatever you want with it."

Marlee then used a pencil and put a small X on the homes they had visited. It didn't take long. When they saw how many houses were left, silence filled the room.

"We should start there," Cooper said as he pointed to the house farthest from the road. Then he looked at Clayton and Danny. "The two of you can't be near this. Neither can Ryan. No one knows Marlee, so she can get away with going door-to-door. Same with me."

"Right," Jace said, his voice heavy with sarcasm. "If you think no one knows you, let me be the one to tell you that you're full of shit."

Clayton's lips thinned as he nodded. "Jace is right. None of us can do this."

"I might not go to the doors, but I'll be driving Marlee," Cooper stated.

Marlee steepled her hands on the table. "That is perfect."

"It's going to take you forever to do this alone," Danny said.

Marlee shrugged, smiling. "I've always done everything on my own. I'll be fine."

"Actually, there might be someone else we can ask," Jace said.

Cooper's brows drew together. "What are you concocting?"

"We need someone like Marlee. I'm thinking Maddy would do great."

"Audrey's sister?" Clayton asked.

Jace smiled. "The very one."

Cooper twisted his lips. "Jace has a point. He can be her driver."

"I'm sure we can come up with at least one more by tomorrow. If there are three teams out there, we'll cover more ground," Danny said.

Cooper walked to Marlee. "Looks like we've got a plan."

"Sure does," she said, linking her fingers with his.

Chapter 32

After spending five hours going door-to-door, Marlee still didn't have anything. Cooper finally made them break for lunch. She was in a poor mood the entire time. She tried to pull herself out of it, but she wasn't very successful.

"I'm sorry," she told him on the ride back to begin working again. "I just feel like time is running out, and every house I visit and find nothing, the more I feel as if everything is slipping through my hands."

Cooper smiled at her and grabbed her hand as he drove. "I understand. What do you do on other cases when you get like this?"

"Work harder and longer," she said with a twist of her lips.

He chuckled softly. "Does it work?"

"Rarely," she admitted. "Most times, I run myself into the ground. It takes me weeks to heal from that. I know better. I should work smarter, not harder. But saying it and implementing it are two different things."

"That's why I'm here."

She turned her hand over so their palms touched. "I'm really glad you are."

Their gazes briefly met before he turned off the main road and wound his way back on the side roads. His smile said so much. Marlee wished they could have a day for just them. Lying in bed talking, watching a movie, cooking together. Whatever. But she didn't have those kinds of days often.

Regardless, she was getting to know Cooper quite well. She'd learned early on after the police academy that you could learn a lot about a person under pressure, as they were now. Cooper was levelheaded even when he was angry. He didn't let his emotions rule him, which was something she *really* needed to work on.

He'd learned a lot in the military, and it showed. She wanted to work with someone like him. Before she realized it, her lips were parted, the words to ask him if he wanted a job right on the tip of her tongue. But she stopped herself at the last second.

Cooper had a life in Clearview. His mother was here, as well as his very close friends, who were also his family. People didn't walk away from that easily, if ever. He liked her, cared about her even, but was it enough for them to try their luck as a couple while working together? Marlee had seen such a couple self-destruct when she was still with the force. How in the world would she and Cooper fare any better traveling all over, searching for murderers and kidnappers?

"We're going to find these assholes," Cooper said into the silence.

She jerked her head to him and nodded when he looked her way. "I know."

"Do you?" He parked the vehicle in front of their next house and turned to her. "I know this is frustrating. We could be wrong about our location, but that doesn't matter. I'll be with you to help for as long as you want me."

She looked down at their joined hands. "Leads may take me away from here."

"I know."

Marlee had tested the waters with those words, and she was surprised—and pleased—by his response. She lifted her eyes to him. "You'd do that?"

He drew in a breath and looked out the windshield for a moment before turning back to her. "My father's accidental death left our family with a tidy sum of money, as you well know from your background check on me. I've done a multitude of jobs and never found anything that seemed to fit. I'm lucky, I know. The money allows me to be picky. My mother is a master when it comes to investing, and she taught me. I make more with my investments than I do with any job. So, I spend my time helping my friends when they need an extra hand." His look in his forest green eyes intensified as he removed his Stetson and set it on the dashboard. "When I meet someone like you, I'm able to devote however much time you need. I'm here. And willing."

She wanted to throw herself against his body. They had spent the night in her motel room, and she had actually slept for the second night in a row. As good as that was, it wasn't as nice as waking up next to Cooper with his large frame curled around hers in bed.

"I want you so bad right now," she admitted.

His smile was slow. Seductive. "Woman, you have no idea how much I want you. It was everything I could do last night to allow you to sleep when all I wanted was to taste your body once more."

"Keep talking like that, and I'll straddle you."

He took her hand and brought it across the way to rest on his hard cock. "If there's any doubt to my words, the proof is right here."

Marlee scooted closer, hating the center console in the truck that kept them separated. She brought her lips to his and softly kissed him. She laid her free hand on his cheek and sighed. "This, what I'm feeling now, what I've felt since I first met you . . . it terrifies me."

His hands cupped her face. "There's nothing to be scared about. I've got you."

She wanted to believe him. It would be so easy to hand her heart to him. Oh, who was she kidding? He already had it. She wasn't sure when it had happened, but it had. Quietly, softly. He had scooped it up as easily as he smiled.

"Trust me," he urged her. "I won't hurt you."

Marlee licked her lips, eager to press her mouth against his again. "You can't promise that."

"I didn't say I wouldn't piss you off," he said with a smile. "I said I wouldn't hurt you."

She laughed softly and gave him a brief kiss. "Oh, I've no doubt I'll make you angry."

"It takes a lot."

"I have a knack for it," she stated. "Truly. It's a gift."

He shrugged while smiling. "No one is perfect, right?"

"I don't even know what we're talking about here."

"Yes, you do," he insisted.

Marlee suddenly sat back in her seat and looked forward. "I barely know you."

"You do know me, though. Do you know everything? No. Just as I don't know everything about you. That's the fun part. We get to keep figuring it out."

"But what if I'm not what you think I am."

Cooper was silent for a moment. "I think you're a woman who is dedicated to finding the lost and hunting criminals. I think you're a woman who forgets to take care of herself because she's looking out for everyone else. I think you're a woman who has one of the biggest hearts around. I think you're a woman who is used to doing things on her own but could use someone with her. I think you're a woman who doesn't need anyone. I think you're special. One-of-a-kind. And you're the woman I want to be with."

She had yearned to hear these words, but now that Cooper had said them, she didn't know what to do. All she kept thinking about was how close he was to everyone around him. She couldn't continue to do her job and stay in one spot—be that in Texas or California. And speaking of California, there was her parents.

"Say something," Cooper urged.

"Nothing has ever felt more right than being with you." Marlee turned her head to meet his gaze. "These past few days have been the best of my life."

He smiled widely. "And I wasn't even on my best game. Just wait."

"Maybe in another life, this could work."

His smile died slowly.

She looked away and grabbed her clipboard. "You have deep roots here, ones that have been tended to for decades. My parents are in California and need me more than I can even be there to help. Then there's my job. I'm all over the place, but never in one location long enough to call it home."

Silence met her words. She couldn't look at him because she was afraid of what she'd see in his eyes. Once she did, she knew she'd crumble. She had to stand strong. Because while things might be good now, if he came with her, he would eventually get homesick and return. He'd probably come back to her, but it would be shorter and shorter each time. She didn't begrudge him that. Her line of work was difficult, and that was on an easy day. And there were very, very few easy days.

Marlee opened the door and stepped out of the vehicle. She closed the door and started walking, even as it felt as if her heart were breaking into a million pieces. It had been the right decision. She knew that.

Then why does it feel so wrong?

There wasn't an answer. The fact was, her real chance at happiness sat in the truck behind her. And she was throwing it away.

To save him. To save myself the heartache that will eventually find its way to me.

Yeah, she was a coward. She didn't even want to take the chance that everything might turn out fine with Cooper. Because that would mean putting her heart on the line, and she wasn't strong enough to do that. Everyone thought that she was stronger than most because she did her job alone.

What no one realized was that she was the weakest of all. She was scared of everything, so she closed herself off.

Marlee was nearly to the front door of the house when her phone vibrated in her pocket. She pulled it out and saw Stephanie's name. She'd forgotten about the message she'd left earlier that morning. Marlee quickly answered. "Hey. Thanks for returning my call."

"Not at all. I'm sorry it took so long. It's crazy in the office today. Not sure how long I can stay on."

"Understood. Did you happen to do a search on Kate Sommerset? I know it's a fake name, but I've not been able to locate her real one."

The sound of a can being opened came across the line. "Wish I had better news. I've got nothing for you."

"Nothing?" Now that was just odd. If anyone could find something on a person, it was the FBI.

"Sorry. Things are insane here. What was it about this woman that caught your attention?"

Despite all the years that Marlee had discussed her clients with Stephanie, something made her uncomfortable now. "The fake name. It was easy to find, but not the real one. Usually, that means the government is somehow involved. But if that's the case, then why make it so easy to pick it out as a fake?"

"I wish I had answers for you." Stephanie then took several drinks of the beverage that Marlee could hear over the phone.

Maybe it was all the stress of everything, but Marlee felt that the entire conversation was off somehow. Her gaze moved to a window with the blinds open to see someone sitting at a table on the phone with a can in their hands. "Thanks. I won't keep you."

"Good luck."

The line went dead. Marlee returned her phone to her pocket, her gaze never leaving the figure. Was it a coincidence that the person through the window had laid down a phone at the same time Marlee's call ended? Sure. But she didn't believe it.

Every instinct she had yelled at her. Marlee looked at the front door before she turned her head to look at Cooper. He stared at her, trying to determine what she was going to do. She motioned with her finger for him to go around to the back of the house.

Without question, Cooper exited the truck and quietly pushed the door closed. He bent low and went around the back of his truck before he ran toward a small cluster of trees near the road. Marlee returned her attention to the house. She knew Cooper could handle himself. She didn't have a gun on her. She had, however, grabbed two of her knives that morning when getting dressed. She'd put one in her boot and the other in her coat pocket. She gave Cooper her largest knife, and when he indicated that he'd be fine, she didn't give him an option. She made him take it.

Marlee's legs were stiff as she turned back to the house and began walking up the path to the door. This house was closer to the road than most, but it had more land surrounding it than those nearest to it.

Her heart pounded slowly like a drum slamming against her rib cage. A chill raced over her the closer she got to the door. She glanced at the window, but the person was gone. It was difficult to tell if it had been a man or a woman. The distance hadn't helped either. Marlee knew Stephanie. They talked about once a month, but they had also met in person a few times during Macey's case. Though it had been years since Marlee had seen her.

There was no such thing as coincidence in Marlee's book. But if it was Stephanie, why was she in town? Why hadn't she said anything? And why was she at this particular house?

The more Marlee thought about it, the more insane it sounded. But she couldn't shake the feeling that something was off. And it all had to do with this house.

Marlee reached the door and lifted her hand. She saw it shake slightly. She steeled herself and gave a quick knock. She plastered a smile on her face as the door was unlocked and opened.

Chapter 33

Cooper kept low as he made his way to the back of the house. He didn't know what had set Marlee off, but it was something. He trusted her instincts. And he was going to make damn sure he had her back.

When he flattened himself against the back of the house near the back porch, he pulled out his phone and quickly sent a text to the group, letting them know what was going on. The day had been quiet. Almost too quiet. None of the three groups going door-to-door about the fake census had come across anything. Cooper had been about to chalk it up to another dead end. Then this.

He didn't want to think about Marlee's words before she'd gotten out of the truck. He should've known that it was too early to talk to her about their relationship. Hell. He wasn't even sure if she thought of it as a relationship. She felt something for him, that much he knew, but that was all he knew. And he didn't like the unknown. Never had. Most likely never would.

Cooper palmed the knife she'd given him earlier. He hadn't wanted to take it. He had one on him at all times. With the knife in hand, he listened. Cooper hated that he couldn't have eyes on Marlee, but she was smart. She could handle herself. His phone began to vibrate, alerting him to incoming texts. He glanced down at the phone to see that his friends were headed their way before he pocketed the cell.

Jace and Maddy were the nearest to him. Clayton was with . . . damn. Cooper kept forgetting her name. It was some college-aged girl whose father worked for Clayton. Cooper shook his head to clear it. Names didn't matter right now. Keeping everyone safe and catching the bad guys was what mattered.

Cooper heard footsteps headed toward him instead of to the front of the dwelling. As he strained to hear, he caught the sound of the front door opening. At least two went inside. He heard a creak and tilted back his head to see the house's window over his right shoulder. He spotted a shadow there as if someone were leaning back against it.

Slowly and quietly, he made his way from beneath the window to stand beside the back door so that whoever was at the window couldn't see him if they looked down. That's when he heard Marlee's voice.

The surprise that flashed in the man's eyes was hidden quickly enough after he opened the door. Marlee might not know who this older gentleman was, but *he* knew *her*. And that made her adrenaline kick up a notch.

"Hi," she said. "I'm with the county, going house to house in an effort to get a new census in place. I wondered if I could take up a few minutes of your time."

The man stared at her with dark brown eyes, his brown hair liberally laced with gray. He was clean-shaven, showing a jawline most men would kill for. He had broad shoulders and muscles shown by his tight shirt. No one that age kept in that kind of shape without reason. She immediately thought military. He just had that look about him. The I-can-get-through-anything look.

She swallowed, waiting for him to say something. Tense seconds passed when she thought he might come at her. That's when she knew that this was the place they had been searching for.

What she needed to do was extract herself and wait until she and Cooper could meet up with everyone else, including Danny and Ryan to bring in the authorities. Of course, she needed actual evidence for that, not just a feeling. But if she went for the proof, there was a very real possibility that she—and Cooper—could be killed.

"Sir?" she pressed when he still didn't answer. The silence was getting awkward. But that might be better than whatever he chose to say.

Marlee took a step back and held up her hands, one holding the clipboard. "That's fine. You don't have to answer the questionnaire. I'll leave now and make sure that no one visits this house again. Have a good day."

The moment Marlee turned, she wanted to run. She couldn't help but think of herself as a sheep with a lion on its tail, ready to pounce. Frankly, it wasn't a good feeling. It took considerable effort not to run, but Marlee somehow managed it. She glanced at Cooper's truck but didn't see him inside. No doubt, he was still around the back. She wanted to reach for her phone to text him, to get him to return to the vehicle immediately, but getting out her phone now wouldn't be smart. She'd have to wait until she got to the truck.

An approaching white Mercedes S-Class pulling into the driveway snared her attention. The car parked, and the door opened as a tall woman with short blond hair got out. She was dressed smartly in clothes that looked more expensive than everything Marlee owned combined. The woman's face was hidden as she opened the back door of the car and took out some shopping bags along with her purse. Then she turned around.

And Marlee finally got a good look at her.

"Stella?" Marlee asked in surprise before she could stop herself.

Stella stood in shock for a heartbeat before she blinked and smiled. She was in her late fifties but looked years younger. "Marlee Frampton? Is that you? What are you doing out here in the middle of nowhere?"

"Working." Marlee's mind was in overdrive as she pulled up as many memories of Stella as she could. Stella had been a neighbor for five years before she moved away for several more and then returned. For some reason, Marlee's mother had taken an instant liking to Stella, and the two had become friends.

But there had always been something about the woman that didn't seem right to Marlee. Macey had said she was crazy, so Marlee had let it go. Yet when she tried to remember the last time she had personally seen Stella, she realized it had been right after Macey died. And not since.

"How long have you been here?" Marlee asked.

Stella laughed and shrugged, but the sound was forced. "Awhile, actually. Oddly enough, I like the quiet. Your mother called yesterday. I didn't get a chance to call her back yet. How is she doing?"

"She's fine. What is it that you do exactly? I asked Mom once, but I don't know that she ever told me."

"I've got the best job. It allows me to move anywhere I want and still get paid. Thank goodness, because I've got wanderlust." Stella laughed.

Marlee didn't join her. She waited for Stella to give her an answer.

Stella cleared her throat. "I work for a law firm. They like to keep tabs on their clients who feel they're in danger as well as others who might cause problems for them.

I hire men," she said and jerked her chin over Marlee's shoulder, "to ensure all that happens without incident."

Marlee turned her head just enough to spot the man from the door standing a few feet behind her. "And I suppose if there is an incident, your men know how to take care of it."

"That they do." Stella moved closer as she adjusted her purse and bags. "Perhaps while you're in town, we can have dinner together. It's been a long time since I've seen you. I'd like to get an update on your parents."

"You could get that by calling my mom."

Stella's smile tightened, and her blue eyes turned cold. "I could, but we both know your mother glosses over things. They're both getting on in years. I'm surprised you aren't there helping to care for them. It would be a shame if anything happened."

"Is that a threat?" Marlee demanded as she took a step closer.

Stella smiled. "Not at all."

"I hope not."

"It was nice seeing you, Marlee. Be sure and tell your mother hello for me."

Marlee turned as Stella walked past her and into the house. The older gentleman stood his ground for several minutes until he walked backward into the home. Only then did Marlee turn and make her way to the truck. She was shaking by the time she got inside. It took her a moment to realize that Cooper wasn't with her. She started to get out to find him when she saw him peek around the corner of the house. As soon as he spotted her, he made his way back.

Once in the truck, he said, "What was that?"

"The house we've been looking for. Drive. We need to get everyone together because we have to move fast."

Chapter 34

When Marlee finished her story, the room was quiet. Cooper twirled a toothpick between his fingers and looked at everyone standing in the middle of Clayton and Abby's kitchen.

"The house was purchased twenty years ago," Danny said as he read from his computer. "By a Stella Pearson."

Clayton ran a hand down his face. "Twenty years? How long have they been operating in this territory?"

"It doesn't matter. What matters is bringing her and the business down," Ryan stated.

Jace leaned his hands on the island and shook his head. "I'm all for going in like we normally do. But this time, they're going to be waiting for us."

"So?" Caleb asked.

Brice shot his brother a dry look. "We all want to kick their asses, but not at the expense of casualties."

"Brice is right. We should call in the FBI," Danny said.

Cooper's gaze slid to Marlee, who stood beside him. Other than telling everyone what had happened at the house, she had been quiet and seemed lost in her thoughts.

Something was bothering her. Something she hadn't mentioned to the others.

He touched her arm, causing her to jump. She looked at him and gave him a small smile. He pulled her against him, and to his surprise, she allowed it. He hadn't been sure she would. "What's wrong?" he whispered.

"The other person in the house," Marlee said loud enough to get everyone's attention. She looked from the others to Cooper. "I told you I got a call from Stephanie."

Cooper nodded in agreement. "Your FBI friend."

"Something about that call didn't sit right."

Ryan raised a brow. "You mean besides her not being able to give you Kate Sommerset's real name?"

Marlee shifted her feet. "Besides that. You see, I could hear a can being opened through the speaker of the phone. While talking to Stephanie, I could see into the house through the window. The shadows prevented me from seeing if it was a man or a woman, but someone was sitting at the table, drinking a canned drink while on the phone. When Stephanie and I finished our call, the person in the house lowered their phone."

"You think Stephanie was in the house," Cooper said.

Marlee nodded. "I do."

"I saw someone when I went to the house," he told the room. "They walked toward the back when Marlee knocked on the door. I didn't get a look at them, but they made sure to move away from the front so they couldn't be seen."

Marlee released a long breath. "I'm telling you all of that to say that I don't think we should call in the FBI. If that *was* Stephanie inside the house, then she's working with Stella."

"Dammit," Clayton said as he slammed his Stetson down on the island. He turned and paced away.

Ryan looked at Danny. "We could ask the judge for

a warrant to search the house, but I've got a feeling we won't find anything there."

"I agree. They'll be using this time to get rid of everything," Danny said.

Caleb squeezed the bridge of his nose with his thumb and forefinger. "Please tell me someone has eyes on the house?"

"Two of my men are undercover," Ryan answered.

Jace widened his stance and crossed his arms over his chest. "What's the plan? Because sitting here and talking about it isn't getting anything done."

"I have nothing but gut instinct," Marlee said. "There is no proof of anything. Stella moves a lot. She'll use that as an excuse. We can't just go in there and arrest her. We have to have something on her, or she'll slip through scot-free."

Cooper smiled as an idea came to him. "Then we make sure we have something."

"As in?" Brice asked.

Cooper swung his gaze to Marlee. "The owner of the adoption agency in Dallas. The one who sent you here. I bet we could make them turn and give up anything they have on Stella."

"That won't be happening," Danny said. "I've not gotten a chance to tell any of you, but Penny Howard's body was found this morning by the Dallas police department. It's been ruled a homicide."

Cooper's breath left him in a whoosh as if he'd been kicked by a horse. "She's known you were here." He faced Marlee, grabbing her arms in his hands. "Stella has known all this time. She had to figure out who sent you here, as well."

"And had Penny killed," Marlee finished. "I agree."

Jace snorted as he straightened. "Anyone want to guess why Stella hasn't just had Marlee killed?"

"Because of us," Cooper said. "All of us."

Ryan rubbed his nose. "We've backed Stella and her group into a corner now. All bets might be off."

"Then we better get ready," Brice announced as he turned to walk away.

Danny's voice rang out, halting everyone. "Hold up! This is police business now. I know all of you have fought for and with each other before, but this isn't something we've dealt with. You need to let the sheriff's department and the police handle this."

"Of course," Clayton said after a tense few moments of silence.

Cooper exchanged looks with Jace, Caleb, and Brice. They were going to do anything but stand down.

Chapter 35

"What are we going to do now?" Chuck demanded.

Stella was shaking as she set the bags down in the kitchen and turned to him. "We do what we've always done. Survive."

"It won't be easy," Stephanie said as she walked into the room.

Stella met the agent's blue eyes and shrugged. "It never is. Did Marlee see you?"

"I'm better than that," Stephanie said in a flat tone.

Chuck snorted as he crossed his arms over his chest. "How many times are we going to underestimate Marlee before she gets to each of us?"

"She has nothing on me," Stephanie stated.

Stella's gaze was on Chuck. What Stephanie didn't know was that his loyalty didn't lie with her or the FBI, it was with Stella. Chuck would turn Stephanie over before he said anything about Stella or anyone else in the company. That's just the way Chuck was. He'd never liked Stephanie, and while he understood what her role was, he hadn't been comfortable with it.

His reasons were valid. Stephanie wasn't the only agent

in the FBI that Stella had dealings with, and she had enough blackmail on all of them to ensure they didn't turn on her. But that didn't mean the rest of her employees were safe.

"Stop," Stella told the two of them. "Stephanie, you need to get out of town. Quickly."

Stephanie shook her head of blond hair. "There's no need. Besides, I was sent by someone much higher up to make sure this meeting tonight goes smoothly. If it doesn't, it could be a nightmare for the agency."

As if Stella gave a damn about the FBI. The only reason she had dealings with them at all was to keep the authorities off her scent. It was the price she had to pay to continue her operation, and she did it willingly. The cost was being at the FBI's beck and call when it served them. As it did tonight.

Stella took a deep breath and faced Stephanie. "I've never failed the agency before, and I'm certainly not going to start now. What I need is to have Marlee and her Scooby gang off my ass. You'll serve better in that department while you let me do what I do best."

For long minutes, Stephanie stared at her. Then she sighed. "Let me make a call."

Once Stephanie was out of the room, Stella turned to Chuck. "Notify the others. We need to get some of them out of the state as soon as possible."

"What location do you want to meet at?"

She thought about that for a moment. "I think it might be time we all took an extended holiday. We need to lay low. Otherwise, Marlee is going to end all of this."

Chuck's nostrils flared as he dropped his arms to his sides. "That isn't going to happen."

"We all knew this couldn't continue forever. She's gotten too close."

"You should've let me get rid of her years ago."

Stella looked away. "Maybe I should have." But she hadn't wanted her friend to lose both of her daughters. It would destroy Diane.

"I've always protected you," Chuck said as he came closer. "Even when you didn't want me to."

Her head swung around, and she met his brown eyes. "I know."

"We could've had a life together."

This wasn't the time to be discussing old feelings, but instead of shutting him down, Stella found herself replying. "I wouldn't let myself."

"Why?" he pressed, a frown marring his features.

"I left an abusive home to live on the streets where I fought for food every day. But I didn't care because I was free to live my life the way I wanted. Then I found myself with an opportunity that I could use not only to pull myself out of the gutter but to also give me a life I never would've had."

Chuck's shoulders lifted as he inhaled. "I know the story."

"Yes, you do. But what you don't know is that when I made the decision to become the woman I am, I knew I would never get to share it with anyone. Not because I was afraid that someone would betray me. Rather because I have to be this cold person who doesn't let feelings get in the way of business. If I let myself love someone, if I dared to open my heart, I feared that what I had created would crumble."

"And you'd rather have the money," he replied.

She put her hand on his arm. "It's not just the money, though that is a factor. It's that I built this company. I put together the teams, hired the employees, developed the contacts. I did that. A woman without a college education. Because what I learned on the streets was much more valuable. Look at what it created for us."

"You," he corrected. "You created this for you. The rest of us just happen to be along for the ride."

He was hurt. Of that much, she was certain. She dropped her arm to her side. "I'm trying to let you know that my decision about us had nothing to do with you. It was about me."

"I see that now. Have you ever been in a relationship?"

The very idea of it made Stella shudder, but she held it back. "No."

"Because of time?"

Why was he pressing her about this? Why couldn't he just leave well enough alone? "The fact is, I don't like anyone thinking they can control me."

"That's not what relationships are."

"Really?" she asked with a quirk of a brow. "Because all the ones I've been in have done exactly that."

"I didn't control you."

She blew out a breath, reining in her anger. "No, you didn't. Because I didn't allow you to get that close. It's how males are, Chuck. You let women think we're equal, and once the relationship is solidified, usually by marriage, then the men start laying down rules. They begin telling women what they can and can't do, and then the beatings start."

"I've never laid a hand in anger on any woman I was dating. Never," he stated in a deep tone.

"You're a decent man. Otherwise, I never would've hired you, much less taken you to my bed. We had a good time together. Shouldn't that be enough?"

"You'd think," he said before he pivoted and walked into the kitchen.

Stella put a hand on her brow. Chuck had never spoken to her like that before, and she wasn't sure what to make of it. She didn't get a chance to think more about it as Stephanie came back into the room.

"It seems that you get your way," Stephanie told her. "I'm leaving and will make sure Marlee is diverted elsewhere. That should give you time to get to the meeting tonight in Houston."

Stella was aware that nothing else was offered. Even if she asked, she wouldn't get it. She had to be happy with whatever the FBI gave her. It was too bad she hadn't developed any relationships with the local authorities in Clearview, because that would have come in handy right about now. There hadn't been a need before, but it was a mistake she would rectify as soon as she could.

"Thank you," Stella said. "Looks like we all need to get busy. Time is of the essence."

Time certainly is of the essence, Chuck thought to himself as he sent out the texts to the other groups. Everyone had their own escape routes wherever they were, and they never left together. It made it harder for the authorities to track them down.

Chuck watched Stephanie get into her car that was hidden in the garage and then drive away. He breathed easier with her gone. But a cloud still loomed over them. Marlee Frampton. If something wasn't done about her, they might as well turn themselves in to the authorities.

Marlee knew their faces. She was smart. That's why she had been out in the area today. As soon as she saw Stella, Marlee pieced it all together. The fact that the police weren't here yet was only because Marlee didn't have any substantial evidence—and she never would.

They were professionals. None of them left behind any DNA. Besides that, Stella had a system designed by the world's leading hackers, just to make sure that no one could crack it. The files there were set to be wiped the moment an incorrect password was keyed in twice.

There wouldn't be any evidence this go-round, but how

much longer until Marlee had what she needed? Since she knew their faces—and Stella's name—it was simply a matter of her following them wherever they went. They might get a month or more in a new city before Marlee showed up but show up the little bitch would.

Chuck looked over his shoulder to see Stella in her office. She'd always traveled light. The only things she had on her were her laptop and a planner, neither of which would give anything to the police to link them to the murders or kidnappings.

"It's hours before your meeting," Chuck said. "I'd advise against staying here."

Stella dropped her cell phone into her purse before she turned to him. "No doubt Marlee has someone watching the house. They'll know when or if any of us come and go."

"Then why did you send Stephanie away?" he asked with a frown.

"Because I wanted her out of my hair and doing something useful."

Chuck didn't like the sound of any of this. "If you think Marlee and her gang will buy any of that, you're wrong."

"It'll send them after Stephanie. If she doesn't want to blow her cover, she won't tell them she's FBI if she's stopped and questioned. Then she can—and will—do what's been ordered and get Marlee to follow another lead. I'm not worried, Chuck, and neither should you be."

"Marlee came to the house. I'm fairly certain every one of us should be fucking worried."

Stella gave him a stern look. "You're the one I count on the most. I need you to make sure everyone gets out of town. Maria will leave with me when I go to the meeting."

"You won't have time for that. Besides, the last thing you should do is stop for anything. I'll take the women."

"Thank you," Stella said with a smile. "You always come through for me."

Yes, he did. And he was going to do it again tonight. Stella might not like what he planned, but she'd get over it eventually.

Chapter 36

The sound of a phone pulled Marlee awake. Her eyes hurt from lack of sleep. She groaned as she reached over and blindly searched for her cell on the bedside table before she knocked it off.

"Want me to get it?" Cooper asked from beside her.

She opened her eyes and leaned over the side of the bed. "I got it."

Everyone had stayed at the East Ranch last night. Most of that time, she and the others had stayed up going over several plans, none of which seemed to properly fit. It had been after three before she and Cooper finally found a bed.

But even then, they hadn't slept.

The moment they were behind closed doors, they reached for each other. Their clothes came off quickly as they found pleasure in each other's arms. Even after what she had told him yesterday, she didn't regret spending the night with him. In fact, she was wondering if her words from yesterday had been said in haste.

Her thoughts ended there when she found the phone, just as the call went to voicemail. Marlee rolled onto her back and looked at the incoming caller ID. "Hmm. That's odd."

"What is?" Cooper asked as he turned toward her and threw an arm over her stomach.

"It's Stephanie."

Cooper's eyes opened. In the next heartbeat, he rose up on his elbow. "Does she often call?"

Marlee shook her head. "Mostly it's me calling her, though she has called me back if she has information."

"Maybe she has information."

"Or maybe she was in that house like I think, and she's trying to divert my attention."

They looked at the phone for a moment. It suddenly dinged, letting Marlee know there was a voicemail. With quick fingers, she unlocked her phone and pulled up the voicemail, putting it on speaker so Cooper could hear.

"Hey, Marlee," Stephanie's voice said. "It's early, I know, but I had an all-nighter at work. You were right about that name you gave me yesterday. I couldn't devote the time needed to it because I was working another case, but I dug into it some more. The woman's real name is Karen Meader. She's got friends in high places. Unfortunately, not high enough. She testified against some bad people, who are now looking for her. Those friends I spoke of, well, they got her a new identity, which was why you couldn't find out anything about her. Wish I could've told you this yesterday. Hopefully, you didn't spend too much time on her. On another note, I saw something come through regarding your particular cases. We're looking into a couple near San Antonio."

Marlee looked at Cooper after Stephanie rattled off an address and the message ended. "What do you think?"

"If you didn't think you saw her yesterday, what would you think of the voicemail?"

"That she did exactly as she said."

Cooper raised his brows as he turned onto his back. "If that was Stephanie in the house, wouldn't she have made this call sooner?"

"I don't know." Marlee blew out a breath and looked at the ceiling. "She could be telling the truth, but she could also be working with Stella."

"I was thinking about Stephanie last night when we were all talking. You said that she was part of your sister's case."

"That's right. That's how we met. She interviewed me as she did everyone. Once I was cleared of anything, I showed her what little I had come up with during my own investigation. She didn't disregard me as others might have. In fact, she was interested in what I had. We compared notes, and she actually showed me what little evidence the Feds had collected."

Cooper put one arm behind his head and used his other to hold her hand. "You like her."

"I did, but that's when I thought I knew her. I believed she was one of the good guys."

"Not everyone in law enforcement is a good guy."

Marlee turned her head to meet his gaze. "I know that. But somehow, I forgot that with Stephanie. For some reason, I believed she was above such things because she's an agent." She rolled her eyes. "God, I sound ridiculous."

"Don't be too hard on yourself. You believed you had a friend, an ally to help you out. Most people would feel the same as you. And for all we know, she was never in our town, and it wasn't her in the house yesterday."

Marlee hoped he was right, but she couldn't be sure. "So, what do you think I should do now?"

"Forget yesterday. What would you normally do?"

"Call her back and thank her."

"Then do it."

Marlee thought about it for a moment and then gave

him a nod. "You're right. Regardless of everything else, I need to stick to what I'd usually do."

She dialed Stephanie's number and kept the phone on speaker so Cooper could listen. Stephanie answered on the third ring.

"Just got your message," Marlee said. "Thought I'd try and catch you before you were too busy to answer the phone."

Stephanie laughed. "That is one thing about this job. I'm always busy. Going one place or another."

Marlee glanced at Cooper as she asked, "They've got you traveling? Where are you headed?"

"Oregon. It is pretty, but damn cold. Oh, well. Duty calls."

"I won't keep you, then. Just wanted to say thanks for the update on the name I was interested in. Thought for sure it was a dead end. You came through for me, though. Thank you."

Stephanie made a sound on the other end of the line. "Don't think twice about it. I'm just glad I could help out. Wish I could do more."

"You do quite a bit for me. I'm not sure why, though."

"Not sure why?" Stephanie repeated with a chuckle. "Marlee, I do it because you're going after the bad guys just like we are. I'm constrained with rules and regulations, and while you are as a PI, as well, it's not nearly as hindering as mine. One way or another, these criminals need to be brought to their knees."

Cooper made a face as if he were surprised by the vehemence of her words.

At one time, Marlee would've been taken in by them, hook, line, and sinker. Now? Not so much. "I'm so glad you feel that way."

"Anything you need, you call me. I've always told you that. I'll help you out any way I can."

"I don't know what to say."

"Just catch the bad guys," Stephanie said and then hung up.

Marlee lowered the phone to the bed. "She said all the right things in the right tone and everything."

"But?" Cooper pushed.

"I think she's lying."

"Do you call her during every case?"

Marlee thought about that for a moment and shook her head. "It's easy for me to do that and get a little edge on the criminals, but I try not to take advantage of that. The few times I did call her, Stephanie always came through."

"Has she really? Or do you just think she has?"

Marlee sat up and rubbed her forehead. "I don't know anymore. When I think about how she could be in with Stella, then I think about all the times I might have caught Stella earlier. So many people would've been saved, and children would still be with their families."

"You can't think like that." Cooper sat up beside her and wrapped an arm around her as he pulled her against him. "It'll drive you nuts. I say follow your instinct. Right now, it's telling you to mistrust everything from those you've trusted before. Listen to your gut."

"You're right. I can't sit here and think about this. I've got to think about how we can take down Stella."

Cooper kissed her temple. "Just make sure not to say anything in front of Danny or Ryan. We don't want to put them in an awkward situation."

"I need to run to my motel room and gather my things."

"I tell you what. You get in the shower, have some coffee and maybe some breakfast, and I'll go get your things."

She smiled, looking deep into his green eyes. "Are you afraid something might happen to me?"

"Maybe."

"You could come with me."

"I could, but you mentioned a shower several times last night."

She wrinkled her nose. "A shower does sound heavenly. All right. You win. But be quick."

"I will." He kissed her lips, lingering for a moment.

She watched as he rose from the bed and hurriedly dressed. At the door, he stopped and blew her a kiss. She wore a wide smile when she got up and made her way into the bathroom. Marlee took her time, lingering in the hot water as she let it loosen her tight muscles. Though, she had to admit, sleeping next to Cooper had done wonders for her both mentally and emotionally.

When she dried off and opened the bathroom door, she expected to find him sitting there waiting on her since she had taken so long. Then she realized that he was probably downstairs having coffee with the others.

Marlee dressed and finished getting ready. After she made the bed and picked up her clothes from the night before, she went downstairs. She heard voices coming from below and was met with smiles from Abby, Clayton, and Caleb.

"Morning," she greeted them. "Is Cooper back yet?"

Caleb shook his head. "Just as he was heading out, Jace came downstairs. They didn't leave until about twenty minutes ago so it'll be a bit before they get back."

Marlee poured herself some coffee. "I'm glad he didn't go alone."

"No one would be stupid enough to try anything with those two," Clayton said.

Marlee smiled, but she couldn't stop thinking of the man she had encountered the day before. That kind of guy wouldn't let anything, or anyone, stop him. He would attack and ask questions later. She inwardly gave herself a shake. Her mind believed there were enemies lurking everywhere. In all her years as a PI, she had only been attacked once. No doubt Stella and her people were getting ready to bolt, not coming after Marlee or her new friends.

Besides, Cooper and Jace were highly trained individuals, not your ordinary civilians. No, she had nothing to worry about.

Chapter 37

"So?" Jace asked as they pulled up to the motel in the pouring rain.

Cooper turned off the ignition and looked at his friend. "You drank coffee and talked about the weather the entire way over here. And now you want to ask a question?"

"Not just any question. *The* question."

"Oh, *the question*. What question is that?"

Jace rolled his eyes. "Don't try that shit with me. You know what."

Cooper faced forward and shrugged, no longer pretending he didn't know what his friend was asking. "I'm not sure. She told me yesterday that I belonged here, and it would never work between us."

"She certainly wasn't acting like things were over last night. Neither of you was."

"Because I don't want them to be."

"You need to call your mom."

Cooper smiled as he glanced at Jace. "I did this morning before you came downstairs. I've been keeping her informed of things, and she was asking to meet Marlee."

"I gather you told Mom you're in love with Marlee."

"Yeah."

"I can guess what she told you."

Cooper turned his head to his best friend. "Oh? What's that?"

"The same thing I'm going to tell you." Jace met his gaze, his expression serious. "I've seen you with lots of women. I knew the instant I saw you with Marlee that she was different. That she was the one for you."

Cooper didn't so much as move as Jace continued.

"We've been best friends for a long time, Coop. We remained close through the years while we were in the military. And you know what? We'll always remain close. No matter where you live. If you want to be with Marlee, and I know you do, then that means your path lies alongside hers, which means traveling away from here."

"I know," Cooper said in a soft voice.

"You two work well together. Think what you could accomplish."

Cooper nodded, unable to find words.

"I'll always be here for you, brother. You know that. Get the girl and take hold of the life that awaits both of you." There was a pause, then Jace got out of the truck, stepping into the frigid rain, and ran to Marlee's door.

Cooper followed his friend. They entered the room and began collecting pictures off the walls, stacking them neatly. Jace had two boxes piled on top of each other as he headed to the truck to load them. Cooper kept packing. He didn't even glance up when the door opened.

"We don't have much left," he said.

"That's nice."

The deep voice wasn't one he recognized. Cooper froze and slowly straightened. He then turned to face whoever it was. That's when he spotted the crowbar in the man's hand that dripped blood on the carpet. The fact that the man was in the room and not Jace put Cooper in defense-mode.

The man smiled sadistically. "Jace never saw me coming."

"You've got one chance to leave before I rip you apart."

"With what?" the man asked. "You have no weapon."

Cooper fisted his hands. "I wouldn't say that."

"I would," he declared and drew out a gun with his other hand, pointing it at Cooper. "Not so cocky now, are you?"

"If you knew who I was, you'd stop running your mouth and do something."

The man laughed. "I know who you are, Cooper Owens. I learned everything about those Marlee was investigating the moment she pulled into town. But all your training doesn't scare me. Because I have much, much more than you."

"What do you want?"

"Marlee. I knew someone would come for her things. I've been waiting all night for one of you to drop by. I'm really glad it was you."

Jace winced as pain radiated through his head. The rain beat a steady tempo on his face, like tiny icicles piercing his skin. He squeezed his eyes shut and tried to push up with his hands. The pain made his stomach roil, and he had to fight not to be sick.

He'd had a head wound before. He knew exactly what was happening. If only he knew how he'd gotten hurt. Had he fallen? He shifted his head and cracked open one eye. The boxes he'd been carrying had spilled, rain pelting the pictures and papers. Yet there was no ice on the parking lot that would have caused him to slip.

Jace forced his body to move as he got to his hands and knees. It took considerable effort because every movement was pure agony. He managed to reach one of the cardboard boxes, toss everything back in, and then put the lid on. It took forever, and he nearly blacked out twice.

As he reached for the second box, the pain became too much, and he had to turn away to vomit. As he finished, Jace glanced up and saw the door to the motel room. He had to get to Cooper. He forgot about the boxes and used the truck to help himself regain his footing. Once he stood, the world began to spin.

Jace grabbed hold of the truck again to remain standing. His legs were Jell-O, and everything kept whirling. He had no idea how much time passed before the Earth stilled. Only then did he attempt to walk. The last thing he wanted to do was fall. He wasn't sure he'd get back up if he did.

Placing one foot in front of the other, he managed to get to the door. He threw it open, ready to attack whoever was inside. Except there was no one. It was empty and everything looked as it should, save for a bullet hole in the wall.

"No," Jace said as he searched for his cell phone in his pockets. When he couldn't find it, he rushed to the phone beside the bed, stumbling and falling upon the mattress. Jace righted himself and dialed Danny, apprehension and his wound, causing his hands to shake.

"We're sorry. Your call cannot be completed as dialed," said an automated female voice.

"Fuck!" Jace yelled as he slammed the receiver down.

He sank onto the comforter and tried to read the instructions on the phone, but his eyes were too blurry. He blinked several times. Thanks to the adrenaline pumping through him, the pain became manageable. Finally, he was able to read the instructions on the motel phone and get an outside line to Danny.

"Mornin', Jace," Danny said happily.

"I need you. ASAP."

His tone shifted to that of the sheriff. "Slow down. Where's here?"

Jace grabbed his head and grimaced as the throbbing intensified. "The motel Marlee was staying at. Cooper and I came . . . I . . . fuck."

"Stay there. I'm on my way."

The line disconnected. Jace looked around the room again as he hung up the receiver. Gingerly, he felt along the back of his head until he found the knot. As soon as he touched it, nausea roiled and had him running to the bathroom to empty his stomach again.

He must have passed out because the next thing he knew, Danny was kneeling beside him, trying to wake him up. Jace raised a hand to let his friend know that he was conscious.

"What the hell happened?" Danny demanded. "Never mind. I've been trying to wake you for about five minutes. I called an ambulance."

Jace started to speak when Karl and Marina filled the doorway. He frowned at his paramedic friends, but before he could ask them what they were doing there, they shooed Danny out and began tending to Jace.

He tried to wave away their hands, but they were too quick for him. "I'm fine. We need to look for Cooper."

"You're far from fine," Marina stated in a no-nonsense tone. "There's blood covering your face and clothes."

Jace couldn't comprehend what they were saying. "I found the bump."

"Not only a bump. A laceration," Karl told him. He grabbed Jace's hands and held his gaze. "We need you to be still. If you want to help Cooper, you need to let us help you first."

Jace wanted to argue with them, but he didn't have the strength. As soon as he stopped fighting, Karl and Marina worked seamlessly. Jace closed his eyes and tried to think back to what had happened. He remembered getting the boxes and walking outside. He even remembered reaching the truck. As he'd stopped to press the boxes against the vehicle to free one hand to open the door, he'd seen a figure come up behind him in the glass. Then, everything went black.

His eyes snapped open. "I was attacked."

Danny leaned against the doorway of the bathroom to give Marina and Karl room. "We figured as much. I also found the bullet hole in the wall. No slug or casing, however. Did you hear a shot?"

"I think he came at me first."

"You?"

Jace blew out a breath while Marina cleaned the blood from his face. "I saw him in the window of the truck before he hit me."

"Whatever he struck you with was meant to kill," Marina stated. "It would've killed others."

Karl chuckled. "It's Jace's hard head that saved him."

"We didn't look for anyone when we got here," Jace said as he lifted his eyes to Danny. "We should have. We know better."

Danny got down on his haunches and shoved his cowboy hat back on his head. "You got your bell rung pretty good. You're going to need to take it easy."

"That's my best friend out there," Jace said as he shoved Karl's hands away.

Marina grabbed Jace's arms and gently lowered them. "You won't be of any help until your pain subsides. You have a concussion and a deep laceration that needs stitches to stop the bleeding."

"Then do it," Jace ordered angrily.

Danny sighed and straightened. "You might as well do it, Marina. He won't go to the hospital."

"Damn straight, I won't," Jace stated.

Karl flattened his lips and got everything ready to begin stitching. Marina pulled out a syringe for a localized anesthetic, but Jace shook his head. He was well accustomed to pain. Deadening it might affect his senses, and he needed to be ready for anything.

"Tell me everything," Danny said.

Jace allowed them to roll him onto his stomach with his face turned toward Danny.

"Ready?" Karl asked.

Jace nodded and took a deep breath. He released it as Karl stuck the needle into his scalp. Instead of giving in to the pain, he focused on Danny and telling the sheriff what he knew. "There were a few vehicles in the parking lot when we drove up. Nothing looked out of place, but we didn't search as we should have. Cooper and I were talking, and I think we both assumed the bad guys wouldn't be interested in us."

"They want Marlee, is my guess," Danny said as he ran a hand over his mouth. "If they know anything, then they know about Marlee and Cooper."

"If they killed Cooper, his body would've been left here."

Danny nodded and removed his hat, turning it around by the brim in his hands. "Then why shoot him?"

"Because Cooper never would've left with them otherwise."

"Would he have gone regardless?"

Jace thought about that for a moment while remaining perfectly still. His wound throbbed uncontrollably, and the feel of his scalp being stitched closed only added to the agony. "No. Cooper would've fought them."

"Then they took him the only way they could. By force."

"In order to get Marlee to come to them."

Danny pulled out his phone as he turned away.

All Jace could think about was finding the bastard who had done this to Cooper and him. Because he would find him. And he would tear him apart.

Chapter 38

Marlee was by herself in the front room at the ranch when her phone buzzed. She had been looking for a sign of Cooper. It was ridiculous for her to worry about him, but she couldn't seem to help herself. She didn't want the others to know that she was a worrier, so she walked away from them to peek outside and look at the drive to see if she could spot Cooper's truck.

She hurriedly reached for her phone, hoping it was Cooper. Only she saw Jace's name pop up. Still, they were together, so that was enough. "Hey, Jace," she said. "I'm getting a little worried, you two have been gone awhile."

"There was a lot to do."

The voice was deep, gravelly, the same as the voice of the man she had encountered yesterday at the house. Her stomach dropped to her feet. She started to turn and run back to the kitchen to tell the others.

"Before you do something stupid, you should listen to what I have to say," the man stated.

Marlee hesitated. She knew men like him. He didn't threaten unless he intended to follow through. Not to mention, he was one of those who murdered pregnant women and cut their unborn babies from them. You had to be the worst kind of human to do that.

"I'm waiting," she finally said.

He laughed softly. "I always knew you were smart. So, here's how this is going to go. If you want your precious Cooper back, you're going to meet me."

"I need to know he's alive. And Jace, as well."

"Sorry, sweetheart. Jace is dead. However, there's still a chance for Cooper."

She took in a steadying breath. "You could be lying."

"I could be, but do I seem the type? You know I'm not. Stella has kept me from slicing your throat for years. I could've killed you a hundred times over. Well, now that you found Stella, all bets are off. You've got a chance here. You can come to me, and I can take your life. Or you can go to your friends and tell them everything. If you do that, I will kill Cooper and disappear. But I'll still come for you. You've done enough damage to our world."

His words were so ludicrous that Marlee had to bite back a laugh. She considered his words. "The men here are trained military men."

"So am I, sweetheart. How do you think I got the drop on Jace *and* Cooper?"

Damn. What was she going to do? But she knew. She was going to do the only thing she could. "Where do we meet?"

He laughed, the sound grating on her nerves. "I knew you'd see reason. Head west for thirty miles."

"That's it? That's all I get?"

"You think I'm going to tell you everything now? Give me some credit. Call Jace's phone when you've done that, and I'll give you the next coordinates. And let me be clear, Marlee. I know you're at the East Ranch. I know the others are there, that the sheriff is at work, and so is the police chief. If you tell any of them or call them while you're on the road to help you, Cooper dies. Do you understand?"

"Perfectly," she answered.

"Then I suggest you get moving because you have less than twenty minutes to reach the destination."

The phone went dead. Marlee's heart beat so fast, she thought it might burst from her chest. She wanted so badly to tell the others, but she didn't want to chance it. If the man knew her location, he could have bugged her phone, which meant he would know if she told anyone. Besides, there wasn't time for her to speak to those at the ranch since he hadn't given her much time to drive thirty miles.

She snuck around the kitchen and waited until everyone was occupied before she grabbed the keys to Abby's Suburban and slipped out the door without even grabbing her coat. The rain soaked her as she ran to the garage. She moved quickly, shoving her wet hair out of her eyes as she looked around for anyone who might try and stop her.

It wasn't until she pulled away from the driveway and got onto the road that she breathed a sigh of relief. The others at the ranch would discover her gone soon enough. Until then, she was going to concentrate on the instructions she'd been given.

Stella paced the house as the hours slowly ticked by. Chuck had left sometime in the night without a word. It was unusual, but she couldn't help but be worried. No sirens could be heard coming her way, so she had to assume she was safe.

For the moment.

The meeting the night before hadn't happened because the couple's plane got delayed due to weather. She should've been long gone from this area. Instead, she was back at the house, waiting for the meeting to happen tonight. And she wasn't happy. Remaining in Clearview felt as if she were giving the authorities time to catch her.

"Dammit, Chuck. Where are you?" she asked aloud.

Cooper woke on his side to find himself in a darkened building. His right shoulder throbbed relentlessly as blood dripped down his arm. He pushed himself up into a seated position, gritting his teeth at the pain. He needed to stop the bleeding. By the puddle of blood pooled on the floor, he had lost a significant amount.

He reached for the knife he always carried in his pocket, but it was gone. So was the one in his boot. A quick check confirmed that his phone was also missing. Cooper removed his jacket as well as the button-down beneath to reveal a white thermal shirt. Sweat beaded on his skin and dripped into his eyes as the pain consumed him.

With no other choice, he tried to use his one good hand and his teeth to rip his shirt. It took several attempts before he got the fabric to do as he wanted. The moment he had the tiniest of tears in the material, he tore off the bottom part all the way around. He worked fast to then wrap it around the wound and tie it tightly. He rested for only a moment before he put his shirt and jacket back on. Then he climbed to his feet.

By the looks of things, he was in an old structure. Probably one of the many buildings downtown that the city council was trying to bring in money to revitalize. He walked until he found a door, only to discover that it was chained from the outside. The three other doors he found were also locked.

The bastard who had shot him had wanted Marlee. There was no way for Cooper to tell any of his friends that he was alive and fine. Which was exactly what the man wanted.

"Be smart, Marlee," he whispered like a prayer.

His thoughts turned to Jace. He had no idea if his friend was alive or not, and that was like a knife to the chest. With Jace and Marlee in danger, Cooper needed to do something. He couldn't sit back and allow anything to happen to them. They were too important to him.

He grabbed the door he stood before and yanked on it again and again, hoping the chains would give way. "Come on, guys! Find me! You can find me!"

Cooper pressed his heated forehead against the cold metal of the door. "Y'all have to find me," he whispered.

Chapter 39

Clayton slowly lowered his phone to the island after the call with Danny and looked around at the faces staring at him intently. He couldn't believe this was happening. Not again. Not after what they had gone through with Danny. But no matter how much he wanted to deny it, Clayton couldn't. The truth was there before them.

A knock sounded on the back door, right before Ryan opened it and stepped inside. His face was as hard as granite when his brown eyes met Clayton's.

"Someone say something," Caleb stated, looking between the two.

Abby walked to Clayton and put her hand on his back. "Honey? What is it?"

"Where's Marlee?" Ryan asked with a frown.

Clayton's gaze scanned the area, looking for Marlee's auburn curls. "She was just here."

"We need to find her. Now."

Brice held up his hands and faced Ryan. "Why? What is it you and Clayton know but won't tell us?"

"Everyone fan out and look for Marlee," Abby ordered in her best mom-voice.

Clayton saw both Brice and Caleb hesitate before they turned and began calling for Marlee. Clayton's gut churned. They had been lucky so many times before. Had their luck run out? Was this the time their ever-growing family couldn't pull out a miracle at the last minute?

"She's gone," Caleb said as he came from outside. "Marlee must have taken the Suburban."

It didn't take long for everyone to reconvene back in the kitchen. Their family and friends had stood in this very spot so many times. They had shared good news, bad news, sad news. They'd celebrated, mourned, and rejoiced. There had been more happy times than bad, at least. That was life. Clayton understood that. But this . . . this was too much.

Brice slammed his hand down on the island. "Dammit, Clayton. You or Ryan better start talking."

Clayton glanced at his wife to find Abby's blue eyes full of tears, because she knew him better than anyone. And she felt his pain. He nodded and cleared his throat. "That was Danny. He was at the motel because Jace called him. From what Danny has been able to piece together—"

"Piece together?" Caleb asked, his brow furrowed. "What the hell does that mean?"

Ryan put a hand on Caleb's shoulder and calmly said, "Let Clayton finish."

Clayton gave Ryan a nod of appreciation. "Jace went out to load up some boxes from Marlee's room when he saw someone's reflection in the truck window. He woke later on the ground. He'd been struck from behind."

"Oh, God," Abby whispered and reached for Clayton's hand.

He held on to her tightly and met his brother-in-law's gaze. "Jace managed to make it back inside the room, but Cooper wasn't there. He used the motel phone to call

Danny. Danny told me the hit Jace took was meant to kill."

"Fuck me," Brice murmured.

Caleb put his hands on the island and dropped his chin to his chest as he squeezed his eyes closed. "Is Jace all right?"

"Marina and Karl are with him now, stitching the wound," Ryan told them. "They're trying to get him to a hospital, but he won't go. He's alive, but the hit was brutal. Jace's memory of everything is piecemeal."

Caleb lifted his head and said, "Which means, no one knows who hit Jace."

"And Cooper?" Abby asked.

Clayton shook his head. "Nowhere to be found. There was a bullet hole in the wall of the motel room, but no shell or casing."

"Whoever did this wanted us to know they shot Cooper," Brice said.

Ryan crossed his arms over his chest. "That's right."

"Was there blood anywhere?" Caleb asked.

Ryan snorted. "It was everywhere. We're not sure how much of it is Jace's since he was bleeding profusely, or if it's Cooper's or whoever attacked them. Unfortunately, learning those details is going to take time."

"Time we don't have," Abby whispered.

Clayton pinched the bridge of his nose with his thumb and forefinger. "Whoever took Cooper must have called Marlee. That's the only reason I can think of for her to leave without telling us."

"Unless they threatened Cooper," Caleb said. "If Audrey were threatened, that would get me to do anything."

Abby nodded. "He's right."

"Someone call her," Ryan suggested.

Clayton had been so wrapped up in everything that

calling Marlee hadn't even crossed his mind. Before he could reach for his phone, Brice was already dialing the number.

"It's ringing," Brice told them. After a few minutes, he lowered the phone to the island. "It went to voicemail."

Abby turned to find her phone. "Then we all call her."

One by one, they placed calls to Marlee, but she didn't answer.

"I think it's time we tracked her," Ryan announced. He then made a call to the police station.

Caleb looked at Clayton. "What do we do now?"

"We wait," Abby replied. "We let Danny and Ryan do what they do best, and we wait for when we can help."

Brice sank heavily onto one of the stools. "What are the odds that this will end happily for us?"

"I don't want to think about that," Caleb answered.

Brice swung his head to his brother. "Well, I have to."

"We do what we do best," Clayton told them. "We be there for each other and our friends who are going to need us. Speaking of, has anyone called Betty?"

Ryan hung up the phone. "Danny had a sheriff's deputy bring her to Jace. They're hoping she can talk some sense into him because he wants to be brought here."

"That wouldn't be a bad idea," Abby said.

Clayton looked at her. "Jace needs to be in a hospital."

"I agree with Abby," Caleb said. "Jace was attacked. We have no idea if anyone else will be, as well. This ranch has always been our go-to when we need to regroup or gather."

Clayton pulled Abby against his side and kissed the top of her head. "You're both right. Call everyone. Get them here."

"Clayton, the kids," Abby said.

Ryan held up a hand. "I'll get them here immediately. Same with Naomi and Nate."

Brice let out a loud sigh. "I don't know how much more of this I can take."

Clayton was used to everyone looking to him for guidance, but this time, he wasn't sure he knew what to do—much less say. He couldn't shake the feeling that they were going to lose Marlee or Cooper. Maybe even both of them.

Each time her phone rang, Marlee fought not to reach for it and talk to them. She couldn't be sure if someone had put a tracker on her phone, and she didn't have time to look through it and find out. So, she decided to be cautious and assume that the asshole who had taken Cooper wasn't lying.

She had less than thirty seconds to spare when she finally reached the thirty-mile mark and jerked the vehicle's wheel to pull over. She slammed on the brakes, but that sent her phone flying off the center console to the floorboard.

Marlee let out a string of curses as she bent over, using her hands to search for it. She happened to glance up and saw that she was moving. With another string of curses, she put the SUV in park and opened the door to find the phone. Once she had it, she hit redial on her last accepted call.

"Cutting it close," the man said as he answered.

She closed her eyes while trying to get herself under control. Getting angry with him would get her nowhere. "I'm here. What next?"

"You're going to ditch whatever vehicle you're in. Do it somewhere it can't be found easily. Destroy the phone while you're at it. Then start walking north."

Marlee looked in the direction he mentioned. "It's nothing but woods. And it's raining."

"Then bring an umbrella. But get moving. Time is running out."

"I have another time limit? What is it this time?"

The man laughed. "Why would I tell you and make it easy?"

"Where north do I go?"

"I recommend you get a move on. Tick-tock."

Marlee let out a scream of frustration when the line went dead. She slammed her hands repeatedly on the steering wheel as tears coursed down her face. Her hands shook as she thought about her parents. She wanted to send them a quick text, but she didn't dare. Cooper's life was on the line.

She sniffed and wiped the tears from her face. No matter how much she wanted to tell her parents goodbye, she couldn't. And maybe that was for the best. If she told them, it might do more harm than good. Both of her parents were in a fragile state right now. A call from her, telling them that she might die, could be the very thing that killed them.

Marlee took in a steadying breath and glanced around for a place to dump the Suburban. She put to memory exactly where she was and shifted the vehicle into drive then pulled back onto the road, looking through the rain for somewhere to put the SUV. She drove about half a mile before she found what she was looking for. The ditch was so steep that it would be easy for a car to go off the side where no one could see it, especially with the rain.

She backed up, thankful that the road was all but deserted at the moment. Then she put it in neutral and got out, immediately drenched and missing the warmth of the interior. She turned the wheel just enough to send the Suburban down the embankment and into the ravine. But if she thought it would be easy, she was sorely mistaken. She pushed against the large SUV with all her might, struggling to move it even an inch. Finally, she realized she didn't have the strength to get it to budge.

"Shit," she murmured, shivering as she got back in and out of the wet and cold.

Marlee left the door open as she put it in drive and let her foot off the brake. The Suburban began to move. She raised her foot off some more, and the vehicle picked up momentum. Just before it went over the side, Marlee jumped out. Except her feet slipped on the pebbles on the shoulder, and she landed hard, the phone slipping from her hands. As soon as she fell, she rolled, the back tire of the SUV barely missing her foot. She heard a crunch as the vehicle ran over her phone.

She pressed her forehead against the pavement for a moment to catch her breath. She had managed to keep from being wounded and had destroyed her phone as she was supposed to. She jumped up and ran across the road. She moved into the trees but worked her way back to where she had been when the man had told her to head north. She wasn't a runner by any means, and soon, she had a stitch in her side. At least she was no longer shivering.

No matter how much she hurt, she didn't stop to even walk. She kept moving as fast as she could. Once she got to where she'd taken the call, she then pivoted north and ran even faster. All the while, hearing the man's *tick-tock* in her head.

And regretting not telling Cooper that she loved him.

Chapter 40

With nothing but time, Cooper walked the entire warehouse. The rain pelted the metal roof, causing a loud din of noise. The warehouse wasn't overly large, and unfortunately, it appeared it had recently been cleaned out. It was obviously one of the buildings the city council wanted to begin renovations on. Which meant he had absolutely nothing to use as a weapon or to free himself.

And with that realization came all sorts of thoughts. Things he wished he had told his mom, stuff he wished he had done with Jace, Caleb, and Brice. But most importantly, how he wished he had told Marlee how he really felt.

Cooper hated not knowing if Jace was alive or dead. By the gunman's reaction, there was a good chance that Jace had been killed, and that tore Cooper up. His best friend had needed him, and he hadn't been there to help. If anyone should have known to look around the property for potential threats, it was Cooper. Why hadn't he?

Because he'd been too wrapped up in thoughts of Marlee and helping her solve the case so they could figure out what their next step was. That's what had gotten his friend killed. Cooper would have to live with that for the rest of his life.

He leaned back against the wall and closed his eyes. His abductor hadn't wanted him dead—at least not yet. There was a real chance that outcome was coming sooner rather than later. Otherwise, why lock him up? It had to be to lure Marlee out. But Cooper knew she wouldn't fall for anything like that. Nor would any of his friends allow it. They'd keep her protected.

That was the only thing that kept him from going insane.

Cooper glanced at his shoulder that still throbbed. The tourniquet he'd fashioned hadn't stopped the bleeding entirely. He could feel it leaking into his shirt, but at least his lifeblood was no longer pouring out. He closed his eyes for a moment and slid to the floor.

Instantly, his mind conjured an image of Marlee from the night before when they had gone to bed together. Neither had asked the other, they had simply gone. They hadn't talked with words, even though there was so much he'd wanted to say to her. Instead, they had spoken through touch and kisses.

The feel of her hands on his body had been heavenly. She'd brought him pleasure the likes of which he'd never experienced before. He'd wanted to give her that same feeling. Watching her climax, seeing the pleasure flow over her face, hearing her cries of ecstasy, and feeling her clench around his cock was something he wanted to revel in for the rest of his life.

After, she had curled up beside him, her head on his chest, and her arm flung over him as he played with her hair. In seconds, she was fast asleep. He hadn't woken her to speak then. It had felt too good to just hold her. Sometime soon after, he had fallen asleep, as well.

Cooper's eyes snapped open. He'd heard something.

He was sure of it. At least, he thought he had. He'd been in a state between sleep and wakefulness so he couldn't be positive. It might have been a dream, but he thought there had been a loud bang.

He climbed uneasily to his feet and looked around the warehouse again. Once more, there was nothing. The rain had tapered off a bit, however. Cooper decided to try the doors again. Maybe someone would pass by and hear him. It was too bad the windows were so high up, or he might try and climb out one.

The first door was the same as before. The second one caused him to hesitate before touching it, however. He was sure there hadn't been wires there the first time he tried to escape.

Cooper squatted down beside the door and investigated the wiring that ran from the bottom up to the top corner. The moment he spotted the switch for the bomb, he took a step back. Had that been there before? He'd been too riddled with pain and the desire to get out to be sure.

He quickly checked the other two doors once more, but neither of them appeared to have been tampered with. So why this door? There had to be a reason. Was it the only one his friends could use to free Cooper? Right now, that didn't matter. What mattered was that he needed to stay near it to make sure that no one tried to open it.

"Where are you?" Stella asked the moment the call from Chuck came in.

The deep voice she recognized said, "I'm taking care of a few last-minute details."

"Is everyone out of town?"

"Martin is helping me with a few things, but he's just about to leave. We'll be the only two left. And after the meeting tonight, we'll be gone, too."

Stella looked around the house. She was leaving with

nothing more than her suitcase that was already in the
car, but the place felt empty. As if this was the last time
she would ever see it. And that was likely the truth. The
houses she had were all paid for and furnished, so she just
had to show up.

"Stella?" Chuck called.

She licked her lips. "Sorry. I'm just unsettled by the
meeting being pushed back and the rest."

"By the rest, you mean Marlee."

Stella rolled her eyes. "Yes, I mean Marlee."

"Has anyone been by the house?"

"No one. It's like she didn't tell the authorities. Or
maybe she did, and they're just waiting to come at me in
one huge rush."

Chuck made a sound. "No one is going to touch you. I
give you my word."

"You can't make that kind of promise."

"I did, and I have. Now, stay there until I arrive. Okay?"

She sat on the couch, feeling better than she had in
hours. "Okay. I'll be here. Just hurry. The sooner I get out
of this place, the better."

"I'm in total agreement on that one."

Jace sat on the bed in the motel room, pleased that his
head no longer felt as if it were split open. The pain was
still there, but it had lessened enough that the room wasn't
spinning anymore. The aspirin he'd taken had done very
little to diminish the pain, but since that was all he was
willing to take, he couldn't gripe about it. Karl and Marina were still there, skulking around him as if waiting
for him to fall on his face.

Which was a very real possibility.

Dammit.

He looked over to find Danny talking to one of his
deputies. Danny glanced his way, his face lined with con-

cern. Jace pushed to his feet to go to him, but the sheriff held up a hand, telling him to wait.

Being hurt sucked. Jace didn't want to wait, but he also wasn't sure if he could actually walk the twenty feet to the door without someone's help. It reminded him too much of his time as a prisoner of war—and no one wanted him to go down that road. Thankfully, his thoughts halted as Danny approached.

"Did you find Cooper?" Jace asked.

Danny shook his head. "Not yet. Do you know if Marlee was headed anywhere this morning?"

"Cooper wanted her to remain at the ranch. That's why both of us came to the motel."

"That's what I thought."

"What's going on?"

The sheriff put his hands on his hips and looked down. "Marlee is missing. It seems she took Abby's Suburban without telling anyone."

"The asshole that hit me and took Cooper must have called her."

Danny raised his brows and nodded. "That's exactly what we think happened. And it looks like he did it with your phone."

Jace thought back to when he'd tried to use his phone. He'd assumed it had fallen from his pocket when he was hit, and he hadn't wasted time looking for it. "The guy took it from me, and I didn't know it."

"Hey, you were hit hard on the head. You can't expect to think of everything."

"I should've told you I didn't have my phone," he argued.

Danny quirked a brow at him. "And I should've asked where it was earlier."

"Please tell me you're tracking my phone and Marlee's."

"We were."

Jace closed his eyes for a second and sighed. "They turned off, didn't they?"

"Right about the time Marlee called your phone. The conversation was brief. We did get a ping on both locations from towers. They're in the area."

"Well, at least there's that." But was it enough?

Danny sat on the second bed and looked at Jace. "Everyone is being brought to the ranch, including your parents."

"The threat is that bad, huh?"

"He tried to kill you," Danny stated in a firm tone. "He shot Cooper and took him, and he lured Marlee out. At the very least, he wants Marlee dead."

"Cooper will never get over it if she's killed." Jace swallowed, his mouth dry. "Not to open old wounds, but do you think this is like what happened to you?"

Danny shook his head. "I've already thought about that and talked it over with Ryan. This is different. I'm not saying they won't torture Cooper, but I think their main target is Marlee. Not that that helps or matters."

"No, it does. What now?"

"We head to the ranch with the others. Your parents are worried sick, and they want to see you. Not to mention, I think it'll help everyone if they can see you're okay."

Jace put his hands on his thighs. "Danny, you've done a great many things for us, and I know you and Ryan are doing everything you can right now. But that's my best friend out there. He's in trouble, along with the woman he loves. I'm going to do anything I can to make sure both of them come out of this alive."

"I know that. I also know that no matter what Ryan and I may tell all of you, you're going to do what y'all always do, which is be there for each other and get the job done."

Jace had thought Danny would tell him to stay out of the way, but he actually got the opposite.

"Come on," the sheriff said. "Let's get to the ranch."

Marlee held on to the side with the stitch in it and desperately tried to keep herself moving. Her mind told her body to run, but her body could no longer respond properly. It was all she could do to keep putting one foot in front of the other. She was so cold, she couldn't stop shivering.

She had no idea how long she had been going north. She never wore a watch because she always had her phone, but with that gone, she could only guess at the time. And with the clouds and rain, she couldn't even figure out where the sun was.

Her head dropped back so she could see through the tree branches, hoping for a glimpse of the sun. Instead, the toe of her shoe caught on something, and she pitched forward. She attempted to catch herself with her hands, even as she saw the big root sticking out of the ground.

Chapter 41

"What about Cooper's phone?" Caleb asked.

Ryan shook his head. "We've already tried it. It's either destroyed or turned off. There's no way to track it."

Jace sat in Clayton's office with the others. It felt wrong that Cooper wasn't with them. Everything about the entire situation was wrong.

Abby had her kids, Jace's parents, Cooper's mom, Naomi and Nate, Audrey, and Skylar in another part of the house. Not that it did much good. Everyone knew why they had been brought there and what was going on.

"Jace?" Ryan asked. "Do you have any ideas?"

He started to shake his head but then stopped. "I do, actually. Cash."

"Why didn't we think of that?" Caleb asked as he looked at Brice.

Danny held out his phone to Jace. "Do you know his number?"

"Yep."

In moments, Jace listened as the phone rang, waiting for Cash to pick up. Just when Jace thought it would go to voicemail, Cash answered. Jace quickly filled him in on what was going on.

"I'm not far. I can be there in a couple of hours. Quicker even, maybe," Cash told him.

Jace gave a thumbs up to the room to let them know. "I don't care how you get here, just get here."

Less than an hour later, someone buzzed for entrance at the gate of the ranch, and Cash said his name. Jace couldn't believe that he had gotten there so quickly, but he was glad Cash had. And the man came prepared.

He walked in carrying a hard, black bag that looked like a cross between a suitcase and a briefcase. His gaze landed on Jace first. "You okay?"

"It looks worse than it is," Jace said.

Clayton held out his hand to Cash. "Jace is lying. It's that bad. Come in. Glad to have you."

Jace took more pills for his headache, hoping it would alleviate the pain, but he knew it was wishful thinking. What really bothered him was that he wasn't any good to Cooper right now, not in his current condition anyway.

He rubbed his eyes and dropped his hand to find Ryan staring at him. The police chief was the kind of man who noticed everything. Which is what made him so damn hard to beat at poker. Ryan gave him a nod before turning his attention to Danny, who was telling everyone that the sheriff's department had set up a perimeter around the county, stopping all vehicles. Other deputies were on the lookout for any signs of Cooper, Marlee, or Stella Pearson.

"Additionally, the department notified OnStar to locate Abby's Suburban," Ryan added. "I'm hoping we hear something from them soon since we can't track the phones."

Jace leaned a shoulder against the wall. "Marlee will have ditched the SUV by now. Regardless, we need to find it. If it's in a parking lot, we can see what other cars are missing. If it's elsewhere, there's a good chance a car was waiting for her or she's on foot."

"I agree with Jace," Cash said. "I had some time to think about this on the way over. If Stella is the ringleader for this criminal activity, then any number of people could be working for her. Is she in custody?"

Ryan shook his head as he crossed his arms over his chest. "We didn't bring her in yesterday because there isn't enough evidence. Marlee has been after these people for a long time, and if she didn't have evidence, then we're going to be hard-pressed to find any."

"But bringing Stella in would at least let her know that we're on to her," Caleb stated.

Brice snorted loudly. "Better than letting her think she's gotten away with all of this."

"Hold up. All of you are acting like we're going to let her go. We've got men on the house. We'll know if there's any movement. Trust me, we're not going to let her leave."

Jace pushed away from the wall too fast and the room spun, but he didn't care. His anger was too great. "Marlee kept telling us last night that Stella was the one. We should've brought her in right away."

"For what?" Ryan demanded. "Only to let her go because we had nothing but the word of a private investigator that she's the culprit? Come on, Jace. You know we can't do that."

Brice cocked his head to the side. "And now that Jace was nearly killed, Cooper shot and taken God-only-knows where, and Marlee missing? What now? Are both you and Danny going to continue to sit there and tell us you can't arrest her?"

"We *can't* arrest her," Danny said. "Until we have evidence that she's involved in the murder of the pregnant women, the kidnapping of newborns, the attempted murder of Jace, Cooper's abduction, or anything else, we can't do anything."

Fury ripped through Jace. Before he could release his words, Cash calmly said, "That's not entirely true, gentlemen."

The room went quiet as all eyes turned to Cash.

Clayton leaned back in his chair behind his desk. "We're all ears."

Cash's pale gray eyes looked from Ryan to Danny. "In order to press charges, you must have evidence. But that doesn't mean you can't bring someone in for questioning and lead them to believe you have evidence."

"I've done that before, yes," Danny said. "It's a thin line we walk, but I only walk it when I know there's evidence to be found."

Jace rolled his eyes. "Marlee knows there's evidence. We just have to find it."

"And if we don't?" Ryan asked.

Danny blew out a breath. "Then we have to let Stella go."

"What other option do you have now?" Cash asked. "You have no idea where Cooper is, no idea where Marlee is, and Stella could leave at any time."

Danny ran a hand down his face. "I can have one of the deputies currently watching the house bring her in."

"Not in," Cash said. "Here. Or somewhere else private."

Jace smiled at Cash. "Now you're talking."

"Whoa. Wait just a minute," Ryan said, his brow puckered in a frown.

Cash slid his gaze to Ryan. "I was called here because there's a problem. I'm giving you a solution to that problem."

"We can't help with that. No matter how much we want to," Danny said in a voice laced with regret.

Caleb glared at them. "This is Cooper. How many times has he helped each of us when we needed it the most? Danny, do you know what he did for you and Skylar?"

"I know perfectly well what he did," Danny answered.

Brice moved to stand by his brother. "Then act like it."

"They are," Clayton said as he got to his feet. "Their positions give them little leeway on these things. All of you know that. Don't take it out on them."

"Cooper wouldn't hesitate to help any of you," Jace said.

Caleb crossed his arms over his chest. "No, he wouldn't. He hasn't."

"Here's where we're at," Clayton told the room. "Danny, Ryan, we need your help, of course. However, this situation calls for more . . . brute force than local law enforcement can give. I cannot, and will not, stand by and wait to find out what happens to Cooper or Marlee. As our friends, we hope that you will continue to help, but we understand if you can't."

Ryan nodded as he looked at the floor. This his gaze lifted to Clayton. "You want me and Danny to tell our people to look the other way—again—while all of you go in guns blazing?"

"We want you to support us as we find our friends," Cash replied.

Jace fisted his hands, waiting for Ryan's and Danny's decision. He couldn't believe they were even debating this. Then again, Jace didn't work for the city or the county, nor did he have others he had to answer to regarding his actions in such an event. If he were caught—and he wasn't going to get caught—he might be arrested.

He then stepped forward and looked at first Danny and then Ryan. "We understand you have jobs and people to answer to. Return to your people and do what y'all need to do. We're going to do what we have to, and if that means either of you arresting one of us after the fact, then that's just how it'll have to be."

"Exactly," Caleb and Brice said in unison.

Ryan gave a nod. "Watch your backs. And don't shoot any of my men."

After he was gone, Danny pressed his lips together. "I've been a friend of this family for a long time. Each of you was there for me and Skylar during our incident. I owe all of you for that. There's nothing I can do to repay that, but I'm going to try. I might not be able to stand with you tonight when you go after whoever this is, but I'll support you. If that means I don't get re-elected, I'm okay with that. Ryan's position is different. But I also know him. He's not going to turn his back on any of us, either."

"No, he won't," Clayton said. "That much I know for certain."

Caleb's face scrunched up in disbelief. "Then why did he leave?"

"So he wouldn't hear anything else said. Just like I'm leaving now." Danny gave them a nod and started for the door. He paused next to Jace and put a hand on his shoulder briefly before walking out.

A full minute passed before Clayton looked at Cash. "I'm hoping you have something to help us."

"As a matter of fact, I do," Cash said with a smile.

Chapter 42

The knock on the back door startled Stella so badly that she jumped and dropped her phone onto the floor. She reached down and grabbed it before she rose from the sofa and headed to the back. She peered through the peephole and saw Chuck.

She hurriedly unlocked and opened the door for him with a smile. "That took longer than I thought it would."

"Lots of loose ends to tie up," he said as he walked past her.

Something about his words made her frown. Softly, she closed the door. "That sounds ominous."

"Let's get moving."

She didn't like that he kept his back to her. Stella said his name and waited for him to face her before saying, "Tell me what you're hiding."

"We've found ourselves in a mess. A mess, I might add, that I warned you would eventually come." He shrugged. "But you ignored me. However, I fixed everything."

"You've never disobeyed me before," she said, crossing her arms.

He gave her a hard look. "We've never been so close to being caught before."

"As I told you, they don't have evidence, or they would've come for me."

Chuck moved closer to her until they stood less than six inches apart. "You might be careless with your life, but I'm not. Nor am I careless with yours. If you go down, we all do. I'm not going to let that happen. Besides, you wouldn't last a day in jail."

"I'm stronger than you think."

"Not when it comes to prison. No one is prepared for that. Especially not someone like you," he said with a sneer. "Let's get moving. You're going to need to change out of those heels into something more . . . practical."

"Practical? What's that supposed to mean?"

Chuck looked her up and down. "I'd also suggest jeans. Do you have a raincoat?"

"I'm not going anywhere until you tell me what's going on."

He moved past her to glance out the window. "We've got a few hours of daylight left, and we're going to need every one of them to get through the woods to the car I have waiting for us."

"What?" she asked, shocked.

He pointed out the window. "Have you noticed there's an unmarked car down the road, watching the house?"

"Yes."

"And you thought we'd just drive past them, no problem?" Chuck asked, bewildered.

Stella shrugged. "They haven't arrested me."

"Why don't you try to drive past them and see what happens? I'll wait here."

She glanced out the window. "Fine. You win. I need to get my luggage out of my car."

"I'll get it," he said and walked away. Seconds later, he returned to place her suitcase in the bedroom.

Stella shut the door behind him and changed. She removed her dress pants and designer blouse and put on jeans and a sweater. The most manageable shoes she had were a pair of booties, but they were better than any of her heels.

When she emerged from the room, Chuck held out a coat for her. "You're going to need this."

No sooner had she put on the raincoat than he grabbed her arm and led her to the door.

"My purse," she said and tried to turn back.

He kept her moving. "I've got your wallet and phone. Everything else can be replaced. We don't have time, Stella. We need to move."

She followed him out. It wasn't long before her suede booties were soaked, and her feet were like ice, but she didn't say a word. At least the hood of the coat kept most of the rain from her face.

"Run," Chuck ordered and took off.

She struggled to keep up with him. Finally, he paused long enough to grab her hand and pull her after him.

Cooper was going to lose his mind. He banged on the warehouse walls, hoping someone, *anyone*, would hear him and come investigate. He pounded for so long that his hand was bloody and bruised, and his voice was hoarse.

Time dragged on slowly. His wound made him weak, and his body demanded that he rest. But he couldn't. He needed to get free and find Marlee and see about Jace. Sitting there doing nothing was the worst kind of torture.

He looked at the wires again. He couldn't see the bomb itself, only the trigger, so he couldn't defuse it. Not that he had anything to cut the wires with anyway. He was utterly helpless, with no way to contact his friends and ask for help.

This was exactly what the man had wanted.

Cooper frowned. If the guy just wanted him out of the way, then why put explosives on the door? That could only mean that, somehow, his friends would be alerted to where he was and would come for him.

If he wasn't able to warn them, then they'd all be killed.

Jace stared at the plan Cash had put together. It was a smart one with them using the same grid they had when Danny was taken. The problem was that they wouldn't have the sheriff's department or the police to help them.

"This is going to take days," Caleb said.

Brice crossed his arms over his chest. "Time we don't have."

"If we could narrow down the search area, that would help," Cash said. "As it is, no one knows where Cooper is."

Clayton shook his head. "It isn't your fault, Cash. We asked, hoping you could come up with a miracle."

"Where is the last place any of us would look for Cooper?" Jace asked.

They turned to him with various looks of confusion.

Brice shrugged. "Here on the ranch."

"Hell, everywhere," Caleb answered.

Clayton made a sound in the back of his throat. "Danny was taken to another county that we never thought to look in."

"Because he was sheriff," Cash replied. He turned his head to Jace. "How long after you were attacked did Marlee leave?"

Clayton threw up his hands. "I don't know how long she was gone. She kept walking out of the room. I assumed she was waiting for Cooper and Jace to return."

"She probably got the call from the guy then," Caleb said.

Cash nodded. "That's my guess. He could've still had Cooper with him. Let's put ourselves in his shoes. That entire ring of criminals has been in the area for a while."

"Yeah," Brice grumbled.

Jace grinned. "Which means he knows the area. I see where you're going with this."

"He would make the most of his time," Clayton continued.

Caleb nodded, a look of excitement crossing his face. "Which means he wouldn't have wasted a lot of time driving Cooper somewhere else."

"He's close, then," Brice replied.

Jace wracked his brain, trying to think about what was near the motel. Then he realized what it was. "Downtown. Cooper is downtown."

"The abandoned warehouses," Clayton replied. "It's a great hiding place."

As they turned to go, Cash said, "Wait."

His tone halted them in their tracks.

Jace looked at him. "What?"

"What about Stella?"

They looked at each other, none of them wanting to speak. Finally, Clayton said, "Danny and Ryan won't let her out of their sight. Let's get Cooper."

The sound of car doors jerked Cooper awake. He peeled his eyes open, feeling worse than he had all day. Lack of food, continual blood loss, and the stress of the situation were taking a toll on his body.

He tried to call out, but his throat was sore from earlier, so his words came out as a croak. Someone was near. If he wanted out, he needed to let them know where he was.

Cooper slowly got to his feet. He tried to beat on the wall again, but his hand just couldn't take it. Instead, he used his foot to beat out Morse code for *SOS*.

"Cooper?"

His name came from a distance, but he heard it. "I'm here!"

He grabbed his throat as pain ripped through him. If only he'd saved his voice. He kicked quicker, hoping that alerted them.

"Cooper?"

That was Caleb. Cooper smiled and kicked rapidly until he heard them approaching the back door.

"Cooper?"

He stilled at the sound of Jace's voice.

"It's me," Jace said, a smile in his voice. "We'll get you out in just a sec."

Cooper tried to talk again but gave up and just started banging on the wall.

"Okay, okay!" Brice shouted. "We get it. We need to look."

It wasn't long before Cooper heard someone curse. He frowned because that sounded suspiciously like Cash.

"Hey, Cooper," Cash said. "We see the bomb. Thanks for the heads-up. Are there other doors?"

"Yes," Cooper said, pressing his face to the door and hoping his voice reached them.

Clayton said, "Stay here, Cooper. We're going to check the other entrances."

The seconds before his friends returned seemed like years. Jace said, "One door is bricked over. The other has too much debris in front of it for us to get to you. We have no choice but to defuse this bomb if we're going to get you out."

"Marlee?" he asked, wondering why he didn't hear her voice.

Brice answered. "We'll fill you in on everything once you're free."

Cooper knew what that meant. Marlee wasn't with them.

"Stand back from the door!" Cash shouted.

Cooper pressed himself against the same wall as the door but scooted down a ways. The entire time they worked, Cooper kept thinking about Marlee and all the different ways she could be hurt. The not knowing was the worst. Was she hurt? Or worse, dead?

Suddenly, the door opened, and his friends poured in. Cooper was soon surrounded. He looked at Jace and saw his pale face and the remnants of blood on him.

"He's got a hard head. Like we've always known," Caleb said.

Clayton urged them out. "We can do this in the truck. I'll call Karl and Marina to the ranch so they can patch you up."

"Tell me about Marlee," Cooper demanded, "or I'm not going anywhere."

Chapter 43

Cooper's gut was twisted in a knot so vicious, he wasn't sure it would ever unravel. Knowing that Marlee had left after the man's call had Cooper seeing red. He would never forget that man's face. And if it was the last thing he did, he'd hunt the bastard down himself.

"Drink," his mom said as she handed him a mug before giving him a kiss on the temple and walking out.

People were talking all around him at the ranch as Marina and Karl cleaned his wound and bandaged him. He was lucky the bullet had gone clean through. Otherwise, he'd be in the hospital. He'd have to go eventually—Jace, too—but right now, there were more pressing matters to deal with. Like finding Marlee.

It had been nearly an hour since Jace had been brought to the ranch. He had a new bandage in place, aspirin to help with the pain, and copious amounts of water to help hydrate him. With a borrowed shirt from Clayton, Cooper found it difficult to sit any longer. He'd been sitting all day.

"I've got to get out there," he said.

Cash met his gaze and nodded. "We're doing the best

we can. It's a large area to cover, and we're not sure which direction Marlee was headed in."

"Actually," Ryan said as he walked into the office, "we do. OnStar came through. We found the Suburban thirty miles west of here in a ditch."

Cooper's stomach fell to his feet. "Is . . . Marlee?"

"She wasn't in the vehicle," Ryan said.

Clayton smiled at Ryan. "Thank you."

"Don't suppose you want to come with us?" Jace asked.

Ryan suddenly grinned. "I was hoping you'd ask. I've got a dozen officers waiting to help, and Danny is meeting us there with some deputies. We'll fan out and begin searching. We need something of Marlee's for the dogs. Cooper. Good to see they found you."

"Yeah." Cooper looked outside. "It's getting dark fast."

"Let's go, then!" Caleb shouted, getting everyone moving.

The drive to the Suburban was the longest of Cooper's life. At least the rain had stopped. He held Marlee's shirt in his hands, wishing it were her instead. He knew Marlee wasn't with the SUV, but it still didn't stop his mind from racing to figure out what she might have been thinking. When they pulled up, the area was roped off, and the road had been shut to any traffic by police cars with their lights flashing.

Cooper got out of the truck and looked down the ravine to where the Suburban was. He tried to put himself in Marlee's shoes to imagine what had prompted her actions.

"What are you thinking?" Jace asked from beside him.

Cooper realized then that Cash, Brice, Caleb, and Clayton were there, as well. He shrugged. "I'm thinking that if the bastard who attacked us is the same one who called Marlee from your phone, then he brought her here."

"Why here, though?" Cash asked. "What's around here?"

Brice shrugged. "It's mostly wooded area."

"Some live out here and lease parts of their land to hunters," Caleb said.

Clayton turned to Cooper. "I hate to say it, but it's somewhere I'd bring someone if I wanted to make sure they were never found."

Cooper nodded and kicked something. As he looked closer, he realized it was the remnants of a phone, but not just any cell—Marlee's.

The K-9s were brought over, and he gave Marlee's shirt to the officers to let the dogs get the scent. As the dogs searched the area, attempting to pick up the trail, Cooper looked around, trying to determine which way Marlee might have gone.

"The trees will make it difficult for a helicopter to see, but this might help," Cash said as he pulled out another of his cases.

He opened it to reveal a drone. As he was getting it ready, the dogs began barking. Everyone jerked their heads across the road to where the dogs were headed, pulling their handlers along.

"North," Jace said.

Cooper didn't wait for the others as he followed the dogs. One deputy tried to stop him, but Cooper ignored him and ran past. The dogs moved fast, covering a lot of ground. Just when Cooper thought they might find her, the dogs lost the scent. Then, they found it and were off again.

After two miles, Cooper was beginning to wonder where Marlee had been headed. There was nothing out here but the forest. As the sun sank into the horizon, he knew they had to find her soon or it might be too late. The fact that the dogs kept the scent was good news. At least, that's what he told himself.

The sound of the drone overhead caught his attention. He looked up and spotted it before he paused and glanced over his shoulder to find his friends following.

"We've got your back, Coop," Jace said as he came up alongside him.

Jace's face was paler than before, and Cooper knew he shouldn't be out here. But he also knew that Jace wouldn't leave. Cooper wouldn't go if their positions were reversed.

"Thanks."

"No need," Jace replied with a smile.

By mile five, Cooper was growing more and more concerned. How far had Marlee been led out into the woods?

Suddenly, he heard a shout. Cooper didn't even wait. He took off running to where the dogs and the police were gathered. He shoved past them to see a form lying on the ground. Cooper's heart leapt into his throat. He kept repeating *No* in his mind because he refused to believe that this person was Marlee. The hood of the raincoat was pulled forward, keeping him from seeing any hair.

"Cooper," Danny said as he walked up.

But Cooper wasn't listening. He knelt beside the body and gently pulled away the hood of the coat to find blond hair.

"Is she alive?" Ryan asked from beside Cooper.

Cooper was so stunned that he remained still, trying to discern what he was seeing. Out of the corner of his eye, he spotted movement and glanced up to see two officers reaching for the body.

"Don't!" Cooper yelled, his hand out to stop the men.

Danny shook his head. "What is it?"

"Maybe another bomb," Jace said, leaning against a tree.

Cooper motioned with his hands for everyone to stay back. "Hold on, let me feel for a pulse."

Silence filled the area. Not even the dogs made a sound as Cooper searched for a heartbeat. After a moment, he looked at the others and shook his head. "She's been dead a few hours is my guess."

"We need to turn her over," Ryan said.

Jace snorted. "I wouldn't touch her until someone searches her. With the bomb that was set for Cooper, there could be another one waiting."

"True. And with the people we're after, I'd rather be safe than sorry," Clayton said.

Cooper said, "Danny. Ryan. Y'all might want to get the bomb squads out here on the double."

Without question, both men did as he urged. Cooper turned his head to look at Jace. He could tell by Jace's voice that he wasn't doing well. Cooper didn't try to tell him to go home, because he knew that his friend wouldn't go anywhere until this was over.

Jace gave him a nod, letting Cooper know that he would make it. Each time Cooper thought about seeing the crowbar in the man's hands dripping with blood— Jace's blood—he wanted to do bodily harm to the bastard.

"What do you see?" Cash asked as he moved to Cooper's side.

Cooper squeezed his eyes shut and returned his attention to the body. "Nothing yet. There are too many leaves, and too much mud and muck to see anything clearly."

Brice cracked his knuckles. "Let me have a go at it."

"Not happening," Cooper told him. "You have your son and wife to think about."

Brice's brow furrowed as he opened his mouth to argue, but Caleb put a hand on his brother's chest and said, "You know Coop's right."

"I have training," Brice said.

Caleb snorted. "We all do, but you have a family now."

Cooper tuned out the brothers and placed his hands on the ground before leaning down to get his face as close to the body as possible to look for any wires. There might not be anything, but given that the dogs had been following Marlee's trail, and the asshole who had taken him had left a bomb on the door, Cooper wasn't taking any chances.

He, along with Cash, slowly made their way around the body. Just when Cooper thought there was nothing, his gaze spotted the wires that hadn't been completely covered by the leaves and the raincoat.

"Stop," Cooper said. He looked over the body to meet Cash's gray eyes. "Found it."

Clayton pressed his lips together. "Dammit."

Cooper slowly and methodically picked up one leaf at a time off the ground until he had exposed the wires. Every second spent doing this took him away from finding Marlee. And with dusk falling, he knew his chances of finding her were running out quicker than he could cope with.

"We've got this," Jace told him. "Get the dogs after the trail again and go find Marlee."

Cooper hesitated as he sat on his haunches. Mud and wet ground soaked through the knees of his jeans as he placed his hands on his thighs. He looked around at the faces of his friends and the authorities who were staring at him.

"I'll go with you," Cash told him.

Caleb stepped forward. "So will I."

"Me, too," Jace said and pushed away from the tree.

Cooper got to his feet and walked to Jace. "There's no one I'd rather have by my side, but I'm going to need you after this. I need you to take care of that wound."

"You're right. I'd only slow you down."

Cooper smiled. "The problem is you'd push yourself too hard." The smile vanished. "There's a real possibility I could lose Marlee. I don't want to lose you, as well."

Jace glanced away as he nodded. "Point taken. Just get that asshole."

"Oh, I will," Cooper promised.

He turned to Caleb and Cash and gave them a nod.

Clayton moved to stand in their way. "You boys know what you're doing, so I don't need to remind any of you to be careful."

"We've got this," Cash told him.

Cooper turned to find Ryan waiting with the K-9 handlers and the dogs. "You coming?"

"As if I'd let you three go alone," Ryan stated with a half-smile.

Caleb let out a sigh. "Let's get this show on the road, then."

With a nod from Ryan, the officers gave the dogs Marlee's scent again. It took them a few minutes until they were able to latch onto it, and then they were off once more.

Chapter 44

The moment she came to, Marlee groaned at the throbbing in her skull. She put her hands on the ground to push herself up, and they sank about half an inch into the mud as she pushed up on her hands and knees. She blinked to try and get her mind straight as she sat back on her haunches. For a heartbeat, she couldn't remember why she was out in the woods. Then it all came back to her.

She choked back a sob and looked around. The light had faded significantly. She could hardly find her way during the day. How was she going to do it at night without a flashlight?

"I'll make do," she told herself as she tried to stand.

It took the use of the tree and a sturdy limb she found to not just get her on her feet but to keep her there. Then she looked at where she'd been lying. Roots from the tree stuck up all around her. She had tripped on one and then fell on another. Marlee reached up and tenderly felt the spot above her eyebrow. The moment her fingertips made contact, pain consumed her.

"Okay. Not doing that again," she said while waiting for the white dots to stop flashing in her vision.

Marlee looked back in the direction she had come. She wasn't sure if she had kept to a straight line or had veered off. Without a compass or anything to guide her, she could be going east or west and not know it. She'd run blindly, worried about covering the distance in the hopes of finding Cooper. Instead, she'd knocked herself unconscious.

Fury and frustration swamped her. Those emotions mixed with her pain caused tears to form, which only made her angry. She didn't want to cry. She needed to focus and figure out what to do next. Despite her training, she was ill-equipped to travel in such an environment without a phone, or to protect herself without a gun.

But she did have her knife. She always had her knife.

With her shoulders squared, Marlee faced the direction she had been going and took a step.

"Where are we going?" Stella asked with a frown.

Chuck kept his gaze on the road as he drove. "I'm getting us out of here."

"Then why are you looping back toward the house?"

"I'm not going to take the chance that those officers saw us leaving."

Stella's head jerked in his direction. "Chuck, no. Leave them. We need to get out of town."

"They'll come after us," he argued. "If they saw us leave, they might have already called in reinforcements."

"You can't know that they did."

"And you can't know they didn't," he snapped.

She blinked and stared at him for a moment before turning her head to face forward. "I'm telling you not to do this."

"Newsflash, Stella. Right now, I'm running things. You had your chance to make the right decisions, and you couldn't do it. So, now I am."

"And that means leaving a trail of dead bodies behind us? They'll come for us for sure."

Chuck slammed on the brakes as he neared the stop sign. She pitched forward violently, the seatbelt keeping her in place. He glared at her. "Dead bodies? You're worried about a couple of policemen when we've left hundreds of dead women all across the country? Where the fuck is your head, Stella?"

Her eyes narrowed on him. "Where it's always been. I'm the one who has kept us out of trouble all these years. Do you honestly think we'd be sitting as nicely as we have been if I let you kill everyone you wanted? Well, *newsflash*, Chuck, but that simply isn't the case. Killing isn't always the answer."

"No. Selling newborns cut from their mother's wombs to the highest bidder is," he retorted.

Stella's mouth fell open.

Chuck didn't wait for the argument to continue. He turned the vehicle toward the two officers watching the house. They were hidden pretty well, seated in an unmarked car, but Chuck had picked them out easily enough. He was going to use the fading light to his advantage. Dusk always made things more difficult to see.

He parked the truck and took the keys. Then he looked at Stella. "You've got two choices. You can get out and fend for yourself, or you can stay here. Either way, I don't want to hear another word about what I'm about to do."

Chuck got out and stalked to the police car with his gun by his side. He came up on the driver first since the window was down as he smoked. Chuck fired two shots, killing both men instantly. He then walked back to the truck.

He wasn't at all surprised to find Stella still inside. She might have a head for business, but when it came to survival, she was clueless.

Neither said a word as he started up the stolen truck and turned around. When he came to the main road, he stopped and looked toward town. There hadn't been any sound of an explosion from his bomb, but there was still a chance that Cooper's friends hadn't found him yet. Chuck really hated to miss all the fun, but he had someone else he needed to find. He turned onto the road and pressed the accelerator.

"We need to get to Houston for the meeting. We don't have enough time to take the long way around," Stella told him.

He noted her calm voice. She was trying, at least. "I'm not going the long way around. I've got something else to take care of real quick, then we'll head to Houston. Trust me, you'll get there in plenty of time to buy new clothes and change."

"I hope so. The only time I've had this much mud on me is at the spa."

It was her attempt at humor, but Chuck wasn't in the mood. It was time Stella truly understood who he was and why she should've listened to him years ago. But she was about to find out.

It didn't matter how fast they moved, Cooper couldn't stop the dread that filled him. The dogs had lost Marlee's scent after only thirty minutes. It took them another five to find it again. Each second felt like an eternity, testing his patience and control.

Then, finally, they were off again. Ryan had given him a pistol. Cash pulled out two and tossed one to Caleb. The four of them, the handlers, and dogs kept moving, each prepared for what they might find.

Cooper wasn't going to stop looking. He didn't care how long it took. He'd find Marlee one way or another.

"I don't need to tell any of you what we might find," Ryan said as they ran.

Caleb shot him a dark look. "We know very well."

"And we're prepared to take the son of a bitch out," Cash said.

A muscle in Ryan's jaw flexed. "You might be a PI, Cash, but my men and I are leading this."

"We understand," Cooper said quickly before Cash could retort. He then exchanged a look with Cash, letting both him and Caleb know that if they found the bastard and any of them had a shot, they should take it.

Cooper didn't care what happened to him after it was over. He was going to find Marlee. But, more importantly, he was going to find the bastard responsible for all of this.

Marlee did her best to move quickly while there was still light, but it was like someone had drawn the shade over a window because, in a blink, the sky was dark. She wasn't afraid of the night, but walking the streets of a city at night was vastly different than being in the middle of the woods, especially ones you didn't know.

It would be easy to give in to all her childish fears that threatened to rise up within her, but she couldn't do that. She needed to be aware of her surroundings and notice any sounds that might be a predator. Cougars had been seen in the area. While she didn't begrudge any wildlife their survival, she really hoped no cougars were nearby with designs on her for a meal.

She smiled, thinking Cooper would've laughed at that. Then tears filled her eyes as she realized that she may never see him again. The man who had given her the instructions hadn't told her much. She'd assumed that she would eventually come upon him and Cooper, and that was just one of the many ways she had made poor choices.

But what else could she have done? Cooper's life was on the line.

Marlee stopped and looked up at the dark limbs above, silhouetted against the dark gray sky. "Where are you?" she bellowed. "I'm here!"

She closed her eyes, hoping there would be some kind of answer. But there was nothing.

Her options were few. She could turn around and, hopefully—eventually—find her way back to the road where she might be able to flag someone down to help her. That didn't do Cooper any good, however. The man holding Cooper had told her to hurry. She had, but the fall had undoubtedly messed things up. And since she had no idea how long she had been unconscious, she wasn't sure if her deadline had passed.

Marlee narrowed her eyes. "A deadline he didn't give me."

Why had she just realized that?

"Because I was too busy being worried about getting to Cooper. I didn't think of the details." Marlee could've kicked herself.

She knew better. She'd been trained in such tactics. But no one she had loved had ever been in such a situation. The man could've intentionally left off a time to lure her into the woods. But . . . why?

Marlee looked around. There were trees everywhere. For all she knew, someone was lurking behind each and every one. It was the perfect place to bring someone if you wanted to kill them. There was a good chance the man didn't even have Cooper. She'd taken his word for it because he was that kind of man. He could've used that to his advantage.

None of that mattered. Marlee wasn't going to backtrack. She had done everything the man had ordered her to do so she could find Cooper. Because she loved him.

She loved him so much that the thought of not being with him left her aching inside, like someone had cut out a piece of her soul. She would walk the breadth and width of Texas if it meant eventually getting to Cooper.

She squared her shoulders and continued walking.

Chapter 45

Everything had changed in an instant. And Stella didn't like it.

She wasn't sure what to make of Chuck. He'd always been her right-hand man, the person who always did as ordered without question. But now, he was someone different. Someone she wasn't sure she could trust—and most definitely someone she was afraid of.

Not that she could do anything about that at the moment. He literally held her life in his hands.

Oh, he'd told her that she could leave, but she didn't believe that for a second. This man was someone she didn't know. This Chuck was someone who killed simply for sport.

For all she knew, he'd always been like this, but had kept it from her. It was her fault. She had looked for people just like him because it took a certain type of person to track down pregnant women, kill them, and cut out their babies. She knew what kind of monster she was and had thought she knew what kind of monsters she employed. Obviously, she'd been wrong.

She didn't ask him where they were going again. Instead,

she kept her hands on her lap as he drove. She noticed the area, keeping details in her mind, even when it got dark. She was shaking, though not from the cold. In response, Chuck turned on the heater. Before, she would've thought he had noticed her needs. But now, it made her shake even more.

"I'm glad you stayed," he suddenly said.

Stella glanced at him and forced herself to smile. "We've been through a lot together."

"Yes, we have. And we'll get through this." He blew out a breath. "I'm sure when we do, you're going to want to talk about all of this. I'll tell you now, there's nothing to discuss. I'm doing what needs to be done for you, me, and the company. That includes everyone who works for you. You'll realize that once you're safe."

She nodded, looking out the passenger window. "I'm sure you're right. It's been ages since I've had to run for my life."

"I always promised I'd protect you. I don't take vows like that lightly."

He slowed and turned off the main road onto what was nothing more than a path created by several vehicles' passage over the years. They bounced along as the truck rolled through puddles of water, some thick with mud.

She thought he might have stashed another vehicle out here for them to switch to, but the farther he drove through the woods, the more she realized that wasn't the case. She tried to tell herself that there was a helicopter waiting for them.

The idea was ridiculous. It would bring too much attention to them. But she couldn't stop trying to make Chuck out to be a decent person in her mind. How could she do that when she had employed him to kill others and kidnap children?

Finally, he came to a stop and put the truck in park.

Her gaze took in the clearing she saw through the trees. He turned off the ignition, cutting the light, and looked at her. She couldn't make out his face, just this outline. He kept telling her that he'd protect her. Surely, that didn't mean he was going to kill her, did it? In truth, she honestly couldn't answer that.

"You can stay here, but I think you'll want to see this," Chuck said.

Stella rubbed her hands together. "I've not warmed up yet."

"Suit yourself." He opened the door and got out, shutting the door behind him.

She watched as he walked toward the clearing with purpose. He had come here for something, but she couldn't tell what from where she sat. And she had seen very little when they'd driven up. As much as she wanted to remain in the truck, Stella found herself reaching to open the door. She softly pushed it closed behind her and followed Chuck.

Stella stood behind two trees and watched when Chuck also ducked behind a trunk. She saw him look up. She did the same and made out the outline of something rectangular in the trees. If she wasn't mistaken, that was a spotlight.

Her gaze jerked back to the clearing. Chuck had set a trap for someone.

Exhaustion and pain weighed heavily on Marlee. Her throat was parched from dehydration, and she was soaked through and unable to stop shivering. But she wasn't going to stop. She had to keep going.

Her mind wandered, going over the conversations she and Cooper had had. Some made her smile, others made her laugh, and many made her stomach flutter. He was special in so many ways, and she'd dragged him and his friends into this mess that was her life. No, it was her life *and* her work.

She rolled her eyes. How could anyone even think about being with her when she had such a job? She was always traveling, digging up information on people she'd rather not know. She chased bad guys in the hopes of getting a win at the end of the day. And for what? Little pay, long hours, horrible health benefits, and few rewards.

Maybe it was time she rethought her future, because she didn't want to end up alone. And if she continued on this path, that's precisely what would happen. She had a chance with Cooper. She knew that now. Only a fool would let that go, and she wasn't a fool.

At least, not most of the time.

Her steps slowed as she realized she'd reached a clearing. It wasn't something she had seen at all yet, so it gave her pause. She leaned heavily upon the stick and tried to get a read on the situation with her instincts, but her head was pounding too hard for her to focus on anything.

Marlee could go around the open area, but why? It was just a clearing. What could possibly happen? Her entire body ached, and if she could shave off even thirty seconds getting to wherever she was headed, she was going to do it. She took one step, then two into the clearing. On her third step, a voice rang out.

"Took you long enough."

She knew that voice. It was the man who had called her earlier. Marlee stilled, debating whether to back up to the tree line again. Before she could, she heard what sounded like a switch being thrown, and then light flooded the area, blinding her. Marlee lifted an arm to block the lights directed at her as she looked in the direction where she'd heard the voice.

"Where's Cooper?" she demanded.

The man's laugh sounded all around her. "I have no

idea, though my guess is he's still locked in the ware-house with the bomb on the door."

Marlee blinked and lowered her arm. "So you drew me out here on my own because you couldn't get to me any other way?"

"Oh, I could get to you," he said and stepped from behind a tree. He wore a smile that made her blood run cold. It was malicious, one worn by someone without a soul.

"Then why here?"

He chuckled, staring at her. "Of all the questions you must have, that isn't the one I'd be asking if I were you."

"Oh? And which should I ask?"

"The one about your sister."

Marlee gasped, her stomach clenching as if she'd been kicked.

The man laughed, his smile widening. "I didn't do it, but I know who did. From what I understand, she fought. Even after he cut her carotid."

Bile rose in Marlee's throat. She wished she had her gun because she'd unload the clip in this man's face.

"Is that hard to hear?" he asked, his smile still in place. "All these years, you've been searching for your sister's killer. And you've been close so many times, I can't be-lieve you didn't find us." The man tapped a finger to his lips. "You know, if I were you and knew how close I'd come, it might make me sick."

Marlee glared at him, hate rising in her like a tidal wave. "Do you get off saying these things to people?"

"Maybe," he replied. "Before today, the closest you got to us was a year after your sister's death. I stood ten feet from you. The man who killed your sister was right next to you, and you didn't even know it."

"And you let me live? That's hard to believe."

"It wasn't my choice," he told her. "I wanted you dead

then. I've been trying to get her to let me kill you every day since."

Her. Marlee knew he was talking about Stella.

The man shrugged. "Had I ignored her orders years ago, we wouldn't be here today. You've ruined things for all of us."

"*I've* ruined things?" Marlee asked with a snort. "What about all those families torn apart by the murders of their wives, mothers, sisters, or friends? And then the kidnapping of the newborns from their wombs? Shall we talk about that devastation? Everything that's happening is of your own creation. Yours and Stella's."

He threw back his head and laughed. "Of course, you'd say that. You, who live in your perfect little house with your perfect family, perfect job, and perfect life. You have no idea what it's really like out there in the world. How savage people are, how bloodthirsty. It's survive or die, and I'm a survivor."

"And if it was *your* wife who was murdered? Your baby cut from her womb?"

"That wouldn't happen to me."

She rolled her eyes. "Boy, are you ever cocky. I hate to tell you this, but your days are numbered."

"Says you?" he asked with a laugh. "You came out to the woods without a phone or a weapon, simply because I told you I had Cooper. Love is stupid and blind, and it has done nothing but bring you to your death."

Marlee shifted her feet. "Maybe so. But if you think any of my new friends are going to let this go, then you know nothing about them. They will hunt you down. Even if I'm the only one you kill—"

"Oh, you aren't. Remember, I got to Jace earlier."

She could only blink at him. He had no remorse in his voice or in his expression. This was pure evil staring back at her. She'd known it when she encountered him at the house. She'd known it when she spoke to him on the phone. And she knew it now.

But it changed nothing. She was still out here. He'd set all of this up, which meant that regardless of what she said or did, she wasn't getting out of this alive.

"You think I was kidding about the bomb where I stashed Cooper?" The man shook his head. "'Fraid not. There's also a trap in the woods by Stephanie's dead body, waiting for them just in case someone gets smart enough and finds where you dumped the vehicle and then follows you out here."

Marlee wasn't at all upset to hear about Stephanie's death since it confirmed what she had suspected about the FBI agent.

The man then lifted a pistol and aimed it right at Marlee's heart.

"Chuck."

Marlee's and Chuck's heads turned at the sound of the voice. Marlee watched as Stella came into the light. Stella kept her eyes on Chuck as she slowly walked toward him.

"What are you doing?" Stella asked.

He gave her a flat look, his gun still aimed at Marlee. "I'm sure you've heard everything I said. You know exactly what I'm doing."

"But why? We can get away."

"You're deranged if you think we'll get away. We might escape this place, but we'll be hunted from now until they catch us," Chuck replied.

Stella shrugged and continued walking toward him. "So what? What we do is dirty enough. There's no need to sully ourselves more."

"More?" he repeated with a laugh. "Right. Because you didn't just send Martin to Dallas to kill Penny."

"That was different."

Marlee looked between the two of them. Stella was

focused on Chuck, but he kept his attention on Marlee, glancing at Stella every now and again.

Chuck shook his head. "It's not different. Marlee caused all of this."

"No," Stella said. "That was me when I began this business. I'm to blame for all of it. Macey wasn't supposed to die. I refuse to allow you to hurt Marlee."

"Are you fucking kidding me?" Chuck bellowed. He lowered the gun and narrowed his eyes on Stella. "After everything that's happened in this town because of her?" he asked and motioned to Marlee with the pistol. "You still want to let her live?"

Stella halted and took a deep breath. "I do."

"Did you grow a conscience when you befriended that old woman? So what if she lost a child? So what if she loses another? That's life. You don't think twice about doing it to others," Chuck pointed out.

Marlee had to agree with him. While she appreciated Stella trying to stop Chuck from shooting her, he had a valid point.

Stella lifted her hands and continued walking to him. "We've been under a lot of pressure lately. We need to get clear of here now. Who cares about some woman who has trailed us? She didn't catch us before, and it was only by happenstance that she did this time. She won't again. We won't let her."

Marlee held her breath when Stella reached Chuck. She wasn't sure what would happen, but Marlee knew it wouldn't be good. Chuck outweighed Stella by quite a bit, not to mention, he had a weapon. The odds of Stella coming out on top were slim to, well . . . none.

"We can be together. As a couple," Stella continued. "Your words earlier weren't ones I wanted to hear, but I've had time to think things over. I don't want to be alone. I want you by my side. My partner in all things. We'll run the company together."

Stella finished by reaching up and cupping Chuck's face with her hands. His head lowered as their lips met. Then there was a loud bang that caused Marlee to jump. Stella jerked, her face locked in a look of surprise as she crumpled to the ground. Marlee watched Stella gasp for breath as blood poured from a wound in her abdomen.

"Do you think I'm that fucking gullible?" Chuck asked Stella. "You had your chance with me, and you threw it away. I've seen the real you today, and it disgusts me. Yeah, I'm going to run the company, and I'm going to run it like it should've been run to begin with. And you know what? Anyone who gets in my way is going to eat a bullet. Just like Marlee."

Marlee's lips parted when the gun swung her way. She didn't have time to think as he pulled the trigger. At the same instant, someone grabbed her from behind and yanked her to the ground.

"Stay there," Cooper whispered as he jumped to his feet.

Marlee could hardly believe that Cooper was there. She could only stare after him as he stalked toward Chuck, firing his gun rapidly.

And he wasn't the only one. Marlee counted several other shots as Chuck ran into the night. Then, dogs were barking and growling, and a few more shots were fired, followed by silence.

Marlee scrambled to her feet and raced to Stella. She slid on her knees beside the woman who was responsible for so much death. Marlee didn't have a phone to call for an ambulance, but she could apply pressure to the wound to slow the bleeding.

"Don't!" Stella said breathlessly.

Marlee looked into her face to see that Stella was at peace with what had happened.

"I . . . deserve this. I'm sorry about . . . Macey."

Marlee wanted to say that she forgave her, but she couldn't get the words out.

Stella smiled. "The password is *Diane*."

"What?" Marlee asked with a frown. "What password, and why did you use my mother's name?"

"You'll . . . know," Stella said.

"Tell me."

But Marlee's order fell on deaf ears as Stella's eyes closed, and her final breath left her body. Marlee fell back on her butt and put a hand to her head. The sound of footsteps approaching made her look over her shoulder. The moment she saw Cooper, she was on her feet again and running toward him.

"I love you. I love you. I love you. I should've told you the moment I knew," she said.

He held her tightly for several minutes. Then he pulled back and looked into her eyes. "I love you, too. I spent the day thinking I might never see you again, and I didn't like what the future looked like. I don't care where we live or what we do, I just want to be with you."

"Good," she said with a smile. "Because I want to be with you. Always."

"Just what I needed to hear," he whispered before he kissed her.

Epilogue

Two weeks later . . .

Life rarely turned out how anyone believed it would. The same could be said for Cooper. He couldn't stop smiling at Marlee, who stood beside him in the church as sunlight filtered through the stained-glass windows. She looked up at him and grinned before mouthing *I love you*. He held her hand, so thankful that they had all survived what could have been a horrendous tragedy.

Cooper's shoulder would take a few weeks to mend, but there was no serious damage. Jace had proven to everyone that he had a hard head and an even longer stubborn streak since he wouldn't take the pain meds given to him by the doctor. He would have another scar to add to the others, but once more, Cooper's best friend had come out of things alive, which was a blessing in itself.

A lot had happened for them over the course of two weeks. Marlee identified the dead body in the woods as Stephanie. Cooper and Marlee went to Stella's house and found her computer. Using the password Stella had given to Marlee, they were able to find all the evidence needed to shut down the operation—including those in the FBI that were in on it with Stella.

The Feds came to claim Stephanie's body, and that's when Danny and Ryan handed them the evidence. Danny and Ryan also ensured that the FBI knew that if something wasn't done to clean up the corrupt individuals in their organization, all of the evidence would be leaked to the press.

Marlee finally got to meet Cooper's mom. The two had hit it off immediately, which pleased Cooper immensely. Then he and Marlee flew out to California to visit her parents for a week. They posed a proposal to the Framptons to see if they would be interested in moving to Texas. If not, then he and Marlee would fly at least once a month to see them. However, her parents were all about being near their daughter and readily agreed to move.

Marlee decided to stay in Texas and set up her company base there. She kept telling Cooper that he had strong roots. He'd told her that she had roots, as well, but she said that his were different. He would've gone anywhere with her, but he was glad he was staying with his family and friends. Cooper had shown her the property he'd been eyeing. She had fallen in love with the land, and plans were already in the works to purchase it.

One thing he knew for sure: Marlee would never stop looking for her niece. And he was going to be right there with her every step of the way.

His thoughts halted as music filled the air. Everyone turned to look at the back of the church as Skylar appeared in a wedding dress, a bouquet of flowers clutched in her hand, and a huge smile on her face. Her gaze locked on Danny as she started walking up the aisle.

While everyone paid attention to the couple as they said their wedding vows, all Cooper could think about was Marlee and when she might want to exchange vows with him. He knew what he wanted to do with his life—hunt bad guys with Marlee. Hopefully, they would also find some missing children to reunite with their families and bring closure to everyone.

They were happy now, and he knew there would be hard times to come—because that was life. But he also knew that as long as they leaned on each other, they could make it through anything.

"You're supposed to be watching the bride and groom," Marlee whispered to him.

He kissed her temple. "You outshine them both, woman. Don't you know that?"

"We were late getting here because you kept talking like that. You need to stop, or we'll have to sneak off."

"I'm okay with that," he said with a grin.

She gazed up at him. "I love you."

"And I love you. You're stuck with me. You better be good with that."

"I'm more than good," she stated. "It's exactly what I want."

They shared a kiss just in time to hear Danny and Skylar announced as man and wife. Everyone shouted for joy and clapped as the happy couple walked down the aisle to start their new life as husband and wife.

"Ready?" Marlee asked as she quirked a brow at Cooper.

He brought her hand to his lips to kiss. "Yes, ma'am."

"Good. We've got a lot of work to do, but first, we're celebrating tonight."

He twisted his lips and brought her against him as they walked with the others out of the church. "And maybe a day or two after. I want it to be just you and me for a few days."

"Oh, that sounds heavenly."

He spotted a closet and pulled her after him. "Maybe we start our holiday early."

Marlee giggled as she closed the door behind them and reached for him.

More Titles by DONNA GRANT!